IMMACULATE
DECEPTION

IMMACULATE DECEPTION

A NOVEL BY

WARREN ADLER

DONALD I. FINE, INC.
New York

Library of Congress Cataloging-in-Publication Data

Adler, Warren.
Immaculate deception: a novel / by Warren Adler.
p.   cm.
ISBN 1-55611-229-7
I. Title.
PS3551.D64I45   1991   813'.54—dc20   90-55235   CIP

Manufactured in the United States of America

10 9 8 7 6 5 4 3 2 1

A.
Cop 1

For Sunny

IMMACULATE
DECEPTION

1

FIONA AWOKE, her senses alert to instant reality. She did not grope for recognition of sounds, shapes and texture. She knew at once what had awakened her. Oak leaves from the twin oaks in the garden, showing their first spring growth, rustling, making sounds like beans shifting in a bean bag.

Then she felt the light breeze through the opened window caressing her left cheek and smelled the gamey odor of the sheep manure the gardener had spread over the rose beds. Opening her eyes, she could see the pale grey slate of presunrise framed by the window.

The texture of early spring always jogged her memories of place. This house and its voices. Daddy calling a cheery goodbye. Mommy's footsteps crunching along the pebbled path of her beloved garden on the way to the shed. Death had not stilled the voices. Death never did. It was the axiom of homicide. People left tracks, left an aura, left flaked pieces of themselves like the invisible residue of dead skin cells.

She stretched under the comforter, toes touching Greg Taylor's hard calf muscles. Her position was partially diagonal. Their strenuous couplings had caused them to shift crosswise in her king-sized bed.

Turning, she observed him in the pale light, then lifted the comforter for a full view of his now fetally positioned body. Hard muscles from calves to shoulders, tight buns, smooth sun-burnished skin, healthy, sexy, beautifully made, a magnificent specimen. Greg would be the first to agree.

I

Resting her head on her elbow, she studied him with her detective's clinical eye. A good genetic match, she decided, at least physically. The odds were that they could make good babies, maybe a bit egocentric, a trifle compulsive, suspicious, distrusting . . . suddenly she was cataloging a long list of their mutual eccentricities and foibles.

Yet lately she had secretly entertained the idea of single parenthood. At thirty-six such ideas were understandable. Her mother, dead seventeen years, would have been appalled at the idea. Not that she wasn't listening to her thoughts at this very moment. Only speculating, Mother, Fiona admonished the periodic apparition, just in case it might be planning to put in an appearance. It would be just like her mother's apparition to catch her in flagrante delicto.

In fact, her mother, in whatever incarnation, would be appalled by her daughter's present life. At the time of her death, Fiona was still every inch the senator's daughter, groomed like a thoroughbred for life among the elite and powerful. Sweetly scrubbed and scented and being turned out for the good life at Mount Vernon Junior College, she was the very model of a good Catholic girlhood, providing boring confessions to old Father Thomas and, swear to Jesus and hope to die, still a true unblemished virgin as her mother's casket was lowered into her grave.

"Respect and dignity is everything," her mother had counseled. It was at the heart of her litany and her life. "No stranger must invade the temple of your body which has been fashioned to accommodate God's image." It was quite a convoluted explanation but she had gotten the message. Only marriage could obviate the status of man as stranger.

Loud and clear, the voice still rose in her mind. She had certainly cohabitated with a fair share of strangers. But she had long outgrown the secret sense of postcoital guilt that used to afflict her.

But the fact was that her mother would approve of her relationship with Gregory Taylor. Not entwined like this, of course. But fully dressed and posed for scrutiny. Greg was tall, handsome and, at least by heritage, Catholic, his mother of good Irish stock. His father had been a renegade Catholic all his life, but he had taken extreme unction to hedge his bet, which would have warmed her mother's heart. Greg, on the surface, would appear to be the perfect prospective mate in every respect.

But then, her mother always trusted the books' cover. Greg was right out of Central Casting for any mother's dreams. Except that he was still married, although separated, pathologically ambitious, devious in the extreme, covetous, greedy, egotistical, self-centered and narcissistic. In short, he had picked up all the native diseases of the nation's capital. And, oh God, she could barely expel the idea, forgive me Mommy, proud as punch of his beautiful specimen. She offered her palm as presentation of a deliciously ivory hard erection, his special pride. And her joy.

Husband and father material? Nada. No more than Daddy. But, at least, Daddy could bleed when pricked. And Daddy, in the end, had proved his bedrock morality and manhood and had died a real hero. He was the first, the very first Senator, to raise his fist against the stupid Vietnam war. For his troubles he was drummed out of the club. How glorious for him? Too bad, Mommy, you weren't there to see the parade. It was wonderful. Wonderful.

Yet, daydreaming aside, Greg could, indeed, provide the spermatic libation that could change the course of Fiona's personal history. Some latent maternal instinct seemed to be growing within her in direct proportion to her now galloping chronology. Perhaps there was some ego in it as well, certainly sentimentality and nostalgia. She was healthy, intelligent and reasonably independent financially. Her house, her parents' legacy, was, aside from being valuable, a place that cried out for a child's sound to fill its comparative vastness.

Such contemplation was taking up serious time in her thoughts, becoming less and less an impractical dream. She had read about others having done it quite successfully and single parenting was a commonplace situation for many. Technologically speaking, she was ready for impregnation. These days she was relying on the old-fashioned diaphragm. Not like the pill. No waiting period required for fertilization.

True, in her own mind, a female single parent alone might not be in the ideal state for child rearing. But surely she had the capacity to provide enough love and caring to satisfy and nurture a child. Was it pure selfishness on her part? She had grown to understand the motives of many of her black single female colleagues who had deliberately had their children. Few had regrets. Their reasons were arguably somewhat simple, shortsighted and naïve. Now we have someone to love and to love us, they told her. It was their universal cry and it had touched her finally. Selfishness aside, a woman's natural role was to bear children, to give life. Wasn't it?

Emotionally, she had not found a suitable mate. Nor would she compromise on that issue. Perhaps, she admitted, she was hung up on her father, was searching for replication. Or maybe she simply had lousy luck in the matter of long term relationships. Of course, it was partially her own fault. Perhaps she was too selective, too overly analytical, too independent.

She had determined that the distribution system involved in mating was definitely faulty, especially in the role she played professionally. It wasn't likely that you could meet the man of your dreams in the Washington Metropolitan Police Department.

Perhaps she was too much of a threat, too strong-willed and painfully frank and honest to be a good wife, but that didn't disqualify her from being a good mother. What she wanted also was a good child, good genetically, physically and mentally. No guarantees on that, but she could not, after all, have just anyone's child. Besides, an attractive specimen had a leg up under any circumstances. The rest, like loving and sharing and decency and kindness, all qualities that she wanted her child to have, were environmental. Up to her. Was she ready?

She contemplated a strategy that might leave the decision partially in the hands of fate. They were going off to Harper's Ferry tomorrow, had booked a quaint room with a canopied bed in a charming little inn. If the deed was to be done, she had decided that it must be done away from her parents' house, away from the constriction of a place that still echoed with her mother's prohibitions. She had gotten over the screwing part, but conception was really heavy duty, another matter entirely.

Despite the fact that she had rationalized the guilt part in terms of her mother, she had not quite jumped the hurdle of the principal deceit. Not telling Greg.

One thing was certain. He would never consent to it. He had children to whom he was devoted and he had often hinted, despite his love for them, that their existence greatly complicated any easy exit from his disastrous marriage. Nor would he react kindly to any confession of conception. That situation was just too painful to contemplate.

And telling him after the fact of birth would greatly compromise her independence and disturb the child's life. It wouldn't do wonders for Greg either. He would be appalled, probably think it was all a ploy to entrap him. She was certain, based on his own testimony in other contexts, that he could be very, very nasty if he thought of himself as attacked, beleaguered or double crossed. He admitted possession of a singular killer instinct.

As for loving him in the truly traditional romantic sense, she doubted that this involvement with him was the so-called real thing. Or, perhaps, she deliberately resisted such vulnerability. One or the other. It was quite possible that he loved her, at least to the limits of his capability, but his agenda did not include another marriage, nor was he planning any imminent divorce from his present spouse. The fact was that she could not imagine him as her husband. He was too shrewd, his mind, although bright, too devious, his value system, to put it kindly, too flawed.

Perhaps she was deliberately painting his moral life in darker colors than they deserved. Most power driven Washington lawyers represented dubious causes and clients if the price was right. Moral compunctions rarely interfered with fees. As registered foreign agents and lobbyists, propriety, patriotism, loyalty and honor were hardly obstacles to yeoman service. They were simply hired guns on sale to the highest bidders.

And Greg served some beauts, killer countries like Libya and Iraq, cults like the Moonies and Hare Krishna, the tobacco lobby, certain well-publicized industrial polluters. He didn't lose a mini-second of sleep about it. Not Greg Taylor, master of justification, rationalization, obfuscation and persuasion. No argument was immune to his convoluted little homilies of logic. A lawyer is a conduit. He merely advocates. Money is neutral. Nothing was hidden. Agents are regulated and policed. Representing the devil incarnate was perfectly acceptable Washington conduct for a lawyer. Somebody had to represent the bad guys. The Constitution says so.

But despite all his obvious character flaws, she was enormously attracted to him physically. In that department they were explosively compatible. All right, she admitted, sometimes his smug contentiousness was trying, but there were glorious compensations. To keep the peace, they had both learned the value of surrender on issues that separated them.

Not that she was any Joan of Arc. But in her musings, maybe she had to accept him as unthinkable husband material to further explain the impending deed of using him to impregnate herself.

She had even worked out a tentative compromise for her conscience. One day she would tell him. Perhaps when the child was ready for college. Or later. She would work that out. As for the child's own inquiries as to the identity of his or her daddy, she would come up with a plausible explanation, one that, she hoped, would not backfire emotionally. But all that was getting ahead of oneself. Wasn't it?

Greg stirred beside her, stretched in his sleep and turned on his back, showing his handsome face, years younger in repose. Yes, we would make a helluva pretty baby, Mommy, that I could guarantee. She lifted the comforter again. Take a gander at that, Mommy. Does God's look like that? If he does, then I promise you I will run, not walk, back to the bosom of the Church. She could not restrain a giggle.

Lightly, she touched his chest, put her palm flat between his pectoral muscles, then lightly traced a single finger downward, lingering briefly at his navel, then following the hair trail south. Is that something, Mommy? See how it obeys natures commands, rises to glory. Dear God, a thousand hosannas for the joy of this life. She felt suddenly an enormous sense of power and it felt, well, delicious.

The telephone's ring put a quick damper on her mood and she dropped the comforter. Pity, she thought. Curtain going down on joy. Quickly she transformed herself, stepped over the line into her other life.

"Yo," she said.

"Got one with your name on it, FitzGerald," the Eggplant said, his voice still hoarse with sleep. Luther Greene, Big Bad Black Rabbi of Homicide, head of the division. He had the knack, like those who can divine water in the ground, for absolute accuracy in finding the perfect inappropriate moment. "Eggplant" was a sobriquet with obscure origins, but somehow it had stuck, implying pigheadedness, which was accurate, and brainlessness, which was not. But it worked for her and her colleagues at MPD as a vent for frustration as well as something that signified on occasion, familial affection.

"You can't, chief," she whined. He had promised her three unassailable days off. It would have given her a five day weekend. And Greg had rearranged his busy schedule to oblige. Was this to be God's sign, her mother's message to cease and desist? She tucked such a thought back in the guilt box of her psyche and closed the lid. My life, Mommy, she berated the specter. Such interdiction was hardly fate intervening. It was a common malady in the cop business.

"I feel bad about it FitzGerald. I really do," the Eggplant said, not without sarcasm as he cleared his his throat.

"Bullshit," she said, the accent very heavy on the last syllable. It was, she knew, to be taken as a comment of deep disapproval, not a lack of respect. Actually, Luther Greene, was a man beleaguered and bedeviled. But he had developed a strategy to cope with harassment. As a captain of homicide, he wore a mask portraying him as a ruthless, bureaucratic, by-the-book son of a bitch. But when he took it off, which was rarely, he showed a subtle and singular view of human behavior, revealing the cynicism and optimism at war inside of him. Also the qualities that gave him the uncanny sixth sense of a persuasive leader. He knew what buttons to press to motivate his people, and collaterally get the best out of them.

She felt Greg stir beside her.

"Tell him to fuck off," he said. Apparently, he had gotten the full import of the conversation from Fiona's reactions.

"Wait'll you hear, FitzGerald," the Eggplant said.

7

"It's sadistic," Fiona snapped, although she knew that there was no reprieve. The Eggplant rarely backtracked.

"One of your tribe, a congresswoman. Name of Frances McGuire." He waited for her reaction.

"Talk about stereotyping people," she sighed, knowing, of course, what he meant. A woman, Irish and, more to the point, a politician. "My father was a senator, remember." It struck her as facetious. But it probably reinforced his perspective that Frances McGuire was, indeed, a member of Fiona's tribe.

"Tell the bastard to wait 'till Monday for chrissakes," Greg said. He had raised himself on one elbow and started twirling the nipple of her left breast. She let him for a moment, then slapped his hand away.

"Murder?"

Harper's Ferry, once such a compelling idea, faded quickly. She would have to pick another time to do the deed.

"That or suicide. We're not sure. Blake and Harris are on the scene. I'm leaving in a minute. It's your meat and I want you on it, Fitzgerald. You call Cates and shake your ass."

"Where?"

"4000 Mass. Avenue. Apart. 4J."

She was already off the bed, standing naked in the faint morning chill, locked into the idea, no longer the reluctant dragon. A prominent congresswoman. Nothing routine about this one.

"Christ, Fiona. This is not just an intrusion on *your* time. What about me? And our weekend?" She put a hand over the mouthpiece and offered a hurried explanation.

"I'm sorry as hell, Greg. We've got a dead congressman." She paused and smiled to herself. "Woman," she added. "Congresswoman." Normally, she rebuked fellow cops who made the error, less on principle than to razz their machismo. "Feeemale, sans Johnson, bro," she would tease. She looked at the pouting Greg and shrugged apologetically.

"Give the stud a raincheck, FitzGerald," the Eggplant quipped. "And move it. We want to get there before any press party."

He hung up. What he meant, of course, was that he was going

precisely because there was bound to be a press party. The Eggplant, ever the thespian, loved the role. Probably dressed to the ears in his brown striped Sunday suit, shoes spit-shined, white shirt crisp, shiny gold tie clip pulling together a high collar over a red silk tie. Hambone, she smirked.

"Only good legislators are the dead ones," Greg said moodily.

She wasn't sure whether this remark was meant to be cranky dark humor generated by pique or serious political comment. She decided on the former.

"That's a sickee, Greg."

"I was speaking figuratively," he muttered. "Who was the lucky lady?"

"Frances McGuire."

His reaction surprised her.

"Frankie McGuire," Gregg mulled, shaking his head. His face contorted into a sardonic smile which puzzled her. "So the bitch bought it."

"You knew her?"

He seemed to be smirking. His reaction was baffling.

"Only in passing, which was more than enough." She caught the hate in his voice. "Holy Roller, papist variety."

"My, the man is cryptic this morning," she said. "You're talking gibberish."

"Right-to-Lifer, baby." He reached out and patted her on the belly. "If it was up to them, you don't own this anymore. Plant the seed of mankind in there and you're just a meat wagon. Only you're not allowed to drive it yourself until the goods are delivered."

"What the hell are you talking about, Greg?"

"The corpse. Lady Goody-Good-Good. Abortion, Fi." His vehemence shocked her, a real rant.

"That's politics. Not a motive," Fiona said.

"That was my wife Amy's big number. The Right-to-Life. High sounding right? Moralistic. Self-righteous. God's work. Save the child. I lived it all. Frankie was a combat general. Amy, a battalion commander."

Normally, Greg kept his enmity toward his wife repressed most of the time. But occasionally the vitriol would spill over and seep out of him like stagnating pus.

"Ticks me off," he sighed. He made a motion as if he were symbolically brushing away the idea of it.

"I'd never have known," Fiona said, ruffling his hair, trying placation.

"Stay away from causes," he said, grabbing her fingers, kissing them, making an effort to recover their sexy loving mood.

"This is Washington, land of the cause of the month," she said, hoping the way she said it would lighten his mood. He continued to kiss her fingers, but she could see his thoughts were drifting and he looked pained and vulnerable.

"Fanaticism is corrosive, Fi. It eats away at a person. I lived with it. A bitch, I tell you, a real downer. I saw how it changed Amy. Forced vindictive reactions in me." He shook his head. "After awhile even the pros and cons of the issue become obscured by the obsession." Looking up at her, he reached out and embraced her around the waist with both arms. She could feel the sprouts of his morning beard against her flesh as she caressed his face.

"I get low marks on organized causes," Fiona said. "And in my business I have only one cause."

"What's that?"

"The truth. That's as lofty as I get."

She pecked him on the cheek and maneuvered herself out of his embrace. Then she moved with a saucy swing of her hips into the bathroom. Jumping into the shower, she turned on the spigots, getting under the spray before the temperature was comfortable.

"Ouch."

Greg was beside her under the shower just as she got the taps right.

"Somebody really murder her?" he asked.

The Eggplant had said he wasn't sure, that it could be suicide. But murder meant bigger grosses publicity-wise and greater glory. For her as well. A suicide was a one-shot.

"Apparently there's some doubt about it," Fiona replied, lathering the soap bar. "That's my job, Greg. Get at the skinny."

She got a good lather going and began spreading it over her arms. He grew suddenly reflective.

"Funny if they actually got to her, rubbed her out. What gorgeous irony." She stopped soaping and looked at him directly. "Some pro-choicer who got carried away. Show the world there's a real war going on." He stuck his head into the shower stream. "Which side are you on?"

"The side of justice," she said with mock pomposity. On that issue, her defense mechanism was to straddle the political issue. Aborting her own child would be a trauma. Perhaps it is for all women. Beyond that, she refused to be judgmental.

He took the soap from her and started to lather her up. She let him. It felt too good.

"Now that's a cause I can really get into," she murmured, playfully biting an earlobe. He was soaping her in all the right places. She took the bar from him and began to lather him where it counted.

"At least I know where you stand," she murmured.

"And I demand to be heard," he whispered placing his tight athletic body where it would do the most good.

2

BLAKE AND HARRIS were both scowling at her. A black odd couple, Blake was fat and sloppy, his clothes always two sizes too small, emphasizing his bulges. A huge tire of flesh hung over his low slung belt. Harris was thin, ascetic looking, with tiny mice eyes and a patch of moustache like Adolf Hitler's. He looked sinister while Blake normally wore a jolly face. When they weren't torn by jealousy and hate, they were the perfect good guy, bad guy pair.

"The white princess gets the caviar," Harris snarled.

"Not my idea, bro," Fiona said, offering a smile. She could understand their attitude.

"Eggplant's orders," Cates said in his lilting Trinidadian English. Like her, he was a department mismatch with his jet black shiny skin pulled tight over Caucasian features. Barely thirty with a degree in criminology, he was marked Uncle Tom by appearances. He was still struggling with winning respect on the basis of sheer competence and brains.

"Anyway, it ain't caviar. Just plain grits. The lady iced herself," Blake said, showing a big shiny smile.

She offered no response and walked into the bedroom where the Eggplant, dressed exactly as predicted, was conferring with Flanagan who ran the technical team. But her eyes quickly concentrated on the bed where the inert form of Frances McGuire lay in mock slumber. Her body, though, was positioned for sitting, pillows propped, the quilt drawn neatly to her waist, its edges tucked under the mattress. Her large full breasts jutted out under the bodice of a lacy nightgown. She was not centered on the bed, more to the left, probably to catch a better light from the lamp on the night table.

Coming closer, Fiona's nostrils quivered, picking up the smell of wine and she noted a puckering of the quilt near her left hand, as if something had spilled and dried. Fiona sketched a mental image in her mind.

The woman had one of those very Irish faces, light reddish hair, sprinkles of reddish freckles everywhere on her face and arms. Fiona was certain that the rest of her body was also covered with similar constellations. The skin on the face had a curious polished look. Her nose was snubbed and, although they could not be seen, Fiona was certain that her eyes were green. This was a genuine redhead. Looking closer at the neatly brushed short-bobbed hair, she could see the beginnings of grey among the radishy untinted strands.

Age, she figured, somewhere around late forties, although she looked years younger.

The Eggplant approached the bed and held up a glass encased in a plastic envelope.

"Probably cyanide. Has an almondy smell," the Eggplant said.

"You think suicide?" Fiona asked.

"No way," a voice boomed, directing her gaze to a darkened corner. A rotund man rose from a chair. He was balding with a chinless face, all fat, with no neck visible. Instantly she was reminded of a childhood toy, a Shmoo, fat and weighted at the bottom. Impossible to kick over. She chuckled at the sudden recall of this random image.

He needed a shave and had large buck teeth that made him seem as if he were perpetually offering a smile. As he moved toward her, she noted that he was one of those people whose fat grew only in front. From the rear, he probably looked like a thin man.

"This is Harlan Foy, the congresswoman's administrative assistant."

Fiona put out her hand. The man ignored it.

"I can't believe it. She had everything to live for. Besides, I was with her until seven last night. We had a speech scheduled on the floor Monday. It's, it's just so unbelievable."

The man was sweating profusely, his puddled chins quivering.

"People's minds snap," Fiona said, remembering scores of other explanations to unbelieving friends and relatives. She turned to the Eggplant.

"No note?"

"You see," Foy said. "That proves it."

"Sometimes it turns up in the mail in a letter to a close relative or the authorities, often the police." Fiona observed the woman's hands, which looked like they had been sculpted in wax. There was a wedding ring on the finger of her left hand, a simple gold band. "Or to a husband. Or a child."

"She did not kill herself. I'd stake my life on it," Foy said.

"One death is quite enough," Fiona said, instantly regretting the rejoinder. She must curb these little wisecracks, she rebuked herself, keep them inside. No sense offending people needlessly. Cates had shot her his Mother Hen look of admonishment. The Eggplant shrugged, above it all. He wouldn't have been here in the first place if he hadn't smelled press. They'd be here, sure enough, at just about the time the body was being hauled away. Information seepage. She always marvelled at the timing. Hoping for a clear case of murder, she knew he was disappointed.

"It is our job to determine," the Eggplant said with an unmistakable air of rebuke. Also an obvious twinge of disappointment.

"We don't jump to conclusions," Fiona said, true to the tribal instinct. When attacked from outside, the Homicide Division circled the wagons. The subtext here was that the poor bastard was a very unreliable source. By taking her life, Frankie had fired him. Worse, she had done it without consulting him, hardly the proper behavior for a member of Congress toward her administrative assistant.

"It was Mr. Foy who called us," the Eggplant said, offering a tiny sop to compassion.

Foy nodded, chins quivering like pale gelatin. The effort seemed to wind him and he suddenly turned ashen.

"Why not sit down in the other room, Mr. Foy," Fiona told him. "We'd like to talk to you in a few moments." She had, after all, been assigned by the Eggplant to supervise the crime scene. This meant absolute take-charge and despite the boss's presence that was exactly what she intended to do.

Foy, forlorn and bent, like a man twice his age, shuffled out of the room, but gathered enough strength to throw them an exit line.

"No way it was suicide," he muttered.

Blake and Harris had followed her into the room, watching the byplay with Foy as they slumped against the walls as Flanagan's boys went about their professional business, gathering potential evidence, dusting for prints, taking photographs of the crime scene. A uniformed cop was posted at the door.

She turned toward Blake and Harris who looked at each other. Since the boss was present, they had little choice other than to pull out their notebooks. Blake began.

"Harris and I arrived at the scene at five-thirty. Foy had called fifteen minutes earlier from the apartment."

"This apartment?" Fiona asked.

Blake's leer told her her answer. The Eggplant seated himself on the chair vacated by Foy and listened. After all, he needed to bone up for his impending television appearance.

"You don't mean to imply that they were lovers?" Cates asked. A year under his belt and still impetuous, Fiona sighed. Blake had looked at him with the contempt an old pro reserved for a perceived amateur.

"He probably had a key," Fiona piped, choosing to give Cates the put-down herself. "Perfectly logical. AA's are everything to a congressman. Chief honcho, valet, bottle washer, rabbi, the whole nine yards."

"Foy had gotten a call from the congresswoman's husband, John J. McGuire, a contractor in Boston. Couldn't get the wife on the phone. Called all night. Called Foy twice. Foy had dropped her off at the apartment building the night before. Finally, when McGuire called again, Foy got worried and came up here. The guard in the lobby knew him and he let himself in and found this." Blake pointed vaguely to the body. "We found her just as you see her, except that the wineglass has been removed."

"The one I showed you," the Eggplant said. Flanagan's boys would have taken their pictures exactly as the scene had looked before anything was touched.

"Then you got here," Harris hissed, meaning that he and Blake had put everything on hold. "You got it now, white princess."

"Hey, Harris," the Eggplant said. "None of that here."

"You know what I mean," he muttered.

"Go play with your Johnson," Fiona sneered, hurling it at him. She had learned how to deal with these men. Good men with fragile egos, conditioned to the female put-down. Work was a good place to get even with what they got at home and from the beginning she had had to fight back. She was a prime target, a white upper class woman, a honky princess. Later she would have to have a talk with both Harris and Blake, bring them back, restore egos. Cupping their Johnsons, both men pimp-walked away showing their contempt for her.

When they had gone, the Eggplant stood up, pointed a finger at Fiona's nose.

"You wire me in on everything, FitzGerald. Everything. I want to know all theories. I want to be apprised. You get it?" He lapsed deliberately into black talk. "Apprahzed" was the way he drawled it.

"Apprahzed," she mimicked.

He ignored the mimicry and turned to look at the dead woman, studying her as he rubbed his chin. He was, of course, easy to satirize, with his obvious ego, his love of publicity, his sometimes toadying reaction to harassment by those above him in rank, his insistence on absolute loyalty, fealty and protection by those in his command below his rank and his naked ambition to be police commissioner which explained everything else.

At times he could be so transparent it was infuriating. He knew, of course, that he was called "the Eggplant" behind his back and it probably puzzled him as much as them.

In fact, he had the one talent without which a homicide cop was functionally a detective illiterate. He had instinct. And he had it in awesome abundance. She could tell it was operating at full throttle now as he studied the dead woman. Finally, he shook his head.

"Not what it seems," he muttered.

"Maybe," she said, offering no judgment but glancing at Cates whose expression told her clearly that he did not agree with the Eggplant's assessment.

"There has never been a murder of a congressman within the boundaries of the District of Columbia in the history of the Republic," the Eggplant mused.

"You really think murder?" Her eyes cut to the dead woman in the bed.

"You tell me, FitzGerald," he shrugged. "The ball is in your court." She felt butterflies of doubt flutter in her stomach.

The absence of a note beside the body left open a small window of speculation. Every homicide rookie learns in his first week that not all suicides leave notes, although those who took poison averaged out the statistics of say, jumpers, who were the least prone to give their reasons for checking out on life.

Certainly it had all the obvious earmarks of suicide. Like most women, Frankie, as she referred to her now in her mind, had groomed herself for her planned exit. Combed hair, clean nightgown primly drawn to her ankles, a neatly made bed, no clothing carelessly discarded, the room spotless and neat. What about her own detective instincts? Fiona wondered. So far no messages received. Not yet. Give it time, she assured herself.

On cue, just as Flanagan wrapped, a uniformed policeman came in to tell the Eggplant that the press were in the lobby.

"Done?" the Eggplant asked rising from his chair, beginning the preening process.

"Fini," Flanagan said. "And the meat wagon awaits downstairs," he added. He'd been on enough murder scenes to know how to set the props for the Eggplant. Show the body being wheeled into the ambulance. Good picture opportunity for the lead-in.

The Eggplant straightened his tie, drew back his shoulders and patted his jacket. Fiona turned to allow him a private look in the mirror. The technicians from the ambulance brought in a wheeled stretcher and skillfully transferred the body, covered it and strapped it down.

"Benton been notified?" Fiona asked Flanagan, referring to the medical examiner, who was also her closest friend in the department.

"He's sharpening his knives."

She smiled at Flanagan then winked as the Eggplant strutted toward the door. His was not quite a pimp walk, more like black cool, but it did send out its message that Luther Greene was one important dude, indeed. As he walked, he snapped a look toward Fiona, made a mock gun out of his finger and pointed.

"What will you say?" she asked, looking for guidance. Grudgingly, she trusted his instincts.

"Well . . ." He rubbed his chin. "I'll call it a mystery."

"Everybody loves a mystery," she said, feeling as if she had entered into a conspiracy.

3

"GRANDSTANDING," CATES SAID after the Eggplant had left. "No mystery to me. Just wants more time in the limelight."

"That's showbiz."

She was already focusing her attention elsewhere. Her gaze drifted around the bedroom. The bed. The night table. The knickknacks. The pictures. There was a forest of photographs on the bureau. The obligatory happy family tableau, Frankie and her husband, four mick-faced freckled kids, all teenagers. Three boys and a girl. So she had punched them out back to back in, say, a six-year span.

Speculating, she constructed a life for Frances McGuire. Married young, a girl child brainwashed by the nuns, a good Catholic who made all the shots count. Husband, puffed up and dead serious, a real Irish rooster proud of his dick's work. The photo looked, from the clothing and hairstyles, five, maybe six years old. The other photographs were older. Mom and Dad over in the corner in their silver frame. Old fashioned folks, upwardly mobile shanty Irish, Ma stiff in a corset, Da tight-suited smiling toothily into the lens.

There was a smaller colored picture of the Virgin Mother hung randomly on the wall in a cluster of celebrity pics, the deceased with Reagan, the deceased with Carter. That meant at least ten years in office, five terms at least. There was also a picture of Frankie with the pope. She with her head covered, obviously a private audience shot. Greg had called her the pro-life lady. Was there another stand for an Irish lady in an Irish Catholic district in South Boston? Was the pope Catholic?

She soaked up other details, until the uniformed policeman stationed at the door came in, a young black man with an Eddie Murphy moustache.

"Fat guy's still here."

She had forgotten, her mind absorbed in assembling the scene's bits and pieces. She made copious notes in her notebook, drew pictures as well. Perhaps tomorrow a note would surface, a letter to the husband or the kids, making all her speculations about murder irrelevant.

The fat man sat slouched in a heavy upholstered couch, his body looking as puffy as the large throw pillows that adorned it. Above the couch was a nest of plaques. Knights of Columbus for Distinguished Service, The Royal Order of Hibernians, Honorary Member. A Kentucky Colonel certificate, a plaque from the Boston chapter of B'nai B'rith, an elaborate certificate from the Pro-Life National Coalition and others. A typical politician's trumpeting wall. This was merely a fraction of the collection. Her office would be lined with them. Her home in Boston as well.

"This is a big shock," the fat man said. He looked exhausted and his eyes were shiny and moist in their deep pockets of fat.

"I assume her husband has been notified."

"I called him immediately."

"Before or after you called the police?" Cates asked. They had settled themselves in upholstered chairs facing him on the couch.

"Is that significant?" the man asked.

"Everything is significant," Cates responded. He looked toward Fiona. His thoughts were transparent. If it's showbiz, then I'll play my role. But it's only for the money.

The fat man pursed his lips and scratched his thinning pate.

"I called him first. After all, he is her husband." There was something awry in the way he said it, resentful.

"Then you called the police," Cates said pleasantly. They were sliding him into it, taking it easy.

"And you saw her at seven when she left the office?" Cates asked. They had worked out a system. Whoever chose the easy ones, the other took the hard ones. Cates was on easy.

"Yes. We had gone over the speech points for Monday. She was going up to the District. Catholic Charities. A good group for us. Large and supportive. She could hold a crowd, Frankie could. Everyone called her Frankie. A natural politician. She was only thirty-six when they sent her up."

Made her maybe forty-six, forty-seven, Fiona calculated, remembering now that the *Washington Post* had put her on the cover of *Style* years ago. Pert and feisty, they had called her. She looked a good ten years younger.

"As far as I could see," Foy said. "She wasn't depressed, showed no signs of, you know, anything that might suggest that she would take her own life."

The fat man looked at his hands which were remarkably thin, not pudgy, but small and tapered, white and clean. Without the fat, he would appear fastidious. There was an air of the effeminate about him. The self-study of his hands suggested that he was masking hesitation.

"She could have slipped into a sudden depression. Many people can keep their real feelings to themselves. Maybe something hit her, a dark thought, some terrible mental blow?" Cates coaxed, exchanging glances with Fiona.

The fat man moistened his lips. However gentle the interrogation, it was making him uneasy.

"The Irish are a moody people," he sighed. "Frankie was no exception. She could be tough. She hated to lose and losing made her moody." He looked up from his hands and gathered his thoughts. "She was up last night I can tell you. Happy. She had got the President's men to push once again on the prayer amendment. Good stuff for our district. No. She was really up, back to her old self." Poor choice of words and he was the first to notice. He was running on inertia now, still protecting the lady's political image, doing his job. A congressman's principal chore, above all else, was to run his or her reelection campaign. This took priority over everything. Two years rolled around like lightning. Image making had to be done on the run.

"Back to her old self, you said," Fiona intervened. Instinct and practice could pick out the hard ones, like fruit graders working a conveyer belt.

"I hadn't meant . . ." the fat man began, chins rippling. She could see a palpitating beat in the skin puddle.

"Nevertheless you must have meant . . . ," Fiona said drawing out the sentence, staring into his fatigued eyes. She waited until she could tell the long pause was unnerving him. ". . . that sometime in the near past she was off her feed."

The expression confused him. Getting it finally, he made an effort to retrieve his confidence.

"She was under the weather last week. Probably a bug going around."

"Making her mopey," Fiona pressed. "Sort of out of it. Something like that."

"Yeah, something like that."

"Not all there? Not her usual bouncy self? Like . . ." Fiona paused and fixed her eyes on his. ". . . her monthlies." Fiona smiled benignly, wondering suddenly if the lady was still menstruating normally.

"Something like that, yeah," Foy nodded, obviously hoping this would end it.

"So that when things happen, things go wrong as they always do, her reaction was more touchy than usual."

"Fair to say," he nodded.

"So what went wrong last week that made her more touchy?" Fiona snapped, cracking the whip. Foy blanched. Fatigue had obviously slowed down his obfuscation. Tremors were rippling his chins. She watched him for a long moment, letting his uncertainty work itself out. "She's dead, Harlan," Fiona said, soothingly. "We have no desire to soil her memory. Two choices here. Suicide or murder. Sometimes people just snap. Happens all the time. But murder implies enemies at work, hate and vicious acts."

"I just want her to rest in peace," he muttered, ever the loyal retainer, although it must have occurred to him that suicide meant she'd left him in the lurch, betrayed him.

"Can she?" Fiona prodded gently, invoking the Catholic hereafter, always a sure-fire way to get a good Catholic's attention, stir up the supernatural. Think of her as watching you now, she told him silently. Judging your performance. Only the truth will set you free. And her.

"We were working on a speech for Monday," he mumbled, but with less conviction than before.

"But she wasn't her usual self?" Cates interjected.

Foy shrugged, rippling his chins.

"Something was bugging her?" Fiona coaxed.

"Not easy in the trenches," he sighed. "Getting beat on the head by both sides. Sometimes they don't think we're doing enough. And fighting off the damned liberals . . ." His voice cracked, then faded away.

"You're talking politics not personal?" Cates asked.

"Hell," Foy said regaining his voice, looking at Cates with contempt for his ignorance. "It's all politics. Nothing is personal. We had two issues. They dominated everything. Abortion and prayer in the schools. For us, that was it. Frankie was the Right-to-Life lady. Everybody knows that. And one day we're going to beat those murdering sons of bitches . . ." His face had flushed a deep scarlet. No question about the depths of his commitment. "Sometimes they would actually accuse her of not doing enough. Not enough? Shit."

"Who are they?"

"May Carter, for one."

"Who is May Carter?" Fiona asked.

"You don't know?" Foy looked at her then took in a deep breath of exasperation. "She's on the National Board of Right to Life for chrissakes and she lives in our district. May is a key player. But she never let up on Frankie. Not for a minute. Called every day. You could set your watch by her."

"Frankie didn't like her?" Cates asked.

"Not easy to like, I can tell you," Foy said.

"She like Frankie?"

Foy thought about that and took his time over the answer. It wasn't simple for him anymore.

"May Carter is the living embodiment of a sacred cause."

"What the hell does that mean?" Cates asked, growing testy, stretching his nice guy role,

"It means," Fiona said, drawing from her father's experience.

"That she judged people only by their level of commitment to the cause."

Foy nodded, obviously thankful for the help.

"Also by the level of results. I can also tell you it wasn't easy in a Congress dominated by abortionists and Godless liberals. No matter what Frankie did it was never enough for May." He was silent for a moment, mulling something, straining against the repression of years.

"She's gone," Fiona said softly.

Foy shrugged, the decision made. He sucked in a deep breath. You got it Foy, Fiona thought. Dead is dead.

"We were just as committed as that bitch," Foy hissed, biting his underlip, then raising his eyes, showing his long endured pain. He was the buffer between the hostile world and his charge, the congress-woman, his queen and master.

Fiona imagined she could see more in him than just a lackey's level of devotion. Encased in that mass of frontal flesh was, quite obviously, the beating heart of a sensitive and vulnerable man. Mentally undressing him, she shuddered, then shrugged. In her game, attraction was always a mystery and she had seen her share of mismatches. It was a consideration, a base to be touched. Conventional wisdom and popular images had little relevance when probing the dark side of human motivation. Only free ranging speculation was relevant to the detective's art. Lackey or lover? Grist for the mill.

"We were as committed as May, although it was never enough. Never." Guard down, Foy was letting the pus squirt from the long-festering wound. "Problem was, Frankie never could attain May's level of hate and confrontation. She hated all those who were against the cause and would piss and moan whenever Frankie was seen with the enemy like her colleagues on the subcommittee who didn't share her view. That's the Subcommittee on Health and Labor of which she was a member. She wanted Frankie to be in a perpetual state of war. No intercourse with the enemy. Explaining to May that you had to get along, especially with the leadership, most of whom were the opposition, was like talking into a cloud."

"What enemy?" Fiona asked, picking up on the word.

"Not enemy in the sense of raw hatred. Not that kind of enemy. Let's say political enemy, which did not rule out human friendship."

"Like who?" Fiona pressed.

"I don't know. Bob Preston, the Minority Whip. Charlie Rome, chairman of the subcommittee. That really set May off. Hell, Charlie opposed everything that Frankie stood for, a real bleeding heart that one. But Charlie and Barbara, his wife, were buddies with Frankie. Hell, they live in this building. In fact, lots of important people live in this building. May Carter didn't even like Frankie living in the same building with the . . . the so-called enemy. I tried to explain to the bitch. That's not the way the system works."

Apparently this May Carter had been a thorn in their side and had triggered an avalanche of animosities, which, once the pus boil was lanced, kept him running at the mouth until finally Fiona interposed the essential question.

"Does May want Frankie's seat?"

Wheels within wheels, Fiona knew. A powerful constituency was one thing but wanting to take one's job was quite another.

"Maybe. There's always takers."

"Does she have a chance?"

"She'll be a disaster if she does get it. They'll box her in a corner and let her rave."

"I asked about her chances?" Fiona persisted.

"She'd have to knock off Jack Grady. Been in line for years. Good old party boy. State senator. The idea was for Frankie to eventually go for the Senate with Grady running for her seat." He smirked. "Considering Massachusetts politics we'd all have beards down to here when that could happen. Him and May going at it for Frankie's seat could be Northern Ireland in South Boston. No war like an Irish war."

"So Grady gains from Frankie's death."

"I'm sure he'll think so," Foy shrugged. He paused for a moment. Beads of perspiration had begun to sprout on his upper lip and the ashen skin carried two circles of red flush on either cheekbone. With one finger, he squeegeed off the sweat, wiping it on his jacket. "Problem is Jack's got lots of skeletons. Things you can do in the State

House you can't do in Congress. Opponent like May would go for the jugular."

"Did Frankie and Jack get along?" Cates asked. He was, as always, traveling in her wake, building theories out of this latest cast of characters. He may have believed in Frankie's suicide, but he was determined, as always, to look under every rock.

"You might say Jack was family." A strange gurgle bubbled up from the jelly of his chins. Fiona caught the unmistakable whiff of sarcasm. "He was a buddy of Jack McGuire. Choir boys together sort of thing. Known as the two Jacks. McGuire was the Jack of Diamonds. Grady the Jack of Clubs."

"How come?"

Foy shot her a gaze of incredulity as if she was supposed to know all this Congressional District lore.

"McGuire is loaded. Road construction. Need I say more. Who gives out the contracts? And Grady's committee is Highways. Also appropriation. The two Jacks. Name fits. Grady has one helluva club. Got it?"

"Power boys," Cates said, a statement without a purpose.

"Yeah," Foy nodded.

No mistaking the obvious, Fiona thought. There was no love lost between Foy and both men. Went with the territory, Fiona decided, remembering Ronnie Schwartz, her father's AA, the man in the middle, protector and liar for the great one. Daddy was the sun and the moon to Ronnie, the alter ego. It had clout, true, but the job, by definition, assumed an obliteration of persona in the service of the great one.

"I'm really bushed," Foy said. His face had grown from pure ashen to grey and the little flush marks were fading.

"What about you, Foy?" Fiona asked.

"Me?"

"Not unheard of for an AA to make a run for the seat when a member leaves. Or dies."

Foy, whose body had been immobile on the couch, like a sack of potatoes thrown carelessly, all bulgy in the wrong places, suddenly stirred, the fat quivering.

"Hadn't thought about it," he lied. It was, of course, presumptuous to think that, but she could sense that it was an ever looming option, perhaps just taking root, but quite a powerful urge. Besides, one could sense he would not be the first choice of either Grady or Carter for AA, despite his expertise.

"But it is possible," Fiona pushed. "I mean if you decided after checking it out with the folks back home." A long shot, perhaps. But one never knew. Lyndon Johnson, along with a number of those holding office in the present House and Senate, had once been an AA.

"Anything is possible," Foy said.

"Even Jack McGuire," Fiona interjected, like folding a dropped card back into the deck.

Foy's lips stretched over his buck teeth in a smile of unmistakable sarcasm. Even a gurgle of a laugh rolled out of his throat.

"Jack McGuire in politics," Foy snickered. "You've got to be kidding. Jack hates politics, hates it with a passion, hates it more than he hates the Brits."

"I mention it because it's not uncommon for a spouse to take over a seat upon the death of a member of Congress. Of course, it's usually the other way around. The wives get the seat."

"Not McGuire. He's not one for kissing butts. Besides. . . ."

Despite Foy's fatigue, he caught himself up short. Whatever was in his mind, it did not exit by his tongue. Not this time. For all his candor, he was holding back, holding back hard.

"Besides nothing," he sighed. "I forgot what I was going to say. It's been a rough day."

"Just trying to find out who benefits from Frankie's death," Fiona said. Only then did it dawn on Foy what all this interrogation was really about.

"You don't think . . . Jesus. I didn't mean . . ." He seemed to choke on the words, coughing suddenly, his white face growing red with the effort.

"But it was you who said she hadn't killed herself," Fiona said gently.

"I hadn't meant them," Foy sputtered.

"Who then, Foy? Who then?"

At that point, he groped for a handhold on the couch and lifted himself up.

"Really, I'm exhausted. I'm not making any sense."

"Just remember, Mr. Foy," Fiona said, taking careful figurative aim. "It was you that put the idea of murder in our minds."

4

A S MUCH AS SHE TRIED, Fiona could not fully agree
with the Eggplant's instincts. Cates was even more adamant
in his assessment of suicide and as they drove along Massachusetts Avenue in the April sunshine, he continued to be vocal on
his doubts.

"It strains all logical deduction," Cates said in his melodic accent,
but in a tone that did not mask his British education. Often when
in the company of other cops, Fiona felt him straining to blunt the
clipped lilt of his speech patterns, a process he still hadn't completely
mastered.

Cates knew his precise mannerisms made him seem "uppity" to his
colleagues, mostly black men, the sons of postal clerks, janitors, social
workers and low level bureaucrats who had been pushed upscale to
the "Pole Ees" by tough and determined black mamas and by black
fathers hungry for their sons to earn the respect never accorded to
them.

The fact was that Randolph Winston Cates III, was a Trinidadian
version of the same antecedents. His father, a fisherman, had died in
a boating accident when he was five and, years later, while he was
at school in England, a Trinidadian perk left over from British
colonial rule, his mother married a Washington cab driver and made
young Cates an American citizen. From the beginning of his American experience he had made it clear that he was henceforth to be
addressed as Cates, never Randolph and, especially, never Randy, an
eccentricity that encapsulated his character.

Like Fiona, his personal dignity was his dominant priority but it was always at war with his thirst for acceptance. Like her, too, he was often outspoken, especially at the least tactful moment. And, also like her, he could be tough, icy mean when cornered, but with very delicate insides, requiring extraordinary discipline to tame his inherent vulnerabilities.

The Eggplant, true to his vaunted instincts had teamed them. At first she had interpreted it as an exercise in nastiness and malice, especially since she had just become an expert, through the Eggplant's previous choice of partners for her, in the care and feeding of the black machismo virus, as opposed to the white machismo virus. She was less of an expert on the latter.

Cates with his jet black shiny skin pulled taut over his distinctively Caucasian features carried neither the black nor white viruses. He started out as an enigma to her, then grew into a perpetual challenge and, finally, into a trusted colleague. But he definitely worked on a different frequency than herself which made the association interesting, although often exasperating.

She had turned on the all-news station, keeping it just audible enough to alert them to any news of the case.

"Do people murder to get the political advantage of being next in line for a House seat?" Cates asked. His academic approach to a killer's motivation was always in direct contrast to her own more gut-oriented modus operandi, although at some point, their approaches invariably intersected.

"Political ambition has a powerful drag," she shrugged, again remembering her father. Such ambition had dominated their lives. Getting elected and reelected was everything and she had been privy to many a conversation that, in retrospect, had had a violent undercurrent.

Remarks like "We'll cut the legs off the bastard" or, "Let's drown the son of a bitch in his own bile" or, "We'll club him to death with his girlfriend" were all phrases that stuck in her mind. Often she had heard such things when her father and his political team held endless discussions around the dining room table which was the only place big enough to hold these all-male meetings. She was never allowed to attend, of course, but their loud raucous tones were easy enough to overhear.

Their remarks with their violent images were commonplace, hardly ominous to her then, merely figures of speech coined by the rough Irishmen among her father's coterie, faces flushed by Scotch and excitement as they talked on into the night through a haze of cigar smoke. Politics, her mother had sighed, forever trying to shoo her far out of earshot. Such talk, punctuated by the foulest of language, was not designed to pollute the ears of nice little Catholic virgins, which made her all the more curious and the talk itself all the more fascinating.

How they reveled in it. How they loved the hurly-burly of the political game. It struck her as so Irish, so subject to the paranoia and parody of the Irish spirit, so punctuated with the Irish sense of grudge wars and dark funks and dire consequences that often appeared, out of the blue, hard on the heels of boundless euphoria and blind optimism. Sharp mood swings were the knell of doom to the vulnerable Irish psyche.

It occurred to her years later that all that late night Irish blarney had little to do with governing, but a great deal to do with getting reelected, knocking off opponents and speculating how Paddy Fitz, as her father, Senator Patrick Ignatius FitzGerald, had been dubbed by the media, could become a presidential contender.

Her mother, ever the lace curtain Irish snob, was appalled by the moniker since it reflected a shanty heritage that she had hoped her marriage to him would obliterate. It hadn't, nor did the common man image it reflected propel him into a serious contender. Perhaps in that were the roots of his self-destruction, although she would never call it anything but "high purpose."

It was true that politics was a bloodsport. But random murder for political advantage was hardly an option of American politics. As opposed to political assassination of our Presidents which was frequent enough in America to be embarrassing. The thought triggered an idea.

"Maybe for a cause," she told him. "Comes under the heading of ideological reasons."

"Right to Life?"

"Could be. Don't they call abortionists murderers? These touchy causes make people violent. People on McGuire's side used bombs on abortion clinics. Could be an act of vengeance."

"You're not serious?" Cates asked.

She shrugged.

"Anything is possible."

Although it was purely a tease on her part, she knew he was mulling it over, looking for logic.

"Maybe I'd buy that if it was more violent. A cutting maybe, a real hack job, say, or a shotgun blast, something that made a real political statement. Perhaps even the bloody work of a fanatic, something outside of the committees that ran strategies for causes. A loner who needed to leave a brutal calling card." He tapped his lips with a thin graceful ebony finger, a familiar tick of his when concentrating. "But a poisoning. Its too low-key for ideological motivation."

Peripherally, she felt him look toward her, his expression earnest. He was about to say more, but Fiona had turned up the volume of the radio.

"Representative Frances McGuire of Massachusetts died today. Known affectionately to everyone as Frankie, Representative McGuire will be best remembered for her strong stand against abortion. The forty-seven-year old congresswoman and mother of four was serving her sixth term. She was discovered in the early morning hours by Harlan Foy, her administrative assistant. We talked earlier with Captain Luther Greene, Chief of Homicide, who was on the scene within moments of being notified."

Fiona harumphed and shook her head.

"Hot dog," she whispered.

"We have not yet determined the cause of death," the Eggplant explained. "Considering the prominence of the deceased, we do not wish to comment at this time until we have fully investigated the situation."

The hook was in. Fiona smirked.

"Does this mean that Representative McGuire did not die of natural causes?" the announcer asked.

"We'll know more when we complete our lab tests," the Eggplant said. "As you know, Bill, our mandate is to investigate every death in the District of Columbia. In the case of a distinguished woman such as Representative McGuire we must be extra thorough as we discharge our responsibility."

Dulcet tones investing the case with great importance. And mystery. On television he would see himself as attractive, brilliant, charismatic, a legend in his own mind. Grudgingly, she gave him high marks as a performer. He had certainly mastered that end of the business. She clicked off the radio.

"More like a hambone than a hot dog," Cates sighed as she accelerated the car down Massachusetts Avenue.

"He set up an appointment," Briggs told them when they arrived back in the squad room. He was the Eggplant's factotum and general handyman, a greying white relic of the time when the MPD was white man's turf. He'd struck his bargain with the Eggplant after being passed over for the job as homicide chief. For him it was smooth sailing until retirement a few months down the road. Mostly, he did routine backup stuff for the Eggplant, handling his scheduling and doling out assignments.

He had a big gut and an ego to match and, although he pretended to be scrupulously color blind, underneath, as everyone knew, he was a hard core red-neck bigot. He had often accosted Fiona outside the office to vent his anger at the "junglebunnies" who had robbed him of his career entitlements.

"You ain't goin' anywhere with the cops, FitzGerald. Three strikes and out. You're a woman, you're a honky and a ballbuster. Ain't no room at the top for that M.O."

"Times change, lieutenant," Fiona would sigh.

"Right, babe. Come a time when instead of any whities in the department, like the ten little Indians, there'll be none."

"A cop's a cop," Fiona muttered. She had tried to believe implicitly in the idea. Someday, she hoped, all this black/white animosity would end. It would never end for Briggs. "All this power's new to them."

"I believed once, FitzGerald. There's a black cloud acomin'. Pitch

33

black. Nigger's are out-screwing us, baby. Power in numbers. Whitey's finished in this town's cops. We're just tokens now. And you're a triple. White, woman, snobby smartass."

No point in explaining to the bastard that she was in the cops for the work and the challenge, that she didn't worry about retirement and was reasonably well-fixed financially.

Yet, for some reason, perhaps racial affinity, she was outwardly more tolerant of him than she might have been to others with the same views. The fact was, that professionally, he was a good cop, a smart detective in his prime. His respect had been won for his work not for his views.

Her earliest, and most surprising, discovery at MPD was that the black cops actually related more to a bigoted red-neck than to the effete liberal. Perhaps it was because both understood each other's anger and hatred. What was it that Foy had said? Something about being too friendly with the enemy?

"An appointment with whom?" Fiona asked, responding to Briggs's pronouncement, glancing at Cates.

Briggs pulled out a pocket-sized battered leather notebook and flipped the pages.

"Jack McGuire, the lady's husband." Taylor looked at his watch. "Bouta half hour in the icebox. McGuire will be there for an ident."

"Thanks for the notice," Fiona smirked.

"And the chief has already requested an autopsy," Briggs added. He enjoyed doling out information piecemeal, a cop's inevitable affliction.

"Moving that fast, is he?" Cates said.

In the case of an ambiguous suicide, it was the detective's option to have an autopsy done. Next of kin, if they were available and notified of the decision, usually balked. They were not anxious to have their loved ones mutilated.

"McGuire know about the autopsy?" Fiona asked, suspecting that the Eggplant had deliberately ducked him. Undoubtedly, he had already calculated the case's political fallout, which was just beginning to dawn on Fiona. Congress, after all, still controlled much of the District government's purse strings and there was some currency in protecting the image of those stalwart legislators.

"Not exactly," Briggs answered.

"Who notified him to show for an ident?"

"I did." Briggs tipped his head in the direction of the Eggplant's office. "I just follow orders."

"Then he signed off and left us the shit detail," Fiona said, clucking her tongue.

She turned her back on Briggs and walked over to her battered metal desk, identical with the others in the squad room. As always it was three-quarters empty with most of the detectives out on the street. Mornings were a kind of garbage collection service, scouting the O.D.s, suicides, and homicides and checking out the routines, the natural deaths.

Mostly death came at night, but the cleanup came in the morning. It was also, for some unknown reason, seasonal. The grim reaper worked overtime in the summertime. Not that he ever really rested. Certainly not in the capital of one of the most violent countries on earth.

She called Dr. Benton, but couldn't get him on the phone and had to talk to his assistant, a young woman named Melanie Marks.

"He's been on the tables for the last three hours," Melanie said in her squeaky voice with its broad, pronounced 'brawd', New York, pronounced 'New Yawk', accent.

"We did big business last night." She giggled nervously. When Fiona didn't respond to the humor on cue she grew more serious. "We had seven murders and three O.D.s. They're being taken in priority order."

"What about McGuire?"

"Just a sec." She paused and looked over a clipboard, which she took from a wall hook.

"As we speak," Melanie said.

So it's rush rush down the line, Fiona thought. Means the Eggplant's got the mayor's backing. Maybe some kind of leverage deal in the works. There was no end to political machinations between the D.C. government and its resident nemesis and provider, the Congress of the United States of America.

"We're meeting the spouse there, Melanie. Tell Doc to clean up the lady as much as he can. And keep a lookout for him. Jack McGuire." Jack of Diamonds, she remembered. A man named Grady was the Jack of Clubs.

She had never quite hardened to the corpse identity process, although she was tolerating it better than the first time when she had thrown up and fainted. But the man's head had been crushed by a six-wheeler and the wife had also been carried out. Since then, she had seen equally horrible corpses, broken, mutilated, dismembered and decapitated. It was not exactly the sight of the corpses that made her queasy. It was the reaction of the next of kin. For them it was always awful and it was for them that she bled, although she no longer threw up or fainted.

5

J ACK MCGUIRE, was a big man, puffed up with Irish pride, although this wasn't the moment to judge him on that score. He was red-faced, veiny around the nose, which meant long acquaintance with John Barleycorn, and he had smooth grey hair combed with a dead-straight part about two inches above his left ear. His eyes were chocolate brown, the whites covered with a network of red lightning bursts.

He wore a well-fitted grey suit, rumpled from his morning's travels, and an appropriate black tie. And he made no effort to be ingratiating. He shot Fiona a glance that clearly meant that he was used to power and command.

On the surface, he did not look like a grieving man, more like a man annoyed to have to suffer this interruption in his busy life. He was getting increasingly impatient and nasty, despite their attempts to soothe him with condolences and testimonials to his deceased wife. His reaction was merely to acknowledge their words with a grunt. He was not interested in conversation. Fiona and Cates were obviously perceived by him as mere functionaries with whom he was not obliged to have any peer dialogue.

She and Cates were stalling him in the outer office, waiting for word that Mrs. McGuire had been "reassembled" and returned to the icebox, a large whitewashed room with refrigerated drawers which stored the bodies until disposition.

"You didn't have the right to move her here," he muttered. "No

37

right." He looked directly at Cates, then gazed around the room. Various official personnel passed through.

"Standard procedure," Fiona said. It wasn't quite standard, but standard for a case of this sort, an ambiguous suicide.

"Shithouse," he grumbled. "Whole goddamned city. Bunch of dummies. Do nothing but fuck up the country." He lowered his voice to barely a whisper. Fiona heard it. "Mau Maus." If Cates heard it he did not acknowledge it.

She had opted for tact, knowing that this was to be a traumatic moment. She had wanted to ask many questions, but she had deliberately demurred, postponing them until he had recovered from the aftershock still to come. All efforts to engage him in conversation ended in failure and finally they let him stew in his own anger.

"Ready now."

It was Melanie herself, dressed in a crisp white smock that led the way to the cold room. She was a small woman who knew her job. Along with the smock, she had donned the appropriate expression for the deed. She had often done this chore and was remarkably inured to it. "My father owned a kosher butcher store in Brooklyn," she had explained, although the comparison, when dredged up in memory, always gave Fiona the willies.

Accompanied by Cates and Fiona on either side of him, they followed Melanie to a drawer. She bent toward it and rolled it out, a slab on which was a sheet-covered corpse. Fiona kept her eyes fixed on McGuire. The bright lights picked out the crimson network of veins on his nose.

Waiting for the dead face to be uncovered, his breathing became labored. She had seen it before. A man steeling himself, anticipating the pain, holding on to control. This could not be an easy chore, even for the Jack of Diamonds.

Melanie drew down the sheet to the neck of what had once been Frances McGuire. Surprisingly, she appeared even younger than she had looked on the bed, the bones beneath the skin more clearly defined, the freckles faded. They let the spectacle sink into Jack McGuire's consciousness. He was clearly moved. He crossed himself. His forehead rippled and tics began in both cheeks. His eyes moistened and fluttered and his lips trembled.

"Is this your spouse Frances McGuire?" Cates asked.

"That's Frankie," he whispered, bowing his head. When he lifted it finally all the crimson network on his face had turned blue and his complexion matched the sheet. Melanie quickly slid the drawer closed. McGuire stood there for a moment, looking mutely at the drawer's metal faceplate. Then he shook his head and walked slowly out of the room.

"Goddamn," he said when they had returned to the waiting room. "She didn't have to do that."

"Do what, Mr. McGuire?"

The Irishman lifted his eyes. The blood had returned to his face, filling the veiny tributaries and putting color back into his skin.

"What the hell does that mean?"

"I'm sorry, Mr. McGuire," Cates said. "These questions have to be asked."

He looked directly into Cates's eyes, narrowing his own, attempting to stare him down.

"You mean you don't think she committed suicide?"

"I think we'd all be better off if we sat down quietly in that office," Fiona said, pointing to the empty office off to one side that was reserved for such discussions. McGuire hesitated, looking confused, but he followed Fiona into the room. Cates joined them. Fiona pulled out the chair from behind the desk and the three of them sat facing each other.

"There was no note found in her apartment," Fiona began.

"Did you receive one?" Cates asked.

He looked at them and shook his head.

"You may get one in the mail in a couple of days," Fiona said. "That should dispose of the matter. Any of your children receive a suicide note from their mother?"

"No. They would have told me."

"That's a drastic step, suicide," he sighed. "Can't understand it."

"The thing is, Mr. McGuire," Fiona said, "we can't be sure."

"Not sure."

"We might have a better idea when we receive the autopsy report."

"Autopsy?"

39

He rose to his feet, seething, his face blood red with anger.

"Autopsy? Who the fuck gave you permission to perform an autopsy on my wife?"

"We have that right, Mr. McGuire," Fiona said, gently. She had been through this before.

"We'll see about that," McGuire said, standing up, pointing a pudgy finger in Fiona's face. She noted a ring with a diamond on his pinky. Royal Order of Hibernians. She recognized the symbol. "I want your badge number." He shifted his attention to Cates. "Yours, too. There'll be hell to pay. I swear it."

They swiftly withdrew their card cases, Cates from his pocket and Fiona from her pocketbook. On each was the person's name, the homicide division, address, telephone and badge number. He seemed startled by the speed of the reaction, took the cards and put them in a side pocket of his jacket.

"We have to ask questions, Mr. McGuire. You can't blame the messenger," Cates said.

He muttered and grumbled, then began to pace the little room. He was a strong bulky man, rough-hewn. Probably hell on his workers.

"Did she have any reason to commit suicide, Mr. McGuire?" Fiona asked.

His reaction was silence, but she wasn't sure he was stonewalling, just unsure and confused.

"Did you notice anything different about her recently?" Cates asked.

"Different?"

"Was she depressed?"

"Depressed? Frankie? Hell, no. Not her. She got angry, but never depressed."

Fiona caught the undercurrent, the unmistakable hint of sarcasm. She cut a glance at Cates.

"Why not her?" Cates pursued.

"Too tough, Frankie was, to let herself get down. She could shrug things off. Nothing bothered her. Not Frankie."

Again she caught an undercurrent. This time a tinge of regret, as if he would have welcomed a streak of vulnerability in his wife.

"In a suicide," Cates said, measuring his tone, "something usually bothers a person who commits it."

McGuire seemed to draw into himself, reassessing his words. Then he shrugged and responded.

"What the hell reason would she have? She had it made. Hell, she was a member of Congress. Her father was a bartender for crissakes. Her mother was a maid, a chamber maid for Hilton. She had dough. Four kids. All grown now. She was a celebrity. She had clout. What the hell else did she want?" He stopped pacing abruptly and stared into space. His eyes glazed. "All in all a good woman. A good mother. A God-fearing woman." He paused for a long time with that glazed spacey look, then slowly got hold of his sense of place again. "She had no good reason to do this. None. She was master of her fate. No good reason."

"Are you implying that someone else did it?" Fiona asked gently. It was in essence the same question that they had asked Foy.

"Someone else?"

"A murderer," Fiona emphasized.

"Frankie murdered?" He seemed aghast. "Why would anyone want to murder Frankie?"

"Could have been for ideological reasons. She was the number one enemy of the abortion gang," Fiona said, her tone implying a commitment. Do I really feel like that? she wondered. At that moment, she fully comprehended the power of the issue's politicization. What would it take for her to abort her own child? She shivered at the prospect. And other women? What did it take for them? Was that the issue? It was so personal, so intimate. She shrugged it away.

"Politics is politics," McGuire said. "I've seen some bruising scraps in my day. But murder . . ." He shook his head.

"Then you are convinced it was suicide."

"Looks like it, doesn't it?" he said after a long pause, speaking the words through clenched teeth. By then, he was in full control of himself again, his obviously shrewd mind working in high gear.

"Did you have any hint of it?" Fiona asked.

"Hell no. She was always a lady in charge of herself. She was tough, headstrong. She always knew where she was going."

"Then it is out of character," Fiona coaxed.

"Yeah. I'd say that," McGuire said. "But people have been known to . . ."

"Snap," Cates said helpfully.

"Listen, she was my wife of twenty-seven years. I married her at twenty and we had five kids together. They're all busted up about this, I can tell you. It wasn't very white of her to do this to them. Hell, we could have helped her. But how the hell do you get a hint of it. How the hell do you do that?"

He started to pace again, genuinely troubled. As he walked his lips moved, as if he were cursing silently to himself.

"What was your marriage like, Mr. McGuire?" Fiona asked suddenly.

He bristled at that one.

"None of your fucking business what my marriage was like. I won't have our personal lives explored by anyone. That was our business. Next thing you know you'll be accusing me."

"Of what, Mr. McGuire?" Fiona asked.

"It's unthinkable. You oughta be ashamed."

"You're jumping to conclusions, Mr. McGuire," Cates said.

"Next thing you know you'll actually be asking me where I was last night."

He was sputtering off again into a temper tantrum. They let it work itself out.

"It would be a legitimate question under any circumstances, Mr. McGuire," Cates said. "Look, we're investigating the possibility of foul play. A routine investigation. Also if your wife committed suicide she had to have her reasons. We need to get close to that as well. Wrap things up. A domestic motive is quite common. She must have been unhappy about something. The first question that always comes to mind in a case like this is: Was she happy in her marriage?"

Of course he was uncomfortable with the question, but Fiona could feel the wheels working to devise a proper answer. He had already telegraphed the message. How could anyone be truly happy in a marriage where the partners were separated most of the time? That was more like an arrangement. Perhaps, she thought, the proper question would be: Was she unhappy with the arrangement? It was a question that quickly found her voice.

"Arrangement?"

"Did you spend much time together?"

"No we didn't. How could we? She was in Congress and I had a construction business to run. No way we could. But we've been doing that for years so it was no hassle. We got together when she came back to Boston."

"Like how many times?" Cates asked.

"I don't count things like that." His defensiveness telegraphed another message. This was no happy marriage. She had to come up to service her district. Probably quick trips, except during campaigns when the family banded together to help her get reelected. All part of the game.

"Was she happy with this arrangement?" Fiona asked, pressing forward now, watching McGuire marshall his defenses.

"She didn't complain," McGuire muttered. "Besides we did talk on the phone." He bit his lip, then in a strangely swift change of mood, his eyes seemed to catch fire. It reminded Fiona of those comic strip drawings where a light bulb suddenly appears above a character's head saying "bright idea."

"It was me that tried getting her last night. Hell, just check with the apartment lobby desk. I must have called four, five times. I finally had to call Foy." His head rose in a repetitive nod of self-confirmation. "Yeah. We talked on the phone."

"And you?" Fiona pushed. "Were you happy with the arrangement?"

He shook his head and smiled sardonically.

"I don't get the point of all this. I'm the victim here. I just lost my wife. It looks to me like she committed suicide. Whatever the motive, she's dead and while I'm in mourning I really think it's an imposition for you to ask those questions. I'm leaving." He started toward the door and turned. "And I want my wife's body to be sent to the Capitol. Foy is handling it all. There's going to be ceremonies day after tomorrow in the rotunda to honor her. We don't need to be harassed by questions about our personal lives. If you think that

Frankie was murdered, it's up to you to make a case for it. Personally I couldn't believe that in a million years. Frankie snapped is all. She pushed herself too hard. It's a damned shame that we didn't see it coming. Maybe she was just too sick at heart about what she was about to do to write a note. Thought this would be the best, the easiest way out. If that was her wish, then we must respect it. Just don't subject me to this. I don't need it in my life and my kids don't need it either. Frankie was a great lady and in two days we'll honor her memory in the Capitol of the United States, then I'll take her home and bury her next to her folks in our family plot in South Boston."

He pulled the card out of his pocket and read the names. He turned to Fiona.

"And you, FitzGerald, a good Irish girl should know better than to press too hard on a grieving man of the same persuasion. Maybe this one . . ." He nodded toward Cates. ". . . doesn't know better, but I certainly expect you to observe decency and respect. You got any clues that are legitimate and might make me or you change our minds, I'd be happy to hear it. In the meantime get my wife's body the hell out of this shithouse, post haste."

Bully Irish all right, showing his authority, giving them his ass. He had drawn himself up to his full height and walked with exaggerated dignity out of the office and the waiting room. They let him go. It was pointless to argue. They had no facts, not even theories. There was a great deal to say for his argument. If it was, indeed, suicide, which it probably was, then he had a right to balk at those questions.

No, all was not right in the marriage of Jack and the late Frankie McGuire. How could it be?

6

DR. CHARLES BENTON, the Chief Medical Examiner, had the unconscious habit of making cathedrals out of his fingers and fitting the forefingers and middle fingers into the cleft of his chin. It had always seemed to Fiona to be an elaborate but suitable pose for this very wise and very gentle man.

When she had started in homicide, they had established an instant rapport and she had spent long hours with him in the sunny little parlor of his Northeast Washington row house which he had shared with his beloved late wife. Here, she had often unburdened herself, told him of her fears and aspirations and, mostly, her disappointments, especially with men.

"My priest and confessor," she would chide him after one of her many visits. "Catholic habits never die."

"More like a free shrink."

He would chuckle wryly and show his still white even teeth, remarkable for a man of sixty. Often when they were together, she would study his face, which she found endlessly fascinating. He was a light skinned black man with hair as white, but not as fine, as cotton and eyes as blue as a South Pacific lagoon. A good Cajun mix, he had joked in the faintest cadences of a Louisiana drawl.

To be with him was comforting and comfortable. He was, she was certain, a rare find, especially for an orphan girl like herself living astride two worlds, as remote from each other as Earth and Mars.

Most of his emotional life was invested in his past and he had, unlike her, no pressing problems in his contemporary existence, despite the heavy pressures of his job. This gave him the ability to make dispassionate judgments and insights, not blemished by personal baggage. He feared nothing, knew most of the strategies of survival in a bureaucracy and his access to the secrets of the dead had provided him with a wisdom that she was certain few men possessed.

She saw his face now through a haze of cigarette smoke, his only apparent vice. Shafts of early afternoon spring sunlight had begun to spear through the open slats of the blinds in his office. The tobacco smoke could barely mask the medicinal odor that clung to him in this environment. It always came as a pleasant surprise to note that for some reason he had never brought the odors of his job home with him.

He was tired, she knew. It took nearly a full week to complete the work of Washington's normal weekend orgies of blood. Special cases like that of Frankie McGuire added to that burden.

Yet, despite the press of work and the endless parade of corpses, not once had he ever referred to these corpses as "stiffs" or "dead meat." To him, they were all people, their humanity still articulate in their revelations, their dignity still intact. Often he had said that a human being's soul continued to live as long as others retained their memory of them as a living person.

Cates had gone to check on the memorial service planned for Mrs. McGuire and Melanie had run out to get them sandwiches, although lunchtime had long passed.

Fiona had explained to Dr. Benton what she had come about, but there was always more to it than a mere report. In these business dealings between them there existed an elaborate gamesmanship in which the psychological implications of the victim's pathology were invariably broached. It gave every inquiry a cat and mouse quality with roles reversing frequently. Always she started out as the cat. Invariably she ended up as the mouse.

"A first for me, Fi. I've never done a member of that august body. Luther was quite adamant about scheduling. Used her VIP status to take her out of turn, put her at the top of the list. I told him that rank has its privileges but that they normally end at the moment of death."

He undid his cathedral of fingers, took a deep drag on his cigarette, blew smoke into the air, then looked at the glowing ash.

"Shame on me," he sighed. "Me, who knows more than anyone the true color of a healthy lung." He shook his head, took another deep drag, then punched out the cigarette.

"The speed of it caught me by surprise," Fiona acknowledged.

"I always respond to Luther's persuasiveness." He would under no circumstances ever refer to him as the Eggplant and there existed between them an enormous professional respect. "He gave me to understand that something was fishy in Denmark. Then he admitted that he couldn't explain it, that something was nagging at him, that his peace of mind was shattered because of it. I'm a sucker for Luther's humility."

"I've never seen it myself."

"Yes, I did her out of turn. It was quite a revelation." He winked at her, teasing.

At that moment, Melanie came in with the sandwiches. She had ordered a tuna on rye and Dr. Benton had his usual peanut butter and jelly on white bread. Beside the wrapped sandwiches, Melanie placed two styrofoam containers of coffee.

"The comfort of habit," he said, unwrapping the sandwich with deft and sure fingers, fingers that she had seen lift out an unbeating heart from a cracked open chest or separate a human liver from its perch among the oily entrails. He bit into the sandwich and chewed carefully, then washed it down with a swallow of coffee. She started on her tuna sandwich oddly unruffled by the gory images that floated in her mind.

"It's all right for you to be curious. But what about me. I've just taken a great deal of abuse from the woman's husband, as if it were me that ordered the autopsy."

"Aside from the speed, would you have ordered an autopsy?" Dr. Benton asked.

She thought a moment, took another bite of her sandwich.

"I don't think so. On the surface it looks like a clear case of suicide. No sign of struggle. Appears to be a classic case of self-inflicted poisoning. Nevertheless, the old Eggplant has a weird antenna. Sometimes picks up strange messages."

"The choice of poison is strange. Cyanide. Haven't seen much of that ever."

"Not exactly your average pharmaceutical."

"Killed the poor woman in seconds," Dr. Benton said. "Excellent choice for quick disposal. Paralyzes the nervous system for a blessed exit. My own method of choice if I were so inclined. Did you know that Goering kept a capsule of it in his anus?"

She shook her head. Her experience with the Hitler era came from books. Goering had died years before she was born.

"Was this a capsule?"

"Doubtful. It was clearly mixed with the wine."

"No container was found," Fiona said. "Of course it could have gone down the disposal." She reconstructed it in her mind, finally utilizing the images she had gathered earlier. "The bottle of wine was in the refrigerator. She poured herself a glass, put in the dose, flushed the wrapper down the toilet, probably nothing more than a folded bit of paper or plastic. Then she replaced the bottle in the refrigerator, carried the glass containing the poison to the bed, crawled in, smoothed out her nightgown and the bedclothes, picked up the glass, took one big gulp and waited until blessed death arrived. The remaining wine fell on the comforter. A single glass. Meaning no company. Suicide for one." Fiona nodded, pleased with her description. Later, after the results of the lab tests, she was certain that her theory would be validated.

"Impeccable logic," Dr. Benton said.

"But no impeccable motive," Fiona sighed. She put aside her sandwich, sipped some coffee, and watched him take the last bite of his peanut butter and jelly sandwich. "All right then. She now arrives on your table. What message, pray tell, has she sent from the grave?"

"A most remarkable organism," Dr. Benton said, his fingers reconstructing his cathedral, the apex of which he tucked back in his chin.

"Remarkable?"

"The woman had the most unblemished organs I've seen in a long time in a body over forty. I wouldn't have given you two cents for an Irish liver. Not a penny. They're invariably semi-cirrhotic. This was clean as a whistle. And the rest of her as well. Good muscle tone.

Nice clean veins, a healthy heart and kidneys. Inside, everywhere, despite child-bearing, she was well, ten years younger at least."

"So much for bad health as a motive," Fiona said half joking. It had never been a consideration.

"A not infrequent one, I might add."

"So she had health. And position and money. Why the hell would she commit suicide?"

"Ah, sweet mystery of death," Dr. Benton said, leaning back in his chair, peering at her through the smooth light tan cathedral structure. Often, he would sit like this for long moments, raking at the mulch of ideas that his pathologist's mind had harvested. She left him to his thoughts, waiting for him to speak.

"A member of Congress, was she?" he asked rhetorically, needing no answer. She knew he was, like a boxer, jabbing at something inside his mind, dancing around the ring, probing the always illusive opponent. Suddenly he broke the cathedral and sat up.

"Tell me more about the political life," he said.

"Not good for marriage," Fiona said, remembering her childhood. "The usual tensions of separation. It's a bitch in that racket, which was why Mother insisted on setting up full housekeeping within commuting distance. Early on when Daddy first went up to the Senate, we kept the house in Yonkers. But she knew that Daddy was too attractive and vulnerable to set loose among all the pretty young things from Pennsylvania and Ohio who migrated down to snare a politico." She stopped short. "Mother of Jesus. Here I go meandering."

With Dr. Benton, her defenses and normal detective's discipline always became unravelled. Theoretical logic in the detection process, she had learned, was always filtered first through the dust-laden light of something deeply personal.

Rarely did she articulate such allusions to her colleagues in the MPD. For a woman, it was considered more than just bad form. It was perceived as typical female emotionalism, that old chestnut so prevalent in a male-dominated world. A pose of neutrality, more like the blindfolded lady of Justice, was considered the operative stance for a woman in her position. Only with Dr. Benton would she have dared offer her most deeply felt personal perspective.

"So you think her act came out of personal unhappiness? A typical condition of the political life . . . domestic-wise." Dr. Benton coaxed.

"It has some logic," Fiona continued. "They had five kids, all grown, and what amounts to an arrangement. Another not uncommon situation for couples of the Roman persuasion. McGuire was proud of the lady, though, and is pushing a big show of it in the Capitol rotunda tomorrow. Cates is checking it out."

"All right then. An arrangement," Dr. Benton said, sitting back once again and reconstructing the cathedral. "An unhappy marriage of longstanding is rarely a motive for suicide."

She nodded agreement.

"Have you considered unrequited love?" Dr. Benton asked. She knew better than to ridicule the idea. His love for his wife, he had told her, was the most compelling obsession of his life. Even in death. It was, she had concluded, more than hopeless romanticism. If Dr. Benton had an Achilles' heel it was this. Even his home had been turned into a shrine for his beloved.

Once, in a moment of depressive grieving, he had confessed that they had eschewed having children on the grounds that it would have threatened a diminution of their love, their sharing. Time, too, had not done a thing to lessen this obsession. His wife had been in her grave for fifteen years.

"Are you suggesting she had a lover?"

"It happens," he sighed. Frankie McGuire? Somehow it seemed off the mark, farfetched, but she did not discount it. Dr. Benton was obviously heading in a specific direction.

"We are talking of a middle-aged female politician, very conscious of her image and about to run again."

But even in her denial, Fiona felt a strange sense of personal testing against her own experience. Did age confer immunity? With some men, she had been reduced to emotional rubble. Nor could she deny the power and exhilaration of being in love and the sense of loss and depression it engendered when the object of it rejected her. It had happened. Yes, indeed. But she had wanted to kill the sons of bitches. Not herself.

Dr. Benton raised his soft brown eyes, gentle as a doe's, and looked at her. She could tell he had again turned inward, that he was chasing a theory along its natural path.

"Suicide is rarely a compulsive act," he said. "Mostly it is a planned response, usually the result of depressive but logical thought processes. In this case, too, careful planning was required. Research as to the expected reaction of the poison, its aquisition, not a common off-the-shelf item, the choice of scene, timing and means of ingestion. If it was suicide, she had worked that out beautifully."

"Then why no note? Why make it a mystery? She was a woman with many responsibilities. She was the most vocal voice in Congress on the issue of abortion, a leader of the pro-life movement, a . . ."

Dr. Benton, swiftly collapsing his cathedral, stood up abruptly. For him it was a rare display of excitement and it startled her.

"Of course," he said. "I'd forgotten." He turned to look at her. "Forgive me Fiona for playing the ferret." He shook his head. "The woman, you see, was six weeks pregnant."

7

THE FLAG-DRAPED CLOSED CASKET stood at the far end of the Capitol rotunda. Chairs had been placed a dozen rows deep in front it. Every seat was filled and a respectful crowd stood behind the chairs and along the rotunda's rim.

From her vantage along the rim, Fiona could see the grim faces in the front row, the chief mourners. Jack McGuire sat between what were obviously two of his daughters. Their arms were interlocked, an appropriately grieving trio.

On either side of the daughters sat the two McGuire sons, straw haired like their father and speckled with freckles like their mother. The girls, in a genetic sex reversal, were beefier with darker hair and no freckles, with cheeks flushed with rouge circles, more like their father, although his radishy skin had been embellished by the brush of John Barleycorn.

Fiona assumed that others seated in the first row and dressed appropriately for mourning were relatives. Also sitting in the first row as if he, too, were a member of the family, was an ashen faced Harlan Foy. Their eyes had drifted toward each other, engaged, then his snapped away with a look of contempt as if Fiona's presence here was an affront to the dead lady.

She recognized the more famous political faces from both Congress and the Executive branch. Some, she assumed, had come out of genuine respect. Others, she observed cynically had rather obvious political motives. A group of violinists in Air Force uniforms played dirge music as the audience gathered. The photographers were also busy. Television cameras had been set up to record the event.

It was a first-class sendoff, Fiona thought, remembering her father's lonely funeral back in Yonkers, the hearse threading its way through the clutter of cemetery angels, the sudden downpour that puddled his open grave as they lowered his casket into the dreary dampness. No last hurrah for this true hero. A sob bubbled out of her chest and, for a brief moment, her eyes filmed over.

They had printed a program on glossy cover stock, complete with Congresswoman McGuire's picture and bio and a short list of speakers.

The Speaker of the House was the first to stand before the microphone in front of the casket. The violinists had ceased their playing. Fiona listened to the platitudes. A good and valiant woman, taken to God in her prime, whose contributions would be remembered by future generations, a woman, above all, who believed with all her heart in the righteousness of her cause, who was not afraid to speak out. The usual script.

He was followed by Harold Hoskins, the Secretary of Health and Human Resources whose theme was conviction and compassion. He read his speech from a little card and was properly laudatory and complimentary. Then came the two senators from Massachusetts, one of whom, tragically, was an acknowledged expert at funeral orations. Despite her role as mere observer, she could not keep her eyes dry as the early trauma of the Kennedy brothers' assassinations rose once again in her memory.

But it was Charles Rome's speech that sparked a special interest. He was a tall slender man with a thick shock of curly grey hair, an eaglelike nose and eyes set deep over high cheekbones. He had the quintessential look of the distinguished stylish gentleman, the kind that might grace a haberdashery advertisement seeking to persuade the older man.

As he moved toward the microphone, a woman in the second row muttered something that sounded unmistakably like the word "shame" and flounced in her seat. A man beside her patted her hand in a comforting gesture. May Carter (who else?) Fiona decided.

Charles Rome was chairman of the committee on Labor, Health and Human Services, the enemy according to Foy, whose picket line sat athwart the road to ban abortion funding, a key target of the pro-lifers.

Chairman Rome had an old-fashioned rhetorical style, complete with body and hand flourishes and dramatic phrasing, a man with obvious powers of persuasion.

"We stood on opposite sides of a great issue," he told the mourn-ers, who listened respectfully, all except May Carter whose posture was one loud harumph. Twice during his oration, she uttered the word "shame".

"Her conviction carried the power of her personality and intellect and those whom she represented were blessed to have such a passion-ate advocate for their cause. Yes, it is true we were at opposing ends of the great fulcrum of democracy, but the true balance was our love for this great country. Above all, on a personal level we did not allow our opposition, sometimes bitter and contentious, to interfere with our great friendship. Barbara and I have lost a dear and devoted friend."

He had the ability to tap into deep emotion and to encapsulate the essence of the political process. He spoke of human beings compro-mising, giving and taking from each other to blunder through, to make the jerry-built system called democracy work. In such a system, he told the group with conviction, it was inevitable and certainly desirable for friendships to be forged, for people of pure heart, as he put it, to rise above the fray. Fiona had, of course, heard it all before. But Rome was a master presenter of ringing patriotic clichés, and it came out of him as if it were being said for the first time.

He was followed by a priest who offered the usual Catholic sermon of resurrection and a ritual prayer for the dead in Latin. As the priest droned on in a singsong tone, Fiona's thoughts drifted back to her discussion with Dr. Benton.

He had explained that he had held back the public revelation of the woman's pregnancy until he had a chance to discuss the matter with Chief Greene. A pregnancy in a woman of forty-seven was not exactly a common event. In a congresswoman who had died by a self-inflicted act or, worse, a possible murder, it was extraordinary.

A number of logical scenarios had come immediately to mind. For Frankie to have a child at this stage in her life would have been a strong career negative, not to mention the physical danger. One could only assume that she had given up any idea of more children and that a new baby would be a massive inconvenience to a woman with other priorities. And, without question, abortion was both politically and morally unthinkable for her. But a suicidal way out of the dilemma was even more morally repugnant than abortion, a cruel twist to the entire Right to Life concept . . . the taking of two lives not just one.

"Could have been the product of an extracurricular liaison," Dr. Benton had suggested. "I've typed the fetus' blood just in case, but even that is never conclusive and the so-called DNA print is too experimental to be valid."

A repugnant image of the deceased woman coupling with Harlan Foy floated into her mind. The possibility existed. It was common practice between intimate office buddies, a neat and discreet solution to safe infidelity. He did, after all, have a key to her apartment. National politics was, she knew, a game which forced the necessity for squirreling away dirty little secrets, many of which grew naturally out of the fact that extracurricular sex was a human consequence of separation.

Such thoughts opened a musty trapdoor in her memory. Daddy was no goody-goody on that score. A bitter female staffer, objecting to the senator's stand on the war, had spewed her filthy confession into her mother's ear. Tales of sexual license, highly detailed, poured out of her, only to be hysterically recycled again by her mother to her denying husband.

Fiona, sitting in her pajamas on a step of the winding household staircase, had heard every word, enough to rekindle memories which, despite the passage of time, had never lost their power to sting.

"It's political vengeance," he had said, dismissing the accusation.

"Liar," her mother had screamed. "Not only in the office. You took her on trips. She gave me chapter and verse. It was revolting. You've defiled me."

"Can't you see her motives?" her father had argued, using his lawyers' skills. "And keep your voice down," he had warned. Fiona, still virginal, had to be protected at all costs. But her mother, usually serene, had erupted beyond control.

"I will not have it. It is an affront, worse, a sin. I can't bear the thought of it. I will not have you consorting with whores."

"I never touched her," she heard her father say, sensing the lie. The man was too attractive, too powerful. What her mother undoubtedly resented most was the forced confrontation. She had always looked the other way, making excuses to herself. Later, after more words, her mother had dissolved into tears, folded her cards and slipped back into self-denial. Her father, she was certain, had admitted nothing.

It was not uncommon for politicians, especially where distance made it too difficult for frequent visits back home and even those on the Tuesday to Thursday legislative run to actually have two families, a mistress, sometimes with children and often complete with a cozy paid-for separate domicile. This was the darker side of the legislative process, revealed in the press only when it was unavoidable, like when the legislator in question was running for the Presidency or being considered for the Supreme Court or some such where a definition of "character" was required.

Washington was tailor-made for clandestine lovers and being a politician's mistress was, ironically, a reasonably respectable position for a woman. The thought brought a hot blush to her cheeks as the unseen accusatory finger pointed square at the center of her forehead.

Despite her cop cynicism, Fiona's early Catholic orthodoxy came out on the side of Mrs. McGuire. Surely it was her husband, demanding his marriage entitlement, that had done the deed. It was Dr. Benton's reaction to that conclusion that dealt a heavy blow to the suicide theory.

"As a politician, a leader in the pro-life movement," he had told her, "wouldn't it have been politically glorious for her to flaunt her pregnancy? Show her commitment by example? 'Look world, I am the recipient of an unwanted pregnancy but I will not evade my responsibility to that unborn child.'"

"Congratulations," Fiona said, surrendering to his view. "You have entered a politician's mind."

Still, their speculations were inconclusive. As the Eggplant had assumed from the beginning, all was not kosher here and further investigation was necessary.

After her talk with Dr. Benton, she had come back to the office. Cates had come in some time later griping about folderol, his English schoolboy word for bullshit, forcing him to beat shoe leather merely to concoct a murder scenario for the ego gratification of the Eggplant. He had reported on the planned ceremonies in the rotunda, then had slumped in his chair and groused.

She had let him rant for awhile, then, in flat tones, she had told him what Dr. Benton had discovered in the woman's dead uterus. It had stiffened him instantly. He did not need to play out the possibilities, absorbing them by osmosis.

"So what did he know . . ." His head moved toward the Eggplant's closed office door. "That we didn't?"

"That might be even more of a puzzle than the other," Fiona had sighed. For an overbearing, egotistical, status-conscious person like the Eggplant to be ahead of his troops was always galling, despite its frequency.

She had motioned with her eyes to Briggs who, as always, sat eagle-eyed and alert for anyone wishing to speak to the Eggplant. He had shrugged his consent, meaning that the Eggplant was approachable. Then she had knocked on the Eggplant's door.

"Come," he had snapped and she and Cates found him, feet on the desk, showing off spit-shined tasseled loafers, puffing a thin panatela and reading *People* magazine. He was an inveterate celebrity worshipper. At one end of his office was a television set, playing without sound, tuned in to the all-news channel.

Without a shred of guilt, he had draped the magazine across his thighs and squinted inquiringly at them.

"I'm here to apprise," she had said, pronouncing it, "apprahze". Ignoring the mimicry, he had nodded. They sat facing him on two wooden arm chairs.

He had listened without comment until Fiona revealed Mrs.

McGuire's pregnancy. Like Dr. Benton she had strung out the revelation.

He had uncurled his legs from the desk and sat up stiffly. The *People* magazine slipped unnoticed to the floor and he smiled a toothy smile.

"Be damned," he had said.

Preempting what he was surely thinking, Fiona had offered the speculations and theories that she had discussed with Dr. Benton.

"Actually it could make the case for suicide even stronger," Fiona told him, again preempting him. Without giving him time for comment, she had filled him in about her discussion with Harlan Foy, although she had edited out, for the moment, the possibility that Harlan might have been Frankie's lover. Too incomprehensible, she had decided, although the Eggplant, listening intently, his head bowed in concentration, had undoubtedly picked up the unspoken subtext.

He had rubbed his chin, stood up and strode toward the window. The upper rim of a spring sun was slipping behind one of the government buildings to the west. After a long silence, he had turned suddenly.

"That woman was murdered," he said. His tone was emphatic, without doubt.

"But how can you be so sure?" Fiona had asked. His surety was exasperating.

"I feel it in my gut," he had replied, punching his flat stomach.

"This is too sensitive a case to build a conclusion on a hunch," Fiona had said, reacting cautiously, being careful to keep due deference in her tone.

"Great case," he had commented using the same fist he had just punched into his stomach to pound a palm. His eyes had moved to the silent TV set. He watched the images for a moment and, she had suspected, he was salivating over the possibilities for his own exposure on the tube. After a while, he had turned and looked sternly at Fiona and Cates. "But you're right. No shooting from the hip. It's political to the core. What I want here is textbook thoroughness, hear? You're on it full-time, overtime and prime time. And nothing, *nothing* goes without me being apprised. (Apprahzed.) The boys upstairs will be

nervous as grasshoppers and the mayor will have a piss hemorrhage
if we make a wrong move but he sure will love the leverage against
those self-righteous Congressional bastards. Only we've got to walk
on eggshells. Those congressmen get very touchy we start mucking
about in their shit."

"Very sensible," Fiona had agreed, exchanging glances with Cates,
who had nodded his understanding.

"And you can dispense with that patronizing bullshit," the Eggplant snapped, reverting to character. He had shot them a snarl,
walked back to his chair, picked up the *People* magazine, relit his
panatela and lifted his feet to the desk signaling an end to the
interview. Cates had risen, but Fiona had continued to sit there
watching him. It was a long time before he reacted. He looked over
the magazine and took a long drag on his panatela.

"I want to know something, chief."

"So?" A stream of smoke had poured out of his mouth.

"From the beginning . . ." She remembered feeling suddenly
embarrassed and had again cut a glance at Cates. Would he think she
was toadying? Such conduct was considered sinful. It was a subject
beyond race and rank. She shrugged it off, had to know. "You seemed
so dead certain it wasn't suicide . . ." She had stumbled for a moment.
Cates had ascribed it to pure gluttony for publicity. But that was a
given, a constant. This was sixth sense, an inborn talent. One of the
great challenges of the job was to best him, cut him down to size.
On a number of occasions, she had actually done it, albeit without
his public acknowledgment. Surely, inside of himself, he had acknowledged her victory.

He had smiled. More smoke had poured from his nose.

"Women," he told her, shaking his head, offering his favorite smile
signifying derision and sarcasm. "I've been studying them since I was
eleven."

"What the hell is that supposed to mean?" Fiona had snapped,
tossing another glance at Cates, hoping the sudden outburst had
redeemed her in his eyes. It was important to show them that she
could give as much as she got, another ritual for gaining respect.

"You call yourself a detective," the Eggplant had said, sighing derisively. "Never yet met a woman who greased her face without a genuine desire to wake up in the morning."

Embarrassment had registered profoundly on Fiona. She stood up absorbing the rebuke. She had missed it. No question. Touché. Her face had grown hot with her blush of shame. Cates, somewhat less moved, had lowered his eyes.

"Happens," the Eggplant had said sighing theatrically, hiding his face discreetly behind the *People* magazine, relieving her of having to watch his smugness.

"Could have been habit," Cates told her. "She may have wanted to look good for St. Peter."

"Jesus," Fiona had replied.

"Him, too," Cates had said, offering not the shred of a smile.

The service in the rotunda had taken all of an hour and the crowd, losing some of its solemnity, began to mill about. A knot of mourners surrounded McGuire and his children offering condolences, shaking hands or embracing them depending on the levels of intimacy.

Charles Rome and, Fiona assumed, his wife Barbara, spoke briefly with McGuire and his children, then moved through the crowd like royalty. Rome had all the bearing and demeanor of a "man of power." She knew the type well. Her father had been a quintessential example, smiling, eye-engaging, erect, commanding, judicious in laying on of hands to manipulate, comfort and charm.

Barbara, the equally quintessential politician's wife, easy in her role as an old shoe, traveled in Rome's wake, spit-polished as a Dresden figure, not a hair out of place, not a crease in her clothing, smile at the ready, complementing her husband's sense of command, showing the kind of distaff charm that underscored the Rome image, spreading the gospel of the Rome power and his worthiness as someone to be idolized and, at the same time, offering a strong hint of wifely influence.

She reminded Fiona of her mother who, in the end, had not adjusted well to her loss of power, had privately and naggingly balked at the senator's stand on the war, had railed at him for going against the grain, for forfeiting his position, for losing his place. Unfortunately, the moral highroad her father had taken, while winning him martyrdom had relegated her parents to exile in a political and social Siberia from which they never returned.

It was this place, the familiar rotunda, where she had sometimes passed the time waiting for her father, playing among the somber statues of famous men and, of course, the context of death, that brought forth this blast of painful memories. The funeral ritual, however distant the relationship of the deceased, always produced personal pain in the spectator. She had attended enough of them in her professional life to understand this truism. In the face of anyone's death, no one, however hardened and aloof, could be disinterested.

As the Romes moved comfortably through the milling crowd, the woman who had heckled his oration, elbowed her way toward them. The man who had sat beside her during the service moved to restrain her but she nudged him away. It was one of those little dramas that one might easily miss if one wasn't, like Fiona, a professional observer.

Fiona followed her on the assumption that any confrontation might offer some insight into the mystery of Mrs. McGuire's strange demise.

"Clear sailing now, Mister Congressman," the woman hissed. She was a tall intense woman, as tall as Rome, with a large bony face and fierce blue eyes that seemed to have burned their way into her cheekbones. Her dyed blonde hair was styled in an old-fashioned bouffant and she wore a flannel navy blue suit embellished with a single strand of pearls which drew attention to a scrawny neck. Her lips were thin, uneven and seemed locked into a perpetual scowl. The way she held herself, her look and persona, marked her unmistakably as single-minded, fearless and determined.

"Surely not now, May," Rome said, touching her arm, which she shrugged away. Barbara's confident look disappeared and she seemed to actually step behind him as if he were a protective shield. Neither had noticed Fiona's proximity. Nor were any of the others aware of the impending confrontation.

"Why not, Congressman," May said sneeringly. "With Frankie

gone you think it's over, don't you?" She watched his face and blocked his way. "Godless murderers. You think there won't be others to take her place. We'll get stronger, more powerful, and beat you and all your liberal abortionist killers. Let me tell you that someone will pick up Frankie's relay stick . . ."

"I'm sure of that, May," Rome said politely, with an air of futility. He started to take a step forward but the woman continued to block his path. "This is ridiculous, May. The least you could do is have some respect for Frankie."

"Respect for Frankie? What respect did you show her?"

"She was my friend," Rome said.

"Double standard hypocrites," the woman muttered. "You're everything we detest. It's disgusting. That committee of yours. Funding murder. Abortion is a sin against mankind. You'll be punished in hell for this."

"Really, May, this is ridiculous."

"Why? Your vaunted system can't be criticized? We must all be ladies and gentlemen about this? Always tea time with the enemy after battle, is it? I never agreed with Frankie's opinion about that and I resent your speaking at this service."

"You expressed yourself on that point, May."

"Jack McGuire was a fool to let you."

"Without me, you wouldn't have been able to hold Frankie's service here. This required a bit of clout."

"If Jack McGuire had any guts he would have rejected it if your help was needed. Your presence here is an insult to her memory."

"You are an unforgiving bitch," Rome snapped, his facade of easy charm collapsing. "Get off your high horse, May. The country is not behind you. Abortion is here to stay."

"We'll never stop until you and your ilk have been crushed."

"I know you're upset about Frankie's death," Rome said unctuously, getting on top of his brief blast of anger. "As always, I'll be glad to debate the point with you or your people. But not here and now."

"You'll hear from me, Congressman. You can bet on it."

He shook his head in mock despair, sidestepped, reached out for his wife's hand and walked quickly out of earshot, disappearing down a corridor.

"Beast," the woman muttered, suddenly becoming aware of Fiona, taking her for one of the mourners and, therefore, automatically an advocate. "The height of bad taste for him to be here. The man opposed everything she stood for. It's people like that murdered Frankie . . ." She paused, looked down and shook her head. "A casualty in a great cause, that's what she was. No other way to look at it. Satan's army is very powerful. Very powerful." Her fierce eyes, dancing behind her cheekbones, burned into Fiona's face. The only sensible action was to offer nothing confrontational. The woman, Fiona knew, took her silence for the advocacy of an ally.

"You're May Carter, aren't you?" Fiona asked.

"I am. And you?"

Fiona fished in her pocketbook and took out her badge.

"Sergeant FitzGerald, Washington MPD."

May Carter lifted her eyebrows, continued to study Fiona's face. Surprise, too, was a police weapon. By then Cates had crossed the rotunda and came up to her side. Fiona introduced him. May acknowledged the introduction with a nod.

"You here to arrest me?" May asked, with little glint of humor in her eyes. A hard case, Fiona thought. Little Ms. One-Note.

"Think we can talk for a few moments?" Fiona asked politely. May hesitated, perhaps remembering Rome's comment about this being not the time and place.

"It's very important, Mrs. Carter," Fiona prodded, noting a wedding band on the woman's finger.

May Carter looked at her watch, then nodded.

"How long will this take?"

"Not long."

They waited until Mrs. Carter said her goodbyes, then moved out of the rotunda. A glance backwards told Fiona that their exit was not lost on Jack McGuire and she noted a puzzled look on his face.

THEY FOUND an empty bench in the little park across from the Capitol building. It was a glorious spring bud-popping day as only an April day in Washington can be, crisp, clear, the light making the neo-Greco facades of the buildings in the Capitol complex shine like new pennies. Hardly the place to probe a question of murder. It was eleven and the lunch hour crowds would soon begin to sprawl over every square inch of the park.

"When was the last time you saw Frances McGuire alive?" Fiona asked as they settled on the bench. In an unspoken strategy it was assumed that Fiona would lead the interrogation.

Mrs. Carter raised her eyes skyward.

"Couple of days. But we were constantly in touch. I'm on the road, out of South Boston, about a week a month. This was my week for Washington."

"How did she strike you?" Fiona asked.

There was a certain awkwardness about the situation since they were all sitting in a straight line. To face her directly, Fiona had to twist her body. Mrs. Carter, on the other hand did not do this, crossing long legs and often answering a question without looking at Fiona directly. This put Fiona at a disadvantage since there was much to be learned from eye contact.

"Why are you asking me these questions?" Mrs. Carter snapped.

Fiona was tempted to provide the usual answer. "Routine." Instead she said, "There is some question about Mrs. McGuire's suicide."

Only then did Mrs. Carter confront Fiona full-face. Her forehead creased and her deep-set eyes probed like lasers. Then, as though a dark cloud had passed over her face, Mrs. Carter brightened, the creases flattened, the lasers shifted.

"I suspected as much," Mrs. Carter said.

"You did?" Cates asked suddenly.

Mrs. Carter chuckled, glanced briefly at Cates, then looked toward the Supreme Court Building across the park.

"There," Mrs. Carter said raising her chin. "Them. Over there. Where nine men decided the fate of a nation of unborn children. Roe v. Wade. A cannonball aimed directly at God himself declaring that a woman can decide, by herself, the fate of life within her. The opening shot of a great war. Since then we have murdered millions. No one can sit still in the face of that. No one. Who will fight God's battle, if not us? The enemy is powerful, ruthless. He will stop at nothing . . . including murder." She seemed to be just winding up, offering the well-honed and surely spellbinding theatrics of her advocacy. The woman was quite obviously obsessed totally by her cause and, because of it, every answer to their questions would somehow be related to it.

Determined to get back on the track, Fiona had interrupted.

"Are you saying that Mrs. McGuire might have been done away with by . . ."

"No question about it," Mrs. Carter interjected, talking now at hyper speed. "Frankie McGuire was our battering ram. Why wouldn't they want to get her out of the way. She was gaining seniority, getting too powerful for them. We're winning, you know. In the end we will win . . ."

"Who specifically did you have in mind?" Fiona asked.

"Oh, they wouldn't be so crude as to stick their own necks out. No way. Probably the work of some hit man. Some stranger who they contracted to do the job."

"Poison is not exactly the weapon of choice for a hit man," Cates said, obviously annoyed and impatient over the woman's drumbeat of polemics.

"Got you confused hasn't it? They're clever, deceitful. They have their own agenda and their own methods." She lowered her voice suddenly and looked around. "I've received hundreds of threats. Keeps me on my toes, I can tell you. But I look at it as acts of desperation, proving conclusively that we've got them on the run. And this thing with Frankie only underlines that fact." She turned once again to look at Fiona full-face. "You'll never catch her killer. Long gone, he is. Probably spirited away on a plane somewhere to Europe or Asia." The assumption made her almost gleeful, as if it was additional proof of the cleverness of the enemy.

"So it's a conspiracy theory then," Cates asked, making no effort to hide his ridicule.

"It's not a theory," Mrs. Carter said smugly. "It's a fact."

"Like some governing body is giving orders, calling the shots."

"Of course. Those lezzies that run the pro-choice outfit and their liberal cohorts. All interconnected. All one cabal." She lowered her voice. "Of course, I could never say this publicly and I'd deny it if pushed. That's not the strategy that will win this fight. Won't give them the ammo to dub us crazy right wing fanatic or religious freaks, part of the pope's army. Our job is to stay in the center. What we're selling is God's choice and that cuts across the spectrum."

It was growing late. Already the lunch hour crowds had begun to pour out of their Capitol Hill offices, sprawling over the park, opening their brown bags. Mrs. Carter began taking quick glances at her clock, pinned to the lapel of her suit.

"So who goes for Mrs. McGuire's seat?" Fiona asked, almost casually. It was an inescapable motive and had to be explored.

"Jack Grady would give his eye teeth for a shot at it."

"Has he a chance?"

"If I don't oppose him," Mrs. Carter said. She snickered. "That was him sitting next to me up there. Quite solicitous, I may add. For obvious reasons."

"Would you run?" Fiona asked innocently.

"Question is where would I be the most effective. Inside or outside. I haven't yet made up my mind. Jack has got some baggage. He and McGuire are old buddies. Jack of Diamonds and Jack of Clubs. Too much scrutiny will do him in. Oh he's a pro-lifer to the core, alright.

No one gets elected in South Boston who isn't. Thing is, a woman gives the Congressional battle more authenticity. Not that we don't need strong men to carry the day. Problem is I know my strengths and weaknesses. I don't have Jack's blarney charm. Some people think I'm too severe." She turned her laser eyes on Fiona and for a brief moment her guard went down showing the real person beneath the fanatic. "You know what I mean. I'm a realist. An aggressive man is dynamic, forceful. An aggressive woman is just a pushy bitch." She bit her lip and as swiftly as it had gone, the guard came up again, armed to the teeth. "Anyway, the longer I hold out, the more solicitous he has to be. Power is in the perception, you know."

"What about Harlan Foy?'"

"For Frankie's seat?"

Fiona nodded.

"A little too prissy, don't you think? I don't approve of course. It's against God's will to be like that. But not once did I ever suggest that Frankie get rid of him. His life was her. No love lost between us. We argued like the devil and sometimes he tried to bar the door to old May, but he was good backup, damned good backup." She shook her head. "Take her seat? No way. Okay as a number two. But let's face it. Our issue gives him a bit of a credibility gap, don't you think?"

The explanation left Fiona strangely relieved, although it did not absolve Foy entirely. Perception, despite May Carter's interpretation, could be illusory. Foy could not be as he seemed, although she agreed that his running for Frankie's seat was a long shot. But he could not be ruled out on the other. Not yet. He did have access to Frankie McGuire's apartment. Access could not be ignored in a murder investigation. And there were other motives available. Mrs. Carter looked at her watch again, spurring Fiona to press on.

"What about Mr. McGuire, the old Jack of Diamonds himself? Might be able to get the sympathy vote. You know, spouse of the victim. Might sell well as a possibility."

"Sounds like you know the game, sergeant," Mrs. Carter said.

"It's in the air," Fiona said, her gaze connecting with Cates, who smiled.

"The Jack of Diamonds you called him," Mrs. Carter said, throwing her head back, an attitude designed for hysterical laughter. But it never came. "No way." She paused and shook her head from side to side.

"Above all. Not that one. He's not just carrying baggage, he's got cement blocks on his feet."

"I don't understand," Fiona probed gently.

"Listen, he can play the bereaved husband down here. But up there where it counts Jack McGuire has a different agenda." Again she turned toward Fiona. "You're not serious are you? Surely, you know about Jack McGuire."

"Know what?" Cates asked.

"I think you people need a course in detecting," Mrs. Carter said, with obvious sarcasm. Then she looked at her watch once again, stood up and primly smoothed her skirt. "I'm already late. I hope I've given you some help."

"What about Jack McGuire's different agenda?"

"Not for me to say. Least we can do is let Frankie's public image rest in peace."

"And you insist that this was a hit man murder?"

"Makes sense to me." She started to back away, but before she could turn, Fiona touched her arm, the kind of gentle gesture that was emphatic.

"Just for the record, though, Mrs. Carter," Fiona asked. It was, of course, the essential question and Fiona had deliberately reserved it for last. "Was there anything about Frankie . . ." Fiona felt comfortable using the dead woman's nickname. The dead congresswoman was taking on an intimate persona in Fiona's mind, a sure sign of an intensifying engagement. "Was she depressed? Was there something on her mind, something gnawing at her? Something that might have triggered a self-destructive act?"

Mrs. Carter pondered the thought for a long moment.

"Frankie could be moody," she admitted. "She could also be difficult. We used to have words about her being overly friendly with the enemy, especially the Romes. She bucked at that. Depressed? Maybe enough to be suicidal? No. My theory is far more compelling."

"Are you saying she was depressed?" Fiona coaxed. "To some degree."

"Not depressed, exactly," Mrs. Carter said. But she was far more tentative than she had appeared earlier. She was applying her memory now, quite obviously mulling a recent impression. "Will-o'-the-wispy, I'd say. Not quite concentrating. It happens sometime. She didn't seem as focused as usual." To Mrs. Carter, Fiona decided, that might have meant not being as intense about "the issue."

"She didn't confide in you? Did you detect . . . well did you get the idea that she might be holding something back?"

"Frankie?" She shook her head emphatically. "Not to me. The fact is, sergeant, Frankie and I had no secrets between us. None."

With that, she turned and headed back toward the Capitol, wearing her determination like a neon sign.

"**R**OMANTIC BEANTOWN," Greg said in his silky close-to-speaker voice with its blatant tease. She knew from the tone that he had accepted her offer, meaning that somehow his parental calendar was clear. His deal with his estranged spouse was that he took the kids every other weekend. Fiona kept track of that, although occasionally they happened out of sequence. Like now. It was, she was certain, a clear signal from that place where fate was concocted.

The childless weekends had belonged to Fiona when she was not working and there were occasional midweek times when the need arose and time permitted, the latter far more frequent than the former. In the new safe sex environment, one steady was almost a health imperative. She hoped that he was fulfilling his part of the unspoken bargain, although she secretly suspected that he was pursuing a long-term closet "office quickie" relationship with his married secretary, a very frequent Washington arrangement.

She had almost wished he had refused and she was fully prepared to accept it as a message from on high that this, like the Harper's Ferry debacle, was another deliberate squelch of her secret agenda.

"I'd love it, Fi," Greg said, underscoring this whim of fate. She had little doubt now that the window of opportunity remained open.

"You understand that I'll be working. I've got to see people in South Boston on the McGuire case. Means you'll have to fare for yourself part of the time."

"Good. I'll need it for R and R."

A quick scramble of sexy imagery in her mind made her cheeks hot and stimulated other familiar reactions. She laughed nervously.

"Hope so," she said saucily, knowing that the die was cast. No turning back, she vowed. As backup for her resolve, she would leave her diaphragm home. Burn her bridges. This is commitment time, baby, she told herself. She had even checked the calender. Fertility was still in season, she noted. Was this fate smiling? It frightened her.

"Okay, Fi, you're penciled in."

"Ink it, pal. You've got a date with destiny."

"Heavy," he said, his voice whispering now. "I feel this rising sensation."

"Take a cold shower."

Nearly a week had gone by since Mrs. McGuire had died and, already, she and Cates had reached the first level of frustration. Flanagan's sweep of her apartment had uncovered nothing that was useful. A fistful of smudged prints. The maid had apparently done a thorough cleaning and polishing on the day before her death and the only other clear fresh prints besides Mrs. McGuire's and the maid's were Harlan Foy's.

This meant that either the killer, if there was one, had been thorough in wiping off his own prints or that Mrs. McGuire did not ordinarily have many people up to her apartment. To complicate matters further, the only prints on the wine bottle in the refrigerator were those of the congresswoman herself. Notwithstanding that, the Eggplant stuck to his guns.

"Means that the killer was one clever bastard. Those prints were put there after the lady had croaked."

"Comes under the heading of making the facts fit the theory," Fiona argued.

"Keeps the ball rolling," the Eggplant said smiling. He had taken a big drag on his panatela and blew a perfect smoke ring across the room. The media had kept the case alive, although his reported assessments were still noncommittal and extremely cautious.

"We're not ready to say either way," he had been quoted in the *Washington Post*. "We are exploring every promising lead. We want to be absolutely certain before we commit." Talk about vagaries.

"Foy is another cipher," Cates had volunteered. Like Fiona, he was reacting primarily to the Eggplant's instincts in direct contrast to his own. "Mrs. Carter implied that the man was gay. Nothing we can find confirms that. On the other hand, we don't find any evidence of heterosexuality."

"May mean that the man's a neuter," Fiona added. "A not uncommon condition in this town." The political cauldron, she had discovered, could also have a numbing effect on sexuality. Hard work, long hours and a high anxiety level could wreak havoc with a man's libido. On occasion she had encountered this darker side, a message that was not lost on the two males in the room.

"We bow to your greater knowledge, sergeant," the Eggplant said. To his credit, his face was expressionless. In the interests of professionalism, she let it pass.

"Clearly, it's an optional conclusion," Cates said with a touch of pedantry.

Fiona and Cates had interviewed everyone on the congresswoman's staff. Frankie was, by all accounts, pretty well insulated by Foy, who was the staff Mother Hen. He hired and fired, barked out the orders and took on all of the burdens of administration. This left the congresswoman free for the upfront chores, showing the flag, communicating with constituents and colleagues, plying the ideological vineyard and generally pressing the flesh. The staff loved her, tolerated him, which was only natural, but none of them, male or female, could offer any solid proof of the man's sexuality. They offered opinions, of course. But when pressed they retreated.

This was true also when they questioned his neighbors in the apartment house where he lived on Capitol Hill. Suppositions galore. But no hard evidence. The man kept to himself. Never partied. Had no apparent close friends of either sex.

"As far as we could find out, his life was his work and his work was Frankie McGuire," Fiona said.

"Gotta be careful on these things. These repressive sex types can pop their corks with nasty results."

Restating the homicide axiom constituted a subtle rebuke which she resented and she could not restrain a cutting response.

"A poisoning does not represent a popping cork. A poisoner plans."

"A textbook conclusion," the Eggplant said, his eyes drifting to the ceiling to emphasize deep contemplation and illustrating his superiority. She capped a rising anger and forced herself to wait for him to speak again. Cates tapped graceful brown fingers on his thigh, keeping his own impatience bridled.

"All right then. Try this on for size," the Eggplant said still looking at the ceiling. "Foy, the devoted retainer is also the secret lover."

She shook her head as if she had just swallowed something very sour.

"There's someone for everyone, FitzGerald. How many impossible combinations have you seen in your lifetime? The point is that they had easy access to each other. Perfect cover. Who could suspect? Then suddenly. Accident of accidents. The lady, who believed she was over the hill in terms of making babies, suddenly finds herself pregnant. A dilemma for her? Fucking A."

"The point is, what's the dilemma for him?"

"Maybe he wants to marry the lady. Maybe he doesn't want her to pass the kid off as her husband's. Maybe he wants to assert himself in some way."

"When she balks, he ices her?" Fiona said.

"Or some combination thereof."

"It's reaching," Cates said.

"That's what we're here for," the Eggplant said, crushing the butt of his still lit panatela into an ashtray on his desk, already piled high with dead butts. "Keep reaching."

"No worse than Mrs. Carter's hit man theory," Fiona said.

"Can't be discounted," the Eggplant persisted, as he sucked in the smoke from a new panatela. "Lots of crazies would kill for a cause. And this one generates lots of heat."

"All right," Cates said. "It's a theoretical motive." Fiona could tell he was getting antsy. "The point is . . . there are no clues. Nothing."

"Makes it a challenge," the Eggplant said.

"At this point, I vote suicide," Cates said, cutting a glance at Fiona. The eggplant's position baffled her. Yet she was not ready to discount his instincts. Not quite yet.

"The fact is," Fiona said, "your Foy theory notwithstanding, we couldn't scare up a breath of scandal. Not in Washington, anyway. And the Boston crowd are starting to duck us."

The "second thoughts" syndrome was a common affliction, especially if the questions hinted at a potential murder case. Involvement, in general, frightened people. In a case where political ramifications were rampant, like this one, all of the principal players were running for cover. Even the voluble May Carter had become aloof, nonaccessible. The same was true for Frankie's husband. She had managed to talk briefly with Jack Grady, but as soon as the subject was broached, he begged off. A telephonic interrogation was easy to evade.

Even Harlan Foy, the Eggplant's "prime" suspect was now less than forthcoming. But he was, at least, a resident and could, if necessary, be legally coerced. They had not told him about Frankie's pregnancy. Not yet. It was too delicate a point, too much grist for the media mill in a town that leaked like a sieve. Even the Eggplant would hang back on that one until he was certain he had a credible hook.

"Maybe if we were to take a stab at them on their own turf," the Eggplant said. He lifted his hand and rocked it, meaning sneak up on them. Enter by the back door. "You know what I mean. Low key. Nothing to shake the trees."

"Rather be safe than sorry," Fiona said.

"Something like that." The Eggplant muttered. His panatela had gone out. "Budget'll only handle one." He studied their faces. Fiona and Cates had exchanged glances. Occasionally they would allude to their personal lives, but it was the kind of relationship where revelation stopped at the door, although each acknowledged a kind of psychological intimacy.

"You go," Cates said, turning away quickly, as if he had received some message from her eyes.

"Worth a try," Fiona said, hiding her elation. Again fate was beckoning, she thought. A regular Pied Piper, proving once again that there were, after all, no accidents.

10

W AS THIS ALL A DEAD GIVEAWAY? she wondered as the waiter rolled in their dinner on a room service cart. She had splurged on a suite at the Ritz-Carlton, a considerable step up from the lousy per diem the MPD allowed.

The bedroom was all done in peach with a four-poster king-sized bed, the floor covered with thick pile carpets and furniture that was either genuine antique or good copies. The sitting room was done in mauve with peach highlights and both rooms had a commanding view of the Common and the Boston skyline.

A small anxiety fit seized her in the elevator. Would he see through her plan? Be on his guard? She had told him it was her treat and he had been relaxed about it, but she had not quite counted on the lavishness of the hotel and the fawning of the service help.

But after the bellman had left and they had inspected the premises, Greg took her in his arms and gave her one of those extraordinary total embrace kisses, which took her mind off her trepidations.

With some reluctance, she maneuvered out of his arms and ran off into the bathroom. There, she showered and primped and put herself into her new wispy white lace lingerie and peignoir, leaving the room only at the knock of room service serving her pre-ordered dinner. She had ordered pâté de foi gras and medallions of veal and asparagus, and two bottles of Dom Perignon Champagne, both of them leaning in lovely serenity in their sleeves of sparkling ice in silver buckets.

Criminals, she knew, often gambled with fate, flaunting the obvious, reasoning that if they were not found out, they had, therefore, escaped detection for all time. She had no illusions. If he didn't catch on, she was home free. The comparison was apt.

"Am I worth all this?" he asked clinking glasses. She felt the bubbles tickling her nose as she sipped the wonderful moist tartness of the champagne.

"At times. Well worth it," she laughed, hiding her nervousness.

He looked over the glass and studied her with his sea-clear-blue eyes. Her gaze washed over him inspecting and approving.

"This has all the trappings of a special occasion."

"Maybe it is," she teased as the effects of the Champagne began to soothe her.

"You could give me a clue."

"Never."

They were standing near the window watching the twinkle of lights from the buildings that ringed the Common. She did not know much about Boston, but it had historical connotations that pleased her, a seat of history and education that boded well as a place of conception.

He rose toward her and kissed her neck, nibbling for a moment, then moving upwards toward her right ear.

"I think you're terrific," he whispered.

With the waiter gone, they ate the pâté de fois gras and picked at the veal, but by the time they popped the cork on the other bottle of Champagne, the special command performance that Fiona had arranged had reached the end of Act One.

She felt the sudden pull of her inhibitions and, for a moment, it took all of her willpower to overcome her body's reticence. Surprisingly sensitive to her physical reactions, he stopped his ministrations for a moment and whispered.

"Anything wrong?"

She did not answer him, fearing that her words might have a negative effect on him. It was usually the male, after all, that was subject to the involuntary whims of the organism. Perhaps this was still another test. Reaching out, she touched him there. Nothing amiss. He passed with flying colors.

It was only when she fully opened up to him, brought him inside of her, felt her body accepting him, that she finally surrendered completely to the act. It had, she knew, its ritual aspect and she felt it important to show him even more enthusiasm than she usually did, which was considerable.

Because this was for real, a deliberate act, at least on her part, of conception, she coaxed him then retreated, moved in a grinding motion, then reversed herself, prolonging the act, determined to extract the maximum power of a spermatic infusion. But, soon, even the clinical aspects were lost to her in a long spasmodic excruciatingly delicious orgasm. Was this yet another validation?

"Lovely," she said, holding him inside of her, her womb still vibrating from the effect of the coupling.

"My God, Fi. You're awesome."

"It's called the Boston effect. The revenge of lust for all those years of repression," she whispered.

"Compliments. Compliments. I thought maybe a little of it might have something to do with me." He pulled a face with his lips turned down.

"Without you it wouldn't have worked," she teased.

He was silent for a long time, holding her. She felt his breath against her hair. His silence frightened her. Perhaps he had figured it out, she thought.

"You're a powerful piece of womanhood, Fi," he began. Quickly she put a finger over his lips. He was getting too close to the bone, she decided. His subconscious was figuring it out, dredging up suspicions. This often happened in her work. Words as a stalking horse for the subconscious. Then suddenly revelation.

They slept, then awoke, drank more Champagne, made love. She set the pace, slowly this time around, although when the ecstatic moment came, she heard the sound of her voice. A cry of joy. A shout. In a metaphysical sense, she was certain it was a welcoming celebration of creation.

"Got a real screamer on my hands," he told her when they had quieted, resting like two spoons, he in back with his hard arm around her, his hand fitted to her breast.

"That ain't the half of it," she sighed, dying to tell him what she had experienced, what she was absolutely certain had occurred. She wrestled with the guilt of it for a time, then slipped into sleep.

When she awoke at first light, he was still in a dead sleep. She let him. He deserved the rest. Instead, she inspected him with the care of someone who had a vested interest. She noted how well-made his hands and feet were, the fingers long and tapering, the legs curved and shapely. His hair, too, was shiny and healthy, his chin strong, his arms hard and powerful. She imagined genetic combinations, a girl with his eyes and hair and straight strong body with her high-pitched breasts and smooth white Irish coleen unfreckled skin and straight nose, slightly elongated like his. She imagined a boy made just like him with her eyes and well-shaped ears and her fine hair and good cheekbones, not that his weren't gorgeous on their own. She hoped, too, that, if it was a boy, Greg's male parts would be replicated.

After awhile, she began working out practical, but necessary, scenarios. She would have to break up with him at some point, long before her time, and she would take her maternity leave somewhere far from Washington, some place difficult to find in case he ever wanted to work out an exact birthdate. Alright, there was a degree of dissimulation here, but we were playing with a child's life. Not that he would ever acknowledge that he was the father. The point was that even if he did not know, she would not let him down. Above all, she vowed, she would be a good and loving mother.

He was still sleeping when she left the suite. She kissed him gently and left a note in lipstick on the bathroom mirror.

"More later. Rest up."

S OUTH BOSTON was Paddy Pig Irish, an expression her father used whenever he referred to his own Brooklyn neighborhood. Driving through in her rented car, she noted the same familiar reminders, the false shingle facades on the two-story houses, the bars on every corner proclaiming their territorial imperative, O'Neill's, O'Hara's, McCarthy's, The Shamrock, Paddy's, the profusion of Catholic churches, the parade of Irish faces. Since it was Sunday, the streets were sprinkled with spruced up family groups coming and going to Sunday mass.

It was, of course, a place of pride and roots, an embattled ethnic island fortress, tough and cantankerous, a bastion for the sons and daughters of the shanty Irish and the mock shanty politicos who lived there for their own reasons.

My crazy people, Fiona thought, feeling a strange rush of nostalgia and loss as she threaded her way through the streets, following a map opened on the seat beside her. She found the storefront headquarters she was looking for. Above it a shiny new banner proclaimed it as "Grady for Congress" headquarters. Quick work, but then politics was based upon opportunism.

She knew he'd be there.

"He'll be interviewing volunteers there all of Sunday morning," a voice on Grady's home telephone had told her, sounding like someone who had just gotten off the boat from the old sod.

It was still early, although some potential volunteers, mostly teenagers and ladies of uncertain age with blue hair had already gathered inside, where young men and women sitting at battered secondhand desks were doing the interviewing.

As she entered, a smiling young woman holding a clipboard made eye contact and held out her hand.

"I'm Peggy Smith," the woman said. After a very firm handshake, she peeled off a paper from the clipboard and handed it to Fiona. "Just fill this out and someone will be with you in a moment."

"I'm here to see Mr. Grady," Fiona said politely.

"Of course. But we have this routine. We have to sort of get acquainted. Jack is here, of course. But he sees you after the initial interview." Peggy Smith had rolled her eyes to a partitioned area in the back of the store. Fiona nodded, took the paper and moved to a shelf along the side of the wall on which there hung pencils connected by string.

There was always a police advantage to the shock value of surprise. But she wasn't on her own turf and, above all, she had to avoid stirring up problems for the Eggplant. He had sent her there with the understanding that she play the guerilla. If push came to shove, he would probably deny the instructions. Normal procedure would have been to check in with the Boston Police Department, but this case, as the Eggplant knew, was different. Too political. She would have been sidetracked, "handled". Police brass and local pols were protective of each other. More than likely partners in corruption.

The procedure here was simple. The screening process was merely an eyeball look at the prospective volunteer, a brief conversation to determine whether the person was of reasonable intelligence and sound mind, then shunted off for the inspirational kicker, an equally brief meeting with the candidate.

She went through the process with agility, having used her own name and social security number, but making up an address. This nearly blew the scam. The interviewer, a male student at Harvard, had not heard of the street.

"Only a half a block long," Fiona countered. "Nobody knows it's there."

This seemed to satisfy him and soon, making no waves at all, she found herself seated next to Jack Grady. She recognized him at once as the man who was seated next to May Carter.

He was the image of an Irish pol. Central Casting could not have done better. Beefy ruddy face, a mop of curly white hair with eyebrows to match and sky blue eyes that peered out of crinkly laugh pockets. His style was hug and smile, a real hearty hail fellow well met. He greeted her with klieg light brightness.

"Welcome aboard, Miss FitzGerald," he said taking her hand in a double shake, one hand on the forearm, slightly awkward for him since he had to partially rise from his chair to perform it.

"I'm not who I seem, Mr. Grady," Fiona said.

He sat squarely back on his chair, his smile gone, not quite knowing how to handle it.

"You media people never let a man rest," he sighed, slapping the table, the smile restored. He had the knack of puffing himself up with charm.

Fiona opened her pocketbook and pulled out her badge.

"I'm really sorry about this, Mr. Grady," she said lifting the badge for him to see, "but I wouldn't have come this far if it wasn't essential."

Again the smile disappeared. He shook his head.

"I really resent this, ah . . ."

"FitzGerald. Sergeant. Metropolitan Washington Police."

"In the flesh now is it? It's a lousy tactic. Worse, you know damned well that you have no jurisdiction here." He picked up the phone at his elbow. "Do I have to zap you out of town or will you go peacefully?"

"I won't go peacefully, Mr. Grady." He started to push buttons. "And you won't be able to visit my turf without a hassle from us. That's Washington, remember. If I'm not mistaken, the place where you want to go."

"Dammit, I got rights." He still held the telephone, his fingers still poised for action.

"So did Frankie," she said with determination.

"Are you saying what I think I'm hearing?" he said.

"I know what I'm saying. I don't know what you're hearing."

"That you think I have something to do with Frankie's death?"

"You don't think she was a suicide?"

He bit his lip, shook his head, and put down the phone.

"What is it with you people? You think I murdered her to get a shot at her seat. We were buddies, for chrissakes. Jack and I were choir boys together. I've known both of them all my life."

"Did I mention murder?"

He struck her as all puffed up ham, the Jack of Clubs. She could actually see the gears of his mind grind, figuring out the best approach.

"You wouldn't be here if you didn't think so," he said. She could tell he had reconciled himself.

"The truth is, Mr. Grady, we're not sure whether it was suicide or murder. But we've got to wrap it up one way or another. The woman was in Congress. She left no note. The best thing for you and for us, Mr. Grady, is to tie up all the loose ends and file it away once and for all."

He looked relieved at what seemed like her frankness. But he still wasn't relaxed.

"I'm a politician, FitzGerald. I ducked you because there's a downside on this for me. I started out as a cop. I understand the problem and I know this much. If there's any hint of a homicide, which I doubt, everybody knows that suspicion always hangs on the question of "Who benefits?" I know you don't know much about politics, lady, but it's all perception, all done with mirrors. It gets out that I'm even remotely considered as a factor in this, in any way, then I hang up my jockstrap."

There was an air of pleading about his justification but it did make absolute sense.

"I understand. No one but my partner and my boss knows I'm here. I can assure you, Mr. Grady, that both these men are the soul of discretion. I can be trusted and I'm not here to make any trouble for you."

"It's got to be confidential."

"No notes. No tape recorder. All we need to wrap this up is reasonable justification. We've got to talk to everybody that's relevant."

"And because I choose to run, I suddenly become relevant."

"You were a cop. I got my orders. Investigate. Talk to everybody. Look, Mr. Grady, it's a hot potato. Nobody really wants to fool with it. All we need to do is close it out."

On the surface, her explanation seemed very credible, even to her.

"The faster we do it, the better all around." She felt him studying her, beginning to surrender to the idea. Keeping the case open, he must have known, wouldn't do him a bit of good.

"Between us then. Man to man." He showed her a smile.

"Man to man."

He put out his hand. She took it. It was warm and clammy.

"Deal," she said.

12

IT WAS A KIND of coffee shop, with a cracked white Formica counter, red imitation leather booths, chrome-edged brown formica tables and an old-fashioned stainless steel urn that made noise like a steam locomotive.

They sat in a booth with high sides, well out of the line of sight of anyone entering. Grady nodded to the big bellied man behind the counter.

"You want a cuppa Joe, Fitz?" Grady asked. In his mind, she could tell, the intimacy with her was sealed. She nodded and he called the order out to the man. "My regular, Sully."

"Up front," Grady began. She could tell he was comfortable with their so-called deal and he trusted her. "I'd say the lady died of a broken heart."

"Now there's a concrete idea," she mused. Here was yet another babbling Irishman purveying mysterious sentiment and compelling charm. The type was painfully familiar. A figurative image crossed her mind, herself donning hip boots to wade through the effluvia of blarney.

Sully placed two mugs of coffee on the table, one with the distinctive odor of brandy, her father's occasional breakfast ploy. She watched as Grady sipped through the steam and smacked his lips.

"I'm telling you why she did it. Broken heart all the way."

His shaggy eyebrows seemed to roll down over his eyelids, hiding his eyes as he contemplated his own words. Then he nodded, agreeing

84

fully with his assessment. She tried not to look skeptical.

"Look. Who would kill Frankie McGuire? Everybody loved Frankie. Talk to anybody in this district. Frankie McGuire was the Irish goddess. Could do no wrong. Even her enemies loved her. Hell, you should have heard what Charlie Rome said at the service in the rotunda of the Capitol of the United States." She hadn't told him that she was present. He took another sip and pounded his chest. "I loved her. I loved her since the first day I saw her coming down the street after church with that green hat on her red head. Maybe she was twelve. No more. Never gave me a tumble though. It was the old Jack of Diamonds from the beginning."

Was he running something up the flagpole to test a campaign ploy? Wrapping himself around the fallen icon? Mustn't forget he is a politician first and foremost, she warned herself, excavating a mental moat around her to protect her from gullibility. These old Irish blarney birds had the ability to reach inside of you, touch the weak spots. Even his tone and language had subtly changed to meet the requirements of persuasion. Above all, he was hustling her figurative vote.

He took another deep sip and sighed, then seemed lost in deep thought for a moment. After a long pause, he then shook himself alert, his gelatin jowls shivering like a St. Bernard.

"It was me that was going to run that first time out when old Huey gave up the ghost. Was our man in Washington for thirty years. You know how it was in the old days." He looked at her. "Maybe not. But it was me that was groomed to take his place. I had to settle for State senator." He put both his hands up, palms out. "I'm not complaining. Been damned good to me. Damned good." He shrugged and she knew he was reliving it all, reaching far back in time for justification.

Hard to fathom these things, she thought. She had encountered it many times in her business. A person reluctant to talk at first suddenly vents himself and explodes with an unstoppable confession. Of course, she needed to ask questions to fill in the gaps, but she knew it would be wrong to interrupt him, break the spell. He called for a refill and Sully stopped what he was doing and eagerly brought it to their booth. He stood over them, waiting for a response from her.

"I'm okay," Fiona said.

"It was the old Jack of Diamonds. He came to Huey on his deathbed and begged him to give Frankie the Congressional spot. Huey said that if Jack Grady stepped aside he would put his blessing on it. That's the way things are done up here. You being Irish know the drill, all dark and mystical with blood bonds, curses and promises to the death. So McGuire, he wasn't the Jack of Diamonds then, and I wasn't the Jack of Clubs, he comes to me and invokes everything from the Holy Mother to the pope, reminding me about us being spiritual brothers since choir boy days. Hell, we were always thick as fleas. Even now." He lowered his voice and leaned over the table. "Used to filch nickels from the Sunday church box. Him and me were the counters. Put the foxes in with the sheep." He chuckled. "Used to get drunk on the ceremonial wine. In the end he was on his knees begging for Frankie to get the shot and I finally said yes and he said, okay Jackie, I owe you one."

He sucked in a deep breath, expelled it, then took a deep drag on his mug. She could fill in the gaps on that one without further questions. The subtext here was money changing hands, a transaction posing as an emotional experience.

"It wasn't all Jack McGuire's soft tongue though," Grady said, after he had slapped the mug down on the table, a signal for Sully to bring another. "I told you. I loved the woman. Always did. Always will. Not something a wife likes to live with, but Patsy has been a card about it. Not that it ever meant anything more than just words. Like now. The fact is she was a hell of a congresswoman. She gave those bastards a run for their money. And I aim to follow in her footsteps, I can tell you. She'll be running with me side by side, all the way."

More campaign stuff, she thought. Because it seemed to be working, he ladled out some more, thick and steaming.

"Got no regrets, though," he added quickly. "Just picking up the relay stick is all." Sully brought another mug for Grady and refilled hers. At that point, he seemed to have gone contemplative again. He looked into the mug for a long time and when he lifted his gaze toward her she could see that his eyes were moist. "Poor Frankie. We really lost one when we lost Frankie."

Not wanting him to lose the thread, she finally spoke.

"You said broken heart."

"Had to be. I can't think what else. Unless she was sick with some terrible disease that she might not want to face."

"Not according to the autopsy."

He nodded.

"Then it's what I told you."

"Mr. Grady, I really don't understand. Are you saying she had a lover who threw her over?"

"Frankie?" He seemed to erupt suddenly waving a finger in her nose. "That's a foul ball, FitzGerald, a real foul ball. Whatever old Jack McGuire did to her, finding himself a new lady, that doesn't mean that she'd do the same to him. Frankie was a true and faithful wife down the line. Next thing you know the damned media will be dragging her hallowed memory through the slime."

"I'm sorry," Fiona said, peeking through the struts of his quickly circled wagon wheels. She had, indeed, offended their Irish tribal mores. Alright for the goose but never for the gander in their convoluted morality. Irish womanhood derived from the Holy Virgin. The bastards would sooner sew a big "A" on Frankie's shroud than abominate the faithlessness of Jack McGuire. She let herself cool inside for a moment. "I'm not from around here. Just doing my job. I suppose I've confused your meaning."

"Left field, FitzGerald. Frankie would never do anything like that. Not Frankie." His look underlined his contempt for the idea. He took another long drag on his mug.

"Okay. Then educate me. I'd like to close the book on this one." A blatant lie. This case had taken on a metaphysical importance in her life. Fate had exchanged a death for life. When a star falls another is born, her father had told her one evening long ago as they watched a glorious twinkling night sky. Swiftly, her thoughts shifted to Greg waiting for her back at the Ritz-Carlton, Greg the unwitting progenitor. With effort, she forced her concentration back to Jack Grady's speculation.

"If you lived here, you'd know. All right, he flaunts it with that woman. But you got to understand. Jack McGuire flaunts everything. Big cars. Big money. Big boats. Hell, even this new lady's got big . . . you know." He described what he meant with his hands. "Got her a fancy condo near the Common. Half his age, too. Gone on now for maybe six, seven years. Has to be a real burden for Frankie." She noted his sudden lapse into the present tense. "He shows up around election time, unfurls the marriage flag and he and their children parade around like a solid loving family. Like it was one of those Irish promises to the death. You know. Showing courage and crying on the inside but never ever reneging on a blood pledge. One thing about the old Jack of Diamonds. He keeps his word."

Again, she swallowed her resentment and tamped down any personal sentiments. Good old Jack of Diamonds, the Barnum of the rotunda, hadn't kept his word at all, not to Frankie, who was, therefore, entitled to her secret lover, whoever he might be.

"Don't think I'm condoning Jack's conduct. Fact is that Frankie also can be faulted for what's going on. Not natural for a woman to stay away from the marriage bed for long periods. Much as I loved her I think she could have done something to be with Jack more. Should have insisted that Jack go down to Washington with her, set up some business there to keep him busy. Maybe come up here two, three times a month." He pursed his lips, shook his head, then took another deep drag on the mug. "People never know how good they had it until they lose it."

"It was her husband who called on the night she died. He got worried and pushed the panic button. Does that square with this . . . this estrangement."

"Oh, they talked. Had to. Lots between them. Kids. Always a worry on that score I can tell you. And, yet, there was money between them. Things like that. But I can tell you this. He was caught between a rock and a hard place. He was getting pressure from that other woman. He told me himself. He came down to my office one day. Last July it was. Hot as a pistol. Pours it out. Claims he loves this woman, really loves her, needs her, all that jazz. He wants a divorce. The woman, Beatrice, I think her name is. An eyetie. Yeah.

Beatrice Dellarotta. Sticks in your head. Wants to be an honest woman. Wants kids. Time running out. Usual stuff for an older guy with a younger woman. He begs me to talk to Frankie. Me? The guy is desperate. He tells me that he's begging her for a divorce ever since he met the new lady."

"You think it was all coming to a head?"

"First of all. Face facts. Politically speaking a divorce is no asset. Not in this neck of the woods. Also, by now, Frankie is a national figure, a real force. She's the leader of the pro-life people in Congress. She's a ball buster on prayer in the schools. That's potent political stuff for our people. She divorces, she blows her credibility with the real die-hard Catholics, the ones that still support the Latin litany which nobody ever understood except the priests. You don't fuck . . . sorry . . . you don't mess with the committed Irish Catholics on these issues. Sure they talked, but I'll bet most of it was about the divorce. Him nagging. She rejecting."

Everything is politics to these people, Fiona sighed. Her people. Again Sully arrived with a refill and she could see the veins in Grady's face begin to redden.

"And did you speak to her?"

"I sure did. When she came back to the district we talked. Cried like hell on my shoulder. Hysterical she was. Too late by then. Jack was committed to this new one and she knew it. Said all this fame and fortune wasn't worth diddley squat. Values. Frankie had values."

"But you said broken heart," Fiona coaxed. "Over Jack McGuire?"

"She loved him, you see. Loved the old Jack of Diamonds."

"She said that?"

"Her? Too much pride to tell it to me."

"So how can you be sure?"

She was easing him along, her voice soft and coaxing. There was a sense of the bizarre about it, hearing this middle-aged hard-bitten, booze-and-blarney-soaked Irish pol talk about love.

"Love like they had doesn't die so easily. Jack told me himself on the phone, when was it, two, three weeks ago. It's not just political, he says. It's love, he confesses. Says maybe she loves him too much to give him up." Again he leaned over the table. She could smell the booze and his eyes had that rheumy look. "He really took off on her that time. Said a lot of stuff I didn't want to hear."

"Like what?"

"I don't like to be talking about things like this," he said, shaking his head sadly. "And I don't want this great lady's name taken in vain."

"We just need to wrap it up, Grady. Just wrap it up."

"She needs to lie in peace. We owe her that much."

"Problem is, she was in Congress. We can't have a lot of smoke hanging around her death. You understand. It's something that can't be swept under the rug. The important thing for you to know, though, is that everything you're telling me will be strictly confidential. That I can promise you."

She couldn't really. In Washington nothing ever remained secret for long. Nothing. But, instinctively, she knew that this was the time for reinforcement if he was to give her more. Responding, he lowered his voice.

"He said he wished she'd fall out of a window or get hit by car."

"He said that. In those words."

"I couldn't say for sure. But he was some kind of pissed off. Said she went back on her word."

"What word?"

"He didn't say."

She paused, watching him. He was hunched over the mug, lugubriously inspecting its contents.

"You think he killed her?"

Slowly, he lifted his eyes from the mug.

"Jack? You crazy." He pointed a stubby finger at her nose. "You get that one right out of your head, lady. People wish people dead all the time. It was a figure of speech. Typical of Jack McGuire. Man has a fierce temper. Fact is, under it all, there was genuine love there."

That again. She couldn't resist.

"Some love," she said, then retreated, waiting for more. He took another deep sip on his mug.

"Needs nourishment. Like anything," he sighed.

Goes for the girls, too, she told herself, keeping her silence.

"He told me he hadn't touched her in six and a half years. Didn't tell me whose choice it was, but then that was none of my business, was it? One thing he did say was that he was committed to his wop lady." He laughed. "He didn't say it that way. His beautiful Beatrice he called her. Said Frankie was ruining his life. I hated to hear it. I tell you the Lord is unfair, FitzGerald. Me, I would have been loyal and true to Frankie till the bitter end. To the bitter end."

"When did he tell you that? The part about not touching her for six and a half years."

"What did I say? Two, three weeks ago." He closed his eyes calculating. "Day after St. Paddy's day, actually. Four weeks. He called me to apologize for not showing up at the party. We have this party every St. Paddy's day at the house. Wife goes all out. Big bash. Can't remember when Jack McGuire didn't show. He had just come back from a month in the Islands."

"With Beatrice?" Fiona asked.

"Who else? Said he and Beatrice had a bad flight. Too pooped out to come."

He continued, but she listened with half an ear. She was doing her own calculations. Dr. Benton had estimated the fetus as about six weeks old. If Grady was right, that would eliminate Jack McGuire as a fathering possibility.

"When did you see Frankie last?"

"Me?"

He shrugged and raised his eyes to the ceiling.

"Coupla months. We were always on the dais together or some such. Royal Order of Hibernians. That's what it was. We both spoke. Patsy and I drove her back to the house. She still kept the old house where she grew up. She's got these two maiden aunts that keep up the place. We spoke two, three times a month. Politics. You know, she needed something from the State House or I needed something from the feds. One hand washes the other. You know the drill."

Be delicate, she cautioned herself.

"You two were, as you said, platonic buddies."

She watched his reaction, which was not to react at all. Possible, she thought. He was a charmer. Probably had scores of ladies dancing around him. And a couple of favorites that serviced whatever needs the booze had spared. After a long silence, he raised his eyes and looked at her.

"You're flattering me, FitzGerald. It was her choice. Not mine. I told you. I loved the woman."

He grew deeply contemplative. He was clever. Candor was always a good defense. He could be blowing smoke, but she could not rule him out as Frankie's lover. At the very least, she could imagine them together in that way. Not like with Foy.

"Any others putting in for Frankie's seat?"

"Not yet. But anything is possible in politics. Always is. Even Frankie had opponents, but nothing serious."

"Where does May Carter stand in all this?"

The question confused him. She could see his guard go up.

"How do you know May?"

"Hell, I'm investigating a death. They were very close, I'm told."

"Old one-note May. Never could do enough to satisfy her. Not even Frankie. She's a powerhouse. No question about it." She could see him growing progressively cautious.

"Think she might decide to run?" She felt snakelike, slithering silently toward her prey, struggling to quiet the rattle.

"May doesn't run. May endorses."

"Will she endorse you?"

"Always has."

"And if she doesn't?"

"Then it's uphill all the way," he said with some reluctance. "I mean we're all committed to the cause, but May packs a wallop nationally as well."

"And she always supported Frankie?"

"Always."

"Would it have hurt if she stopped supporting Frankie?"

His cup was still half-full, the coffee cooling, which she took as another clue to his caution. He wanted to keep his wits about him. Harlan Foy had hinted that May always kept them anxious about her endorsement and was not very happy about Frankie's willingness to consort with the enemy, like Charles Rome.

"Depends," Grady said.

"On what?"

"On how actively she campaigned against her. The thing about May is that she commands an army of loyal troops. This business of abortion is powerful stuff. Powerful. If she thought that Frankie was losing her effectiveness, then she wouldn't hesitate to fight her. I mean really fight her."

"The question then is, Did she?"

"Did she what?"

"Plan to dump Frankie. Put her support and her troops at the service of someone else, someone more malleable. Someone who she could control more effectively."

"I get the message," Grady said and Fiona remembered that it was an attentive Grady who had sat next to May Carter at the Capitol service.

"Way out of your depth, FitzGerald. You're a cop, not a politician, and I can see the gears grinding."

She tried to second-guess him. Was he thinking that she was concocting a scenario in which Frankie takes poison because May Carter has decided to dump her and she sees her life going up in smoke? Her husband gone. Her kids blaming her. The potential loss of her place in Congress. Could have lighted a fuse inside of her. Set off a massive suicidal depression.

Seeing those gears grinding was nothing compared to still another scenario. In this one, Frankie discovers she is pregnant by a lover, whoever he may be. May knows her husband is no longer sleeping with her. No secret that, not in South Boston. Can't admit that she's pregnant by a lover. Can't have an abortion. Too tough a moral burden to carry. Hard to keep secret in any event. Can't hide her pregnancy. May pulls her endorsement. Her constituents abandon her. A triple bind. Juicy grist for the media mill. Her career, her life, going downhill in a handbasket. Only one way out for Frankie.

She could almost buy that, she decided. But would the Eggplant?

She looked at Jack Grady, the Jack of Clubs, and contemplated the swirling mass of hidden agendas, secret ambitions and invisible motives that moved people to desperate acts. The human mind could justify almost anything. For the greater good, could May Clark commit murder? Weren't wars fought for the greater good? Would Jack McGuire kill for the love of another woman? A story as old as time itself. Remember Helen of Troy, who triggered a devastating war. Could festering ambition drive Jack Grady to murder, despite his protestations of love? And Harlan Foy? What turmoil and agitation lies in the eye of repression?

Call it suicide and be done with it. She urged the logic on herself. There was still no physical evidence or anything to suggest foul play. Yet the Eggplant had persisted.

"You can read anything into anything," Grady said, with remarkable insight into her thoughts. "The woman is dead by her own hand for chrissakes. If you weren't a woman, I'd tell you what you remind me of."

"I'm a cop. Not a woman." Fiona snapped. She no longer felt like ingratiating herself. She had gotten from him all she was able to absorb and it irritated her to know she wasn't any closer to an airtight conclusion, at least one that would satisfy the Eggplant, than when she had left Washington.

"Alright then," Grady said. "The African weejee bird." His lips formed a smug grin.

"The what?"

"It's like you were the African weejee bird," he repeated, his smile broadening. His speech had thickened. With his middle finger he drew circles in the air. "The African weejee bird flies in ever decreasing concentric circles until it loses itself up it's own asshole."

He studied her face for a reaction.

"Then what happens?" Fiona asked.

He shrugged and emptied his mug.

13

THE ROOM WAS FILLED with flowers and her first knee-jerk thought was that somebody had died. There were three kinds of roses, white, red and pink placed on surfaces all around the room. A silver bucket in a fresh load of ice was on a stand near the couch. There was a card propped against a rose-filled vase.

"To the girl of my dreams," it read.

"I don't believe this," she said aloud. Then she heard his voice responding. He had sneaked up on her.

"Believe it," Greg said, encircling her from behind, kissing her neck. She was glad that he could not see her misty eyes. His sudden attack of romanticism had stunned her. Athletically sexual, passionate, physically affectionate. He had been all of that. But a roomful of roses, a cute card and a surprise hello, this was a side of him that he had kept hidden.

Then it occurred to her.

He knows. The idea frightened her.

"I missed you," he whispered in her ear.

Her eyes had dried and she dissolved in his arms.

"Thought you had enough of me last night," she said.

"Never enough."

"I catch your drift."

"Champagne now or after?" he whispered.

"I'd prefer a clear head," she sighed, letting him undress her as she embraced him.

It was late afternoon before they got to the Champagne. After the first sip, she realized that they had forgotten to eat lunch and said so.

"Man does not live by bread alone," Greg said. They wore matching terry cloth robes provided by the hotel. She rested her head against his shoulder and sipped her Champagne. It was perfect, she thought, absolutely perfect. She lifted an arm and caressed his face in gratitude. He took her hand and kissed her fingers.

"It's true you know," he said.

"What's true?"

"You are the girl of my dreams," he said.

"This is getting out of hand," she said, putting a spin of humor on the remark, mostly to hide a nagging emotional discomfort. It wasn't supposed to be like this.

"I know," he said, kissing her hair.

"Snap out of it," she joked.

There was a long silence as they sipped their Champagne. She watched the reddish tint of the setting sun against the windowpanes.

"Getting any closer?" he asked. She had discussed the case with him perfunctorily, satisfying his curiosity within strict bounds of ethics and professionalism.

"Can of worms," she said.

As a lawyer, he knew the constrictions, but he was also a clever manipulator, shifty, with hair-trigger insight and the ability, as they say, to put two and two together. Also, he probably thought he had a vested interest in the case on two counts, his experience with his ex-wife and his intimacy with Fiona.

Giving him any information was a bit of a tease on her part. She could not truly trust him to keep his mouth sealed and it was quite possible he might find use for the information, especially if he needed to dazzle a potential client with his insider clout.

"Well, was it suicide or political assassination?" he asked.

"Political assassination? Now there's a heavy hypothesis."

He simulated a gun with his fingers.

"Bang. Bang. I could have done it without a pang of conscience."

"The Bernard Goetz syndrome. He shoots three black toughs who hassled him in a New York subway and many of us secretly applaud. He is our surrogate."

Many murders, she knew, were surrogate murders, prompted by deep psychological hatreds of mothers, fathers, siblings, wives, husbands, whatever.

"Apt comparison, sarge. Goetz had no cause, no ideology. His victims were also surrogates. For all those black toughs whom he perceived as hassling his life."

She detected a persuasive passion in his tone, a growing vehemence. It seemed odd for postcoital conversation which should have been low key, lazy, laid back.

"And poor Frankie?" she asked, her question still easy, offhand, although she found herself growing edgy. "Would she have been a surrogate?"

"For me she would," he snapped. She could sense his rising anger, which surprised her.

"Why?"

"Religious fanaticism. As if our bodies didn't belong to us. Hell, that fetus doesn't get there by accident. Hiding behind the idea of God to mortgage us body and soul to the State. I hate them all."

"Can't say you haven't got a position on the issue," she said, searching for a way to lighten his mood.

"Controlling your own destiny," he said, the anger still boiling. "That's the name of the game." The idea hit a deep chord in her. She was trying to control her own destiny, at the expense of his. "All they want to do is control us. Always control. That's their game."

There was only one logical explanation for his vehemence. It was, she remembered, his wife's cause and he hated his wife. Therefore, he hated her cause.

That she could understand. Also his reaction. But he had also touched on something that had relevance to her investigation. She deliberately tried to recalibrate the conversation, take it from the specific to the general and out of the personal arena.

She turned her head to look at him. "It's America. A cause is a cause. Is ideological passion enough motive to kill?" It was a lawyerly question and she hoped it would trigger a lawyerly response.

He stroked her cheek, but she could tell that he was having a hard time repressing the emotional baggage he was carrying.

"Done all the time. It's a worldwide epidemic." He patted her shoulder. "Believe me I have observed it firsthand. It's a thin line between the political and the personal, I can tell you."

He grew silent for a long moment. His thoughts seemed to drift and she could tell he was still under the spell of painful old psychic injuries. "It requires strong measures to combat it, to stand up to it and protect yourself against its onslaught. People with causes never admit to the possibility that they are wrong, you see. Beware especially of people who believe that they have enlisted in God's army. Their minds are closed. History has shown they are willing to kill for their ideology."

He reached out and refilled their glasses with Champagne, sipping some and replacing the glass on the end table. She could tell he wasn't finished with his argument.

"There's a complete lack of doubt, absolute surety. Under that mantle you stop at nothing. The cause takes over. You're no longer an individual. Nothing matters but the cause. No matter what it does to the people around you. Soon all those who are against the cause are mortal enemies. Then hate takes over. Give it a mandate from the deity, any deity, and you've got unshakable fanaticism. I abhor all ideology."

"Which explains why you can represent such shitheels as the tobacco industry, Libya and the Moonies."

"You got it."

Suddenly he shrugged and shook himself like an awakening dog. Fiona detected a twinge of embarrassment. Obviously, he had taken the subject farther than he had intended. Certainly, it was farther than she had intended. But he had been a sounding board and she forced herself to come full circle, back to the case at issue.

"So you think it could be a political assassination?"

"I told you. If I had the guts I might have done it myself."

"I'm serious."

"If I were on the other side, I wouldn't have voted for it," he said. "What you don't want to do in this business is create a martyr. Frankie murdered would be an opening for canonization." He paused. "On the other hand, he could have been a lone killer, a fire-in-the-belly killer with the political all mixed up with the personal. Lee Harvey Oswald, for openers."

"You're getting closer to May Carter's thesis. She thinks a hit man did it."

"She may have a point," Greg said.

She had her rebuttal ready before he finished the sentence.

"No way. A hit man doesn't do poison."

"A fanatic then, a crazy."

"Too well planned for the work of a crazy. A crazy pushes, chokes, shoots, cuts, bombs. Not this cat. This killer, if there was one, calculates."

"You're murdering our theories, Madame Detective."

"Maybe," she said, mulling the distinction between politics and ideology. Grady was politics. May Carter was ideology. Her thoughts were spinning now.

"Which brings us back to suicide," Greg said.

"I'm not ready to vote. But if it was suicide then the lady deliberately created the puzzle. No note. No clues." She paused. A yellow caution light flashed in her mind. There was a clue, of course. A live fetus growing inside of her. The irony was disturbing. She shook her head. Maybe this was her message. Death before abortion. The ultimate political statement. An outrageous act to illustrate a point. She shivered suddenly and stood up.

"Something wrong?" he asked.

"She could be laughing at us. All this effort and angst. If she wasn't who she was, it would be over. File closed. And yet . . . when you ask yourself the eternal question. Who benefits? You do get answers."

She could sense him waiting for more. Ethics and propriety intruded, repressing her. The fact was she was not yet ready to truly trust him, which was ironic since she had proven that she herself could not be trusted and had plotted to steal his genetic legacy without his permission. Guilt again. It came at her in waves. Once again, she faced them, braced, and let them crash over her and eddy back on the tide. She clutched her midsection and paced the room.

"And suspects," Greg volunteered, recalling the question, bringing her back to Frankie's death. Suspects, yes, she thought, but no real evidence, no nagging hunches. Only the Eggplant's good batting average on instinct. An errant thought suddenly floated into her consciousness. No, it wasn't the Eggplant's instinct pushing her now.

At the beginning maybe, but not now. Or any burning desire beyond professionalism to discover the truth about Frankie's death. Nor the desire to see justice done on principle. None of the above.

It was the dead baby.

A chill swept through her. It was an issue she had avoided, never daring to come down on either side. She believed intensely in her power to control her destiny, to make responsible decisions concerning her life, which included her body and her mind. The church held her as a sentimental childhood concept, although when she did go to church on rare occasions, she was moved by the soothing sense of spirituality, of being a tiny particle of a great grand design, a rudderless figure in a stormy sea with no power whatsoever against the wind and tides. Yes, it moved her, but it also repelled her.

No, she had not allowed herself to fantasize a predicament where she would ever have to make a choice. She had been impeccable in protecting herself against pregnancy. A passionate woman, she had always kept her wits about her. Even in the most intense sexual situations she had never gambled on fate. Never.

Until now.

She let the sudden chill subside, then drove the idea from her mind. Only then did she cease her pacing and plunk herself down beside him on the couch.

"The thing about this business . . ." she said, forcing her thoughts back to the case, soaking in the comfort of his proximity. She lifted her arm and put it on his bare chest. ". . . in the absence of a confession or even hard proof, you can't make a good case out of mere suspicion. In any homicide there are always beneficiaries. They cover the spectrum."

Grady gets to run. McGuire gets his other lady. Carter gets a controllable congressman. The Eggplant gets to be show bizzy. She gets to go to Boston and make a baby. A giggle bubbled out of her.

"That's funny?"

She shrugged and with her free hand reached for the Champagne glass and emptied it. He drank his and filled them both again.

"Now, down to the business at hand," she whispered caressing him. He lifted her face and kissed her deeply. She felt it beginning again, the tide of pleasure stirring. He had slipped his hand into her robe and began to knead her breasts.

The sound at the door startled them both. It was a loud hammering noise, hardly the discreet knock of the hotel help.

Greg ran to the door and called out, but he did not open it.

"What the hell is going on?"

The hammering continued unabated.

"I'm calling the manager," Greg threatened. It did not intimidate whoever was doing the hammering, although the intervals seemed to be getting longer. Greg looked toward Fiona who shrugged.

"I want that bitch," a gravelly voice shouted in the lengthening intervals between the pounding. The voice had a familiar ring. Fiona came toward the door.

"What bitch?" Fiona called out, recognizing the voice.

"You. The cop bitch," the gravelly voice said. Fiona opened the door. Jack McGuire, red-faced and fuming stood in the doorway. His blue eyes peering from underneath shaggy white eyebrows glared hatred.

"You calm down, pal," Greg said menacingly.

"Out of my way, asshole," McGuire said heading toward Fiona who stood her ground.

"It's okay, Greg," she said calmly shifting herself into a Karate stance in case the man got physical. She found his eyes and stared him down. He got just close enough to wave a finger in front of her nose.

"You come around here trying to make a mockery of my wife's name. I tell you this, lady. You go back to that . . ." Spittle settled at the ends of his mouth and when he spoke sticky strands clung to the corners. ". . . that sewer you call the capital. Your kind is not welcome here." He paused, the flow of his words constipated by rage.

"Make some sense, McGuire," Fiona said calmly.

"You don't have to take this, Fi," Greg said.

In the pause, Jack McGuire seemed to find his tongue again.

"You listen, bitch. This is my turf here. I can have you thrown out on your ass. Like this." He snapped his fingers.

"Who is this jackass?" Greg asked. He had moved behind the man to get in position to defend her.

"He's Jack McGuire. Husband of the deceased."

"Doesn't give him license for this," Greg muttered.

McGuire shot him a look of contempt.

"Disturbed your little shack-up, did I?"

Greg snarled back at him, obviously preparing himself for any physical eventuality.

"Couldn't blame the lady . . . if it was suicide."

"Whatayamean, if?" McGuire sneered. His face flushed as if he were working up another head of anger.

"Under control," Fiona said to Greg. "Really."

She turned to McGuire, studying him. No contest, she thought. The man was heavy, out of shape. With one well-placed blow with the edge of her hand she could break his windpipe. He seemed to consider the odds, then appeared to retreat from contemplating any violence.

"Grady told me," he mumbled between clenched teeth.

"Just what did he tell you?" Fiona asked.

"That . . ." He paused, licked the spittle from the corners of his mouth. ". . . that you were implying that Frankie was . . . well . . . a loose woman. I don't know what you people are up to. But we have children. And she had constituents. Nothing must blemish her memory. Nothing."

He was running out of steam fast and she dropped her hands and tightened the belt of her bathrobe.

"Sit down and have a drink," Fiona said. Who could resist the Irish salutation? she thought. Sure enough, he responded.

"I won't drink that swill," he said, looking at the Champagne.

"We have Scotch," Greg said, his eyes probing Fiona's.

McGuire nodded and Greg went into the bedroom for the bottle he had brought with him.

"Why can't you just let her rest in peace?" he sighed, sitting down on one of the chairs. His festering sense of outrage had obviously exhausted him. Greg came out of the bedroom with a bottle of Chivas Regal and a bathroom glass still wrapped in plastic.

"No ice or soda," Greg said, undoing the plastic. "I could call down."

"Just pour," McGuire said, watching Greg as he unwrapped the glass and poured three fingers of Scotch into it.

"D.C.'s got chummy cops," McGuire said watching Greg as he handed him the glass. He was still in his terry cloth robe which matched Fiona's. He looked at Fiona. "What happened to the black boy?"

"He's doing Frankie's case in D.C.," Fiona said in clipped cop talk. McGuire, she decided, was one nasty bigot.

McGuire upended his glass and drained it in two swallows. Greg watched him and reached for the bottle.

"Why don't you leave it while I talk to Mr. McGuire here?" Fiona said, hoping that Greg got the message. He gave her his little-boy-insulted look and shrugged. He didn't like being dismissed. She couldn't blame him, but this was now an official interrogation and Greg's presence would be an inhibition. He knew that, of course, but still didn't relish the dismissal.

"You want him. You got him," Greg muttered as he left the room.

"Touchy one," McGuire said. He poured himself another three fingers, but only took one small sip before putting it down on the table again.

"I'm here trying to get to the bottom of this, McGuire."

He finished his drink then looked at her, anger smoldering.

"There is no bottom," he said. "She killed herself. People do it every day. She pushed it too hard. It takes its toll. I don't know what set her off. But nobody murdered Frankie. She snapped, is all. There is no other explanation."

"Why, do you think?"

"I don't know what goes on in people's heads." He tossed her a cold look. "Either do you."

She let him finish his drink, pour himself another, take a deep swallow and put down the glass. No point in humoring the bastard, she decided.

"How hard did you press her about wanting to marry Beatrice?"

It took him totally by surprise. But instead of rage he registered confusion and knitted his brows. His forehead wrinkled into deep frown lines.

"The son of a bitch told you."

"They tell me it's common knowledge," she said, as if she had spoken to others. He lowered his eyes and stared at his drink for a long time. He hadn't even bothered to ask: "Who's they?"

"So it's no secret. Big deal." He emitted a cold joyless chuckle. "Yeah. We talked."

"No dice, right?"

"Not at first. But after awhile she changed her mind. Then, all of a sudden she did a turnaround, called the whole thing off."

"Why?"

He hesitated, then shrugged.

"Maybe she wanted me back. Who knows?"

"She said so?"

"Danced around. Led me to believe that was it. But I know better."

"I don't understand."

"Politics. Everything was politics with Frankie. Maybe she thought a divorce would hurt her chances? Hell, she was a shoo-in. But who knows what goes on in the devious mind of a politician."

"That's an old fashioned view, Mr. McGuire. Lots of divorced Catholics are in politics now. Lots of divorced politicians, too. Reagan was divorced. They're all over the House and Senate."

"Tell me. I argued until I was blue. Couldn't budge her. It made no sense. She was entrenched. Nobody could beat her. A real hardhead, she was." He nodded in agreement with himself, then looked up. "But a great lady just the same." His finger came up again and he wagged it in front of her nose. "We mustn't drag her name through the mud now. It's over. She's gone. Nobody killed her. Who would kill Frankie?" His gaze drifted, fixed on the window through which could be seen the lights from the buildings surrounding the Common. "She's at peace now. No one to harass her. Not anymore."

"Who, Mr. McGuire?"

"Who what?" he said after a long silence. Wherever his mind had gone it had come back now. He lifted his glass and emptied it.

"Who harassed her?" she said quietly.

"Harassed her?" he said, his eyes glazed with confusion. "Did I say that?"

"Yes, you did."

"I guess I meant me, then," he said. "Me, always at it with her, especially in the last few weeks, pushing her on the divorce. Nothing could budge her. Nothing. Believe me, I tried every argument I knew. Even more money. I got enough, she said. Hell, she got enough because the Jack of Diamonds earned it for her."

"Grady said she died of a broken heart," Fiona offered cautiously, watching his expression.

"Broken heart? He told you that? Broken over who?"

"You."

"Me? That's rich." He actually chuckled. "Show you the power of P.R. The ever loving Frankie McGuire. Had even Grady fooled. Hell, it was always easy to fool Grady. I suppose he gave you that chestnut about him loving Frankie."

"As a matter of fact."

"Hated her guts he did. Ever since old Huey dumped him in favor of Frankie. Raised hell about that."

"He implied you begged him until he consented to be bought off."

"Half-right, I suppose. I don't beg. But I do buy. On that alone, she owed me one. Frankie owed it all to me in the first place. But it worked out fine all around. Old Grady didn't have a pot to pee in or a window to throw it out of. We got him a chunk of real power in the State." He hesitated. "Changed his life. Good all around."

"You don't mind him running for Frankie's seat?"

"Hell let the son of a bitch have the seat. He's got an ego on him won't quit. Inside he's dancing on Frankie's grave. Perfect timing, too. The Jack of Clubs was losing his clout."

He was straying too far afield now. She had to reign him in, get back to the central question.

"Did you ask her again that night?" He seemed not to comprehend. "Ask her for a divorce?"

"That night?" His eyes narrowed and he rubbed his chin, as if were unsure how to answer.

"That could have set her off. Been the deciding factor. The straw that broke the camel's back."

"That's a heavy load to lay on a person," he sighed.

"I know. But it could provide a conclusive motive for Frankie's suicide and end this investigation once and for all." And put the monkey of guilt on your back all the rest of your life, she thought. It was the kind of knowledge that could be passed on without words. When he reached again for his glass, she noted that his fingers were trembling. He put it down quickly. It was empty and she poured him another, but he held off from taking it.

"Did you speak to her that night?" Fiona pressed.

He shook his head, his eyes staring into space.

"Tried to, but never reached her. It was me that called Foy, remember."

"Because you were worried about Frankie?"

"Worried about Frankie?" He mulled over the idea for a moment, then said: "I wanted to speak with her."

"About the divorce?"

"I told you."

"Was it that urgent?"

"Yeah," he drawled. "To me it was."

She allowed another long pause to happen, then struck out again.

"Where were you on the night Frankie was killed, Mr. McGuire?"

She could see his nostrils widen. He seemed to be searching for something deep inside of himself. Whatever it was, it triggered a sudden alertness. He reached out, took the glass, contemplated its contents, then slapped it down on the table as if to say, as Grady had done that morning, "No more, got to keep my wits about me."

"Builders' meeting," he said. "Greater Boston Builders' Association. I was the principal speaker."

"What time did it break up?"

"About ten-thirty, I think it was. I remember because I was back at the apartment at eleven. Turned on the eleven o'clock news."

"The apartment you shared with Beatrice Dellarotta."

He nodded. He had reached a point where he was almost volunteering answers as fast as she could think up the questions. It also had all the earmarks of a prepared script.

"Why did you call Frankie?"

"I was pushing her, you see. Asking for that divorce."

"At that late hour?"

"She always worked late at her office. I told you. She worked her ass off, a regular workaholic. That's what done her in. But the office wasn't the place for serious conversation. Besides, I think Foy was on the phone, monitoring her calls. He was always there. You couldn't have a real private talk. Not about what we had to talk about. No way."

He was embellishing the script now, ad libbing, backfilling. She let it happen. He looked at her directly, his eyes pleading for understanding.

"She had every reason to let me go," he said. "Every reason." At that he pulled up abruptly and studied his hands. After too long a silence she decided to coax him along.

"Because of you and Beatrice?" she asked gently.

"Not just that," McGuire said. The booze had mellowed him.

"She knew about you and Beatrice?" Fiona asked.

"That she did. Found out two, three years ago. Not that it mattered. We hadn't been man and wife for years before that. She had her life in Congress. I had mine back here in Boston. Common problem for politicians."

"I know," she said. "I'm the daughter of a senator." Often in an interrogation, she had used something in her own background as a bonding mechanism. It relaxed the subject, made him more secure and open. People who hold deep dark disturbing secrets are dying to reveal them. Not entirely cricket, but it did the job.

"There you go," he said finally picking up his glass, sipping sparingly then putting it down. "Pulls a family apart, it does. We're only human. God's flawed children. There was a bargain in it, of course. I showed up with her every election in the district. Many of them knew, of course. But it was the propriety of it that was important. I respected Frankie and couldn't embarrass her. Even Beatrice understood that. Poor Beatrice. It's been hell on Beatrice." He took another deep drag on his drink. "It needn't have happened this way, though."

She wasn't sure how to take that, waiting for him to explain. Again, he hesitated and she had to stoke the fires.

"So that night you decided to have it out again," Fiona pressed, taking a relentless tack. "But you couldn't reach her."

"No. No one answered."

"Did that often happen?"

"As a matter of fact, yes. I was always leaving messages at the apartment desk."

"But last night you didn't."

"Couldn't. It wasn't connected. You see she has to turn this switch so that the desk picks up the messages. When she left in the morning she would turn the switch, then switch it back when she got home later."

"So you knew she had gotten home because the desk wasn't picking up."

"That's it."

"You called a number of times and when you got no answer you called Foy."

"Right. That's what I did. And he went over and found her."

"So no one can say that it was your talk with her that was the immediate cause of her death."

"How could it be? I never reached her. Not that night."

"But you did call her frequently?"

"Yes I did. I wanted that divorce. I was pushing. It wasn't fair. Not to me. Especially not to Beatrice."

"Why especially?"

"She was, well younger. Also traditional. She wanted marriage, family. Frankie was being pigheaded. She would have ridden out the divorce politically. It was vindictive on Frankie's part. I kept asking for a better reason. Politics. Always politics. But I kept at it. Why was it okay before and not now?"

"You were really madder than hell about her changing her mind?"

"She was being a real bitch. It was making me crazy."

He could not conceal his vehemence. Enough to kill? she wondered.

"Why was it so urgent?" Fiona asked.

His eyes widened and his eyebrows lifted, crawling up his forehead to the grey hairline.

"Because of the baby, for chrissakes."

"The baby?" She felt the inner bong as the blood rushed to her head.

"You knew?" she croaked.

"Of course, I knew. I'm the father. Beatrice is nearly four months pregnant."

14

THE EGGPLANT WAS always in a foul mood. It was an axiom of the squad room. Heaven help those who confront him first thing on Monday morning. There were various theories about why this condition existed, but one unassailable truth. His weekends were hell.

His wife Loreen had badgered, coerced, abused, and tormented him. On Monday morning he needed surrogates on whom to avenge himself. On this Monday this need was fulfilled by Fiona and Cates.

"I have motives and scenarios," he shouted, his palm a human gavel as he rapped the desk. "No clues. No closers. This is not a high-school psychology class. Worse, it is not police work."

This was a familiar script, but she detected a difference in the delivery, an undercurrent not only of anger but of fear. He had smoked down two panatelas and had lit a third.

Unable to sit behind the desk and suffer his real or imagined frustration, he got up and badgered them without any obstacles between. This was particularly offensive to Fiona who had to suffer through eye-level confrontation with the Eggplant's crotch as she sat on his battered leather couch crunched by years of abuse by overweight cops.

Eventually, she knew, he would work it out, find his manhood again, repress the weekend pussywhipping until the following Monday. Unfortunately, this was taking longer than usual to happen. The reason for this did not emerge until he had raved and ranted for nearly half an hour.

"As you know," he said, showing the first clear signs of spent ire, "we are a churchgoing family. We consult the Lord on his day of rest for comfort and insight. Loreen insists on such a cleansing. Good for the soul. We go as a family. It is a ritual of high order, of enormous priority. For me to miss this experience creates a needless trauma in my household."

He waved his panatela, wet end up in Fiona's face. She allowed it, avoiding the stink by not breathing through her nose. She could tell he was on the verge of revelation. No point in deflecting his attention by flouncy rebellion.

Besides, she was not taking his rebuke seriously and she and Cates had already exchanged numerous winks whenever the Eggplant looked the other way. Nor did this long-winded outburst try their tolerance. It went with the territory. Everyone in Homicide knew that suffering through one of these explosions was an essential ingredient of the boss's therapy.

"Instead of this exercise in spiritual renewal, my sacrosanct Sunday morning was spent at the mayor's breakfast table. He took his morning coffee and I took his shit."

Serious stuff, she agreed. In the Eggplant's life the mayor was Mr. Everything. By statute, position and inclination, he controlled the police department. It was he who picked the chief, manipulated promotions and generally, by whatever political intimidation he employed, ruled the cop roost absolutely. Normally, the mayor exercised this control through his police chief, but as they soon discovered, the Eggplant's meeting with the mayor was one on one, an event that portended ill for the Eggplant's career plans.

"He wanted to know about the McGuire case. He made it perfectly clear that he did not wish this to be an open case for too much longer, that I had to stop feeding the press tantalizing bullshit. Then he asked me what I had." He shook his head, then turned his eyes away from them. "I gave him smoke. I blew it in a steady stream right up his kazoo."

His ire had shifted now as he telegraphed to them his chief animus, his enormous contempt for the dark machinations of the bureaucracy. He forgot to puff life back into his panatela and he walked to the window and spit out his anger through the unwashed clouded window to the sun-dappled, sharply shadowed streets.

"Lady and gentleman, our asses are sitting on a heavy keg of political dynamite. His Honor, you see, is being leaned on by those high powered dudes in the House of fucking Representatives, those stalwarts who give us their monetary largesse in exchange for our toadying to their whims and caprices." He shrugged and turned to face them again. "This is strictly top-secret. I mean *top*—TOP. Got it?" He waited until they had nodded, then lowered his voice and gave a paranoid roll to his eyes. "My black ass is on the line, folks. He got the word direct from Rep. Charles Rome who brought it down from the Mount of the Speaker himself." Rome's image, as he appeared at the Capitol service, rose in her mind. She remembered his regal bearing, the deep authoritative voice, the doting Dresden doll perfect wife following in his wake.

"This is real heavy-duty stuff. It seems that the Speaker has gotten wind of a scheme afoot to make the McGuire demise appear to be the work of a hit man paid for by the pro-choice people." He stuck the cigar in his mouth and waved his hands. "I know. This is a poisoning. Not a hit man M.O. None of that is relevant. The idea, as I hear it from the mayor, is to make it look like an ideological killing, give it a political spin to further the cause of the pro-lifers. Make hay for their cause. The reasoning goes like this. It's the pro-lifers who are always getting stung by those fanatics burning down abortion clinics. Now they got a chance to show that the real crazies are on the other side. You get my drift?"

The early blind anger had spent itself. The logic of the professional was taking over.

"May Carter stirring things up," Cates said.

He had, of course, been "apprahzed" of their interview with her.

"That's of the 'how'. As I understand it, it's the 'why' that scares the big boys. Political nastiness is bad for both sides. Makes them all look like assholes." He lowered his voice. "As if they need more grist for that mill. Anyway, they say that as long as this investigation drags on without a conclusion, then this other thing, the hit man theory, stirs the political pot unnecessarily."

"Circling the wagons," Fiona said. "To protect their vaunted image. That's always number one with the boys on the Hill." She looked up at him. "Now give us the real hidden agenda."

"The mayor explains it this way. And he ain't no dummy. The majority is holding the line on abortion rights. The issue for hizzoner is Congressional funding for poor girls to get an abortion. That's a powerful goal for the pro-choicers. And there's political currency in it for him. Hizzoner and the congressman sees this ploy, making it look like this was an ideological killer, reinforcing the image that the pro-choice team are murderers. The public opinion factor at work. In politics such pressure bubbles upward. The pro-choice politicians see themselves caught in the middle and when a politician is caught in the middle, watch out."

Her own political experience, through her father, gave her some understanding of the scenario. Like all political stews this one boiled and bubbled with trade-offs, deals, overblown rhetoric, fanaticism, chicanery and hypocrisy. She patted Cates's knee which meant for him to accept the Eggplant's view of it and that she would attempt to unravel it all later.

"And hizzoner wants it finished fast, before the idea of a political killing gets loose," Fiona said.

"You got it. Lance the abscess before the pus spreads in the body politic," the Eggplant said.

"Does that mean no more press?" Fiona asked.

"Can't you see my muzzle, woman?"

"There's one easy out," Cates said, too late for Fiona to stop him. He could walk into fans faster than any cop she ever knew. It wasn't exactly naïveté. Or being still wet behind the ears. Cates worshipped at the shrine of the blindfolded lady with the sword and the scale. On this issue he was without guile or subtlety. He had chosen this work to right wrongs. Nothing so pedestrian as earning a living or "getting ahead" interfered with that calling.

"Call it a suicide, right?" the Eggplant smiled down at him benignly, setting the trap.

"Because that's what it is," Cates said. "We have no real evidence to the contrary. As you put it before. Only motives and scenarios."

"That's what they want, Cates," the Eggplant said. "You got it."

"So where's the problem?" Cates asked.

"Explain it to the pussy, FitzGerald," the Eggplant said, puffing smoke into the air.

"It's not very complicated, Cates." She was sure she had it down the way the Eggplant saw it. He had his foibles and eccentricities but he knew his turf, both the grit of the streets and the steamy underside of politics. The primary mission of the MPD, was to protect the politicians, the bureaucrats and diplomats in the nation's capital, protect their lives and property and their ability to function. The system was politicized, top to bottom. Everything else was secondary, although keeping the peace was a given, an essential part of the equation. It was, of course, a two-way street. One hand, as they say, washed the other. The only common enemy was the media.

Such a primary mission required, above all, discretion, the keeping and use of secrets. Even the lowliest recruit knew that you didn't mess with the big shots, that you kicked certain problems upstairs pronto. Sometimes it got out of hand and was inadvertently pushed into a floodlit media circle. Like that aide to President Johnson who got picked up for soliciting in the men's room of the Y or the powerful drunken congressman who pushed his stripper girlfriend into the tidal basin. No way to hide things like that.

But there were lots of little crimes, silly illegal indiscretions that could have fatal political consequences. A gay pol found in flagrante delicto with his underage closet twinkie. A swinger diplomat caught in a cat house. A second-story job on a house owned by a pol, bought for his mistress. A bureaucrat caught buying a spot of coke. Lots of little crimes. Raids on high stake poker games. Closing down a raucous salt-and-pepper sex and liquor party. Even drunk driving. All political career killers.

An official wink could pile up lots of chits. It didn't qualify as real corruption, like bribery or obstruction of justice. Washington was no place for Batman and Robin.

The trick was to circle the wagons before the Indians attacked. Keep stuff out of the computer. To the Eggplant and Fiona such things were baggage you carried, like your piece and your badge. She would have to explain it all to Cates. He would learn. To get anywhere in the MPD, he had to.

"Double-edged sword kind of thing," Fiona said. "The woman was an icon for the pro-lifers."

"So?"

"She was pregnant by a man other than her husband. She chose not to have her baby by taking poison. To pro-lifers that's a double killing."

"But it's over. The woman has been buried. Who's to know?"

"The cover-up fairy," the Eggplant said.

Cates looked confused.

He was talking political shorthand, knowing she would pick it up. It was the way her father explained things. "I'm simplifying but you get the message." Cates looked at her and shrugged. He was obviously concentrating, carefully following the Eggplant's explanation. The Eggplant looked at Fiona, his signal for her to explain it further.

"When you have two violently opposed forces in politics there can be no secrets. The fact of Frankie's pregnancy is already engraved in the medical examiner's paperwork. The Boston connection is a can of worms, juicy stuff. We conclude suicide by decree, we open ourselves up to an avalanche of inquiries. Why our conclusion? Why did she do it?"

"You got those answers, Cates?" the Eggplant asked.

"So, we're damned if we do and damned if we don't," Fiona sighed.

"Unless we get down to the skinny," the Eggplant said. He shook his head. "I know it. I feel it in my gut."

"But they want you to end it," Fiona said.

"We are looking here for an ending, FitzGerald," the Eggplant said. "A truthful ending. A judgment of murder definitely sours the political stew, agitates the cooks. Some politicians could choke on it."

"But suppose we come up with nothing definitive, a total absence of proof positive?" Cates said.

The Eggplant shrugged.

"My bones say murder," the Eggplant whispered.

He was still being stubborn. At first glance it seemed out of character. She had seen the extent of his brown-nosing. But this was different. Admittedly, he was operating in a narrow sphere, but it was just wide enough to accommodate his instincts, at least for the moment.

"You tell that to the mayor, chief?" Fiona asked.

"Danced around it," the Eggplant admitted. "Both he and Rome were in no mood for anything but suicide."

"And, of course, you explained the consequences of a hasty rush to judgment?" Fiona asked.

"Say what? They were also in no mood for rebuttal," the Eggplant sighed.

"What did they say when you told them she was pregnant?" Fiona asked.

His face froze and he looked at her with his cryptic rheumy eyes. Then his mouth tightened into a joyless smile.

"I didn't," he said, nostrils quivering.

"Talk about cover-up," Fiona muttered.

"Didn't say, therefore didn't lie," he said.

"That's a bad-guy line," Fiona sighed.

"I know."

"Then, why not?"

He looked into space for awhile, then struck a match and relit his panatela, inhaling, then puffing out his cheeks and expelling a smoke stream.

"They weren't ready for it," he said into the smoke's wake. "I'm saving them from themselves, giving them deniability. Not to mention that I don't trust either of them."

There was, she knew, a two-edged truth in that. Lack of trust was only one edge. The other was that he was also playing the loyal flunky, setting himself up as scapegoat if it came out in the wrong way at the wrong time, giving the mayor a chance to deny knowledge and point a finger at a sub-sub subordinate, always the best choice of goat.

"Does Dr. Benton know this?" Fiona asked. She was calculating how many people up to that point knew the truth. Dr. Benton, of course, and his assistant who would have transcribed his notes.

"We had us a little talk."

"He won't hide it and you know it."

"No, he won't. If asked. But for the moment, no one is asking."

"However you slice it that puts us between a rock and a hard place," Fiona said.

"Worse than that. The mayor promised to keep Congressman Rome apprised." Apprahzed.

"Sounds like a little too kissassy political to me," Fiona said, hoping she had put a sneer into her tone.

"Shall I convey these sentiments to hizzoner?" the Eggplant said. She looked downward, surveying her well-kept nails, assessing her cuticles. She just wanted him to be sure that she knew the ploy. Not that it was at all sinister. The case was a hot potato. The House leadership had leverage over the mayor. What good was leverage if it wasn't judiciously exerted?

"So, we're the ones on the hook," Fiona said.

"In more ways than one. More than anything, they want suicide," the Eggplant shrugged.

She did not respond, watching him. He walked to the window again, looked out, blew smoke against the dirty windowpane.

"No way we're going to prove that," he said, his anger rising as he spoke. "No way. Leaves a lot of grey area. If I was them, the pro-lifers, I'd be sitting out there watching and waiting like a line of circling vultures. We say suicide. They say cover-up, that we're hiding an ideological murder for political purposes. And the pro-choicers. We say suicide. They say why, then start poking around and soon we got the press on our ass and more troubles."

He turned from the window. No longer the poseur, he was basic Eggplant now. Telling it the way it was. No frills, no fakery, no bullshit.

"I hate it when they use us hardworking cops to do their political dirty work. Okay, maybe we're not the top of the ladder prestige-wise or money-wise. But we're out there in the front lines putting our substance between them and the bad guys. I'm not talking causes here. Not race. Not liberal, conservative, right wing, left wing. Not abortion, anti or pro. Not nothing but cops."

She looked at Cates who was a mirror of her own frustration.

"So where does that leave us?" she whispered.

He seemed to rear up like a bear on his hind legs, his words almost a growl.

"We've got to find us a killer, preferably one who would be relieved to confess."

Cates and Fiona exchanged glances.

"How much time do we have?"

The Eggplant looked at his watch.

"You got until high noon," he said.

"I should have expected that," Fiona said. "I saw the movie."

15

CATES WAS visibly depressed. They were sitting at one of Sherry's chrome, Naugahyde and Formica booths, drinking more cups of coffee than was good for them. For him, Fiona knew, the McGuire case was a rite of passage.

She had not been thrilled at being paired with Cates. He had no visible street smarts. Worse, he was an idealist, which was charming, but misplaced in his profession of choice.

He was also a bit of an esthete, a totally useless virtue in their line of work. On the other hand, he was efficient, analytical, loyal, trustworthy and compassionate. Not too shabby for a cop. He also moved with the quick sureness of a panther, had a black belt, was a crack shot and fearless.

After three months together, she had stopped bullying him and his respectful willingness to learn how to be better won her respect. Despite the cases they had worked on, he had actually managed to keep himself above the cynicism and disillusionment that was a natural affliction of their work, like lung disease to a miner. Sooner or later, she knew, the affliction would invade his cells. Unfortunately, it was destined to make him less savory as a human being, but a greatly improved homicide detective. She wondered if the McGuire case would see the first penetration of his immune system.

"He's putting our careers at risk," Cates said. "We're civil servants not politicians."

"Where you been pal? Life is politics."

"Not my life," he muttered.

"That's your problem, Cates. You haven't got a devious enough mind. You need a higher level of sophistication. It takes practice to talk out of both sides of your mouth. The important thing is to never lose sight of your objective."

"And what's that?"

"The truth."

Again she felt the pang of guilt about Greg and what she had done, sharper now, an acute pain. She was a dissimulator, a liar babbling platitudes about truth.

She and Greg had come home from Boston Sunday night and he had dropped her off at her home.

Then he had called her first thing in the morning. He knew her habits, of course, the exact hour she rose.

"Missed you like crazy," he said. "Just wanted you to know."

"Mighty cold here all alone," she had bantered, actually patting the left side of the bed which was ordinarily his place when he stayed over.

"Doesn't have to be," he had told her.

A warning signal went off in her mind. What was he saying? He interpreted her silence as encouragement.

"Call it a trial run," he said.

She knew, of course, exactly what he meant. Living together. A scary concept considering what she hoped was going on in her body.

"We'll see," she said. It was what she had dreaded most. He was rewriting the script.

"Not pushing," he said, backing off. "Just falling in love."

"What!"

Love? She hadn't called what she felt by that name. Attracted? Yes. Turned on? Absolutely. But love? She dismissed it from her thoughts. Her objective here was procreation. Not love.

"Talk about it next weekend," he said. She caught a hint of disappointment. You're making a federal case out of this, she thought, but she didn't say it. Finally, he hung up leaving her shaken. He wasn't supposed to do that.

She resented this intrusion on her thoughts. She had kept it at bay all during the Eggplant's morning revelations. But it was her own attack on Cates's lack of deviousness that had penetrated her defenses.

"Seems to me he wants to get us to push due process to the wall," Cates said. "Find this killer at all costs. Even if we can't make it stick. Unless, we squeeze it out of him. Maybe we get ourselves some rubber truncheons."

"I kind of like the idea," she said. "Full of surprises, that dude, considering that he may be better off to just lay down and cry suicide."

"Makes sense to me," Cates muttered. "Despite his big number about cover-up."

"Keep an open mind, pal," she teased.

"Wouldn't have been in this pickle if that self-centered showboat would have kept his mouth shut. A mystery, he called it. Just to satisfy his ego and vanity. No mystery as far as I can see." He brought his coffee cup to his lips, forgetting the coffee was cold. He shook his head and spit a mouthful back into the cup. "He was right about one thing. You did bring back motives from Boston but nothing that contradicts suicide."

"And you, Cates. What did your little sortie turn up last weekend?"

"Not much."

He proceeded to tell her. He had put in long hours and lots of shoe leather. Nobody could research a case better than Cates. He was a stickler for detail.

Among others, he had interviewed the person who manned the apartment house desk that night, a Nigerian. His report to Fiona was brisk, succinct. Mrs. McGuire had switched phone answering back to her apartment when she came home. Up to the time Foy arrived it had been a routine shift. Nor had the man noticed any strangers coming through the lobby. He did his best to recall but he could have missed someone. Tenants of that building were a demanding bunch, the man had pointed out. Always needing something.

"Some security," Fiona clucked.

"He was the night man. A full-time student. Only on the job two months."

Foreign students who worked mostly nights were a Washington subculture. Living on the economic brink, they took lowly jobs as parking attendants, apartment desk men, caretakers, gas pump attendants or all-night waiters.

"But it is a prestige building nonetheless," Cates explained. "Ten congressmen live there. Three senators and a cabinet member. Even our present watchdog, the eminent Congressman Rome, lives there with his wife."

Fiona remembered Rome's words at the service. He had said he was a neighbor.

"I interviewed the people that lived on either side of her and across the hall. All said she was a quiet neighbor, kept to herself. Always pleasant, gave them a ready smile and a hello. They did say, however, that she was often seen in the building with a man. In the lobby. Coming up the elevator. Coming out of her apartment. Chubby fellow with lots of chins."

"Foy."

"The desk man thought, at first, that he was her husband or boyfriend." Cates paused, then smiled archly. He hadn't completed the explanation.

"What made him change his mind?"

"It was the way he said it. A wink. More like a leer. Highly doubtful, he told me. One night the man arrived drunk. The clear implication of the Nigerian was that Foy made a pass."

"When?" Fiona asked.

"The man only worked there two months."

"Maybe Foy wanted the new man to think that. Sort of a a cover ploy," Fiona said. "Best there was. She could then be having an affair with impunity."

"Impunity didn't plant that child," Cates said, a rare joke for him.

"You didn't mention it to the Eggplant. The stuff about the pass at the desk man."

"No." He shook his head as if to emphasize the point. The fact was that Cates hadn't briefed the Eggplant on anything that morning. After Fiona had made her report, he had erupted.

"It wasn't mentioned because you wrote Foy off as a suspect, right?"

"I thought we all did," Cates said, obviously confused by her sudden pressure. "He seems obvious to me. He's effeminate, a pufter boy as we called it in the old country."

"You believe the Nigerian?"

"He had no reason to lie."

"He take Foy up on it?"

"He said no."

"Not like you Cates. To throw in your hand so early. The fact is you have no proof on Foy's sex bias."

She watched his nostrils twitch. Then he shook his head and offered a joyless smile.

"Christ, Fi. If I didn't know you better, I'd say you were trying to make that poor bastard the killer? Deliver the Eggplant his patsy."

She studied him, searching for some excuse to cap her anger. The politics of the situation was getting to him.

"You got a bug up your ass, Cates," she said.

He lowered his eyes and shrugged and she sensed his embarrassment.

"He just got me riled," he muttered.

"The point is that I'm sure as hell not writing Foy off. Not yet. That lady died with a baby growing in her uterus. It wasn't immaculate conception. Somebody did it. As for the man's being dubbed a gay, never believe rumors or hearsay. Only way you know if a man is overtly gay is if he admits it or you catch him at it. As for all the closet stuff, leave that to the psychiatrists. I've seen lots of sissy boys who screw women and lots of macho men who are gay. Watch out for those clichés, Cates. In our business nothing is ever as it seems."

He needed a little more bullying, she had decided.

"All right then, let's ask the son of a bitch," Cates said. "Settle it one way or another."

"And if he says 'Yes, I am,' he's got his alibi."

"And if he says 'No,' he's automatically a suspect?"

"Maybe. Unless he's some kind of a neuter, one of these guys who couldn't care less. Lots of them around, you know." She winked. "I've met my share."

He grew thoughtful. And she felt remorse.

"I know. I'm being a pain in the butt. We're missing something is all I'm saying. We're also working under a severe handicap. We need more troops on this."

"Widen the circle? Hell, he wants to keep it contained. That way he can blame us."

Fiona chuckled.

"Maybe we should get us a little insurance on that," Fiona said.

"Like what?"

"I'll think of something."

"Okay, let's keep Foy open," he said, somewhat grudgingly.

"Let's keep everything open," Fiona replied. "Stick with the objective facts here. Frankie McGuire had sex with somebody and she took no precautions."

"Maybe she thought she was too old to conceive?"

"She probably was. Forty-seven. Normally over the hill for that."

"Let's put it down as an accident. Passion must have gotten the better of her judgment."

"Or his."

"It happens, I suppose," he said, lowering his eyes. She had noted in him a prudish streak. He rarely used the "F" word and often spoke in euphemisms when discussing sex. Like now.

"Was she a whore, you think?" she asked. "A hardup lady on the make looking for young meat." Although his skin color didn't show it, she knew he was blushing.

"Doesn't fit. Not from what I was able to find," he answered crisply, still averting his eyes.

"No way," she agreed. "She was too image conscious, too political. She wouldn't take the chance."

"But she apparently did take the chance," Cates countered. It was a little victory for him and it seemed to burn away any brewing anger.

"Considering the results," Fiona said, "she certainly did." Again the thought of Greg and her own "chance" flashed through her mind.

"There wasn't anything the immediate neighbors said that we could hang a hat on either," Cates continued. "Sometimes, the neighbors told me, she would entertain, have a cocktail party. Mostly Congressional business, constituents, colleagues, some of whom lived in the building. She was seen a lot with the Romes, though. They were a threesome. Occasional dinner and a show kind of thing. Squares with what Foy and May Carter said. Cavorting with the enemy. Something like that."

She knew he was thorough, his interrogations revealing and precise. But there was nothing in them that could satisfy the Eggplant and he knew it. It boiled down to the same dilemma and led to the obvious.

"He's got us chasing rainbows, Fi."

"We could be overlooking something," she said. It was the homicide detective's ultimate cliché.

"I also checked the Boston shuttle. They faxed me a passenger roster for the week before the crime. No Grady. No McGuire."

"Doesn't matter. They both have alibis. Airtight," Fiona said.

"I also checked out May Carter. Hell, if it was a murder it has all the signs of a woman's touch. Poison. A female's weapon of choice."

Good point, she thought. Forty percent of murders were committed by women. Since they weren't traditionally involved with violence and firearms, females used other means. Poison and fire were their favorites.

"Struck out on old May, too," Cates said. "She was at a Right-to-Life meeting in Kansas."

"So, it's back to Foy," Fiona said. She looked at Cates and shrugged.

"Poor bastard," Cates said. The compassion was real, despite his earlier remarks. For a moment it crossed her mind that Cates might be gay. He was surprisingly delicate, with soft sensual thin lips and brooding dark eyes. He was also thin, tapered. One might say he was effeminate. But, no, he had a steady, Arleen, a nurse at the Washington Hospital Center. See, she rebuked herself, how easy it was to fall into the trap of making judgments on appearances alone.

"Maybe we should put it to Foy once and for all," Fiona suggested. "Fact is he's our only suspect."

"And for your second choice?"

Fiona didn't answer.

"The Eggplant's good," Cates said, "but he's been wrong before."

"He's not wrong," she snapped. "It's us."

"Not me." he persisted. "You know where I stand."

"Maybe that's what's wrong. No fire in the belly."

"That's not it," he replied.

"What then?"

"No clues," he said. "Killers can't be manufactured. Not even Foy."

"No they can't," she agreed. "But I've got this theory."

"What theory?"

"Find the father. Find the killer."

16

HARLAN FOY was a forlorn figure of despair as he sat among the wreckage of Frankie McGuire's Congressional office. Packed cartons were everywhere. Pictures, framed citations and plaques were piled high on dusty desks, along with unused computers, coffee mugs and wastebaskets. The walls were barren, except for the outlines where the pictures and plaques were hung. It had, Fiona decided, the appropriate look of devastation and defeat.

Foy was sitting in what apparently was Frankie's desk chair which had been rolled in front of the standard issue leather couch where Fiona and Cates sat facing him. He was pale and haggard with deep black circles under his eyes. Their visit had caught him unawares, a good thing in their line. He was not, of course, overjoyed to see them.

"A bad dream," he sighed, waving his hand. Cates and she exchanged glances. The wave was a decidedly effeminate limp wrist gesture. "So much to do. The congresswoman was very active. There should be a rule. Do not die in office. It's hell on the survivors."

"You still think she was murdered?" Fiona asked. No sense being oblique on that point. Besides, she wanted to set the stage for some tough questions.

"I don't know what to think anymore," he said, folding chubby little hands on his lap and shaking his head, which was disconcerting, since it made his puddled chins shiver like half-frozen gelatin.

"It certainly is not the work of any ordinary hot-entry prowler,"

Fiona said. "If it was murder this one was well-planned by somebody with a big reason." She watched his eyes as she spoke. There was fright in them. She was sure of it.

"I can't see the forest for the trees anymore," Foy sighed. "All I know is I lost a friend, a colleague, an employer. And the world lost a beautiful person."

"You were close?" Fiona asked. "More than just an AA?"

"Very," he said. "Life won't ever be the same for me."

"I thought maybe you were going to run for her seat?" Cates asked gently.

"That took all of five minutes to decide," he said. "A silly little fantasy. It's already been decided, you see. The powers that be have anointed the great Jack Grady."

"And May Carter?" Fiona asked. "Where does she stand?"

"In the end, she'll support old Jack. He's a professional charmer, you know. May likes a boot licker, especially if it's of the male variety. Frankie wouldn't take too much from May. And I got the full brunt of the lady's wrath. No love lost between me and that big bitch."

He wasn't being the least guarded. He must have felt that it was no longer necessary for him to hide his feelings.

"Whatever we did, it was never enough for May. She kept us frantic, I can tell you. If she thinks Jack Grady will do better than Frankie on fighting abortion, then she has another guess coming, I can tell you. That lush will spend most of his time here sucking whiskey bottles."

He was obviously bitter, starting to spew venom. Perfect for their purposes.

"For me, I guess it's all downhill from here," Foy continued. "Naturally, Jack wouldn't think of hiring me. I was Frankie's person, you see. Proud of it, too. Their loss. I know where all the bodies are buried around here. All of them. I did it all for Frankie."

"Private business as well?" Fiona interjected.

"Part of the job, you see. An AA is more like a Man Friday. An everything. I did everything for Frankie. Took care of all her personal things, too. I scheduled her whole life. Made sure she made her appointments, took her meals, arranged for the cleaning woman. I even made sure her clothes went to the dry cleaners." His gaze locked into Fiona's. "And I loved every minute of it."

"Then you knew about Jack McGuire and his lady friend?" Fiona asked. His upper lip trembled and he took his time answering. "It's alright, Harlan," Fiona said soothingly. "She's gone." He could not, even now, let go of his kneejerk protection of her political image, portraying her as the loving wife of the loving husband.

"I knew. Of course, I knew. It just wasn't something one flaunted. Not that it mattered to that turd."

"McGuire?"

"He is a miserable callous son of a bitch. Cruel. I hated that man."

"Did Frankie?" Fiona asked.

"At first, when she heard about his little affair with that . . ." He shivered with disgust. ". . . that little rat, that's what we called her. Beatrice Dellarotta. McGuire and his little rat. Frankie was devastated. Of course, he always fooled around. But this was just too much to bear. And yet, she was a great soldier, Frankie was. She rose above it. Never let it destroy her dignity. Even when the children blamed her, she stood up to it. Her life, you see, was politics. She believed that God put her there to work for what she believed in."

"Why wouldn't she give him a divorce?" Fiona asked.

"The reality of politics. A man might get away with it. But a divorced woman in Catholic Boston. Well, that's another matter. Especially if she wanted to get to the Senate. Maybe she could have gotten away with it. Who knows?"

"According to McGuire, she had consented, then changed her mind."

He shook his head, vibrating his chins. His face had flushed. He reminded Fiona of a circus clown.

"I see there are no little secrets anymore," he said, waving his hand again.

"Oh, there still are a few," Cates said with a touch of sarcasm. Foy cut him a quick glance of contempt and turned back to Fiona.

"Why did she do that?" Fiona asked. "Change her mind?"

She saw him hesitate, thinking it through.

"A dispute about the financial settlement," he said quickly. "Not for her, of course. Frankie was not very interested in money. It was about the children. Yes . . ." He seemed to be convincing himself. But Fiona was already unconvinced. It was, she decided, the first real hollow ring to his words. She exchanged glances with Cates, who nodded. He also had caught the lie.

"McGuire says that such things were not the issue, that the kids were well provided for."

"Well, you're not going to believe him, are you?" Foy said, his cadences prissy. In fact, they seemed to get prissier as the interrogation progressed.

"I'm not sure who to believe," Fiona said, deliberately showing her own vacillation, urging him to convince her of his own position. He was not reluctant to do so.

"If there was any other reason, I would have known. I was her friend and confidante. I knew everything about her. Everything."

"Every little thing?" Cates asked pointedly, again with a touch of sarcasm.

"Absolutely," Foy said with an air of finality.

It seemed time, Fiona thought. She fixed her eyes on Foy. He was, indeed, a poor bastard.

"Did she have any lovers?"

He did not blanch, responding swiftly.

"That's absurd."

"Why absurd? She was attractive. Hardly over the hill. Still desirable. Her husband admittedly hadn't had relations with her for years. Woman have been known to need the blandishments of a man."

"I would have known," he said flatly, retreating from any further engagement on that subject. "There was no way I could not have known. We spent so much time together. No." He shook his head. "It would have been impossible."

"Were you her lover?" Fiona asked.

Not only did his chins vibrate, he seemed to bend by the sheer force of the questions. His body actually seemed to collapse, as if he were a puppet whose operator had suddenly let go of it's strings.

"I've asked you a question, Harlan. Were you her lover?"

"My God," he gulped.

"You were, by your own admission, her friend and confidante. You had the keys to her apartment. She was dependent on you." Fiona raised her voice. "Were you also her lover?"

His nostrils twitched and, with effort, he sucked in short gasping gulps of breath. Finally, gathering his wits, he found words.

"That is impertinent. Worse. It's rotten. Trying to defame Frankie McGuire. It's sick. Sick. You people ought to be ashamed. This was a fine woman, a good Catholic woman, a compassionate, decent human being. How dare you defame her name?"

Suddenly his eyes moistened and tears ran down his cheeks. He was overcome and collapsed with emotion, covering his face with his hands. His shoulders shook. The reaction seemed genuine enough, although she could not draw true pity out of herself. She had seen many a similar breakdown, some authentic, some pure acting.

"It's important, Harlan," she said gently. "It could explain a great deal."

If he heard, he made no sign. She looked at Cates who also seemed unmoved by Foy's emotional display. She detected a certain vagueness in him, as if his attention was diverted elsewhere. It surprised her that he did not jump into the interrogation.

"Are you saying it's not possible?" Fiona asked Foy. She paused, waiting expectantly, letting Foy gather his wits. She was, after all, approaching the climax of this interrogation, the moment of truth.

Foy reached into his pocket and pulled out a tissue, wiping his nose and eyes. Finally, he took a deep breath and looked at them again. He rose in the chair, squared his shoulders.

"Did you know she was pregnant?" Fiona asked bluntly.

This time the blow seemed to strike him in the seat of his pants. He shot up.

"You people are monstrous," he sputtered, waving a fat finger in Fiona's face. "I will not talk to you anymore. I demand my rights. As for that last remark, I demand proof positive. Proof positive." Bubbles of perspiration rose on his upper lip.

"We have it," Fiona said. "It's a fact. And all this anger and histrionics will not change it."

"I want you people out of here," he screamed, stamping his foot. "Out of here."

"She was pregnant," Fiona said coolly when his tantrum had run out of steam. "It is highly unlikely that it was in vitro. Copulation, Harlan. Fornication, Harlan. Stop all this dramatic bullshit. Somebody impregnated her." She stood, working up her own head of steam. She came close and grabbed his lapels, her face up against his. "Do we have to do this at headquarters? Who impregnated her? Was it you?"

He shook his head.

"No. It wasn't."

"You had no physical relations with her?"

"No."

"Are you gay?" Deliberately, she had shot him the question before he had time to see it coming. Cruel work, she thought.

"No, I'm not. I can sue you for that. I have never . . . I am not gay. You should be ashamed. Ashamed to make such an accusation. You people do that to all single men. Make an assumption of gayness. I am not gay. Not on your life. I am a man, a man all the way." His overreaction told the story. Still in the closet. Not bi. Totally gay. Deeply repressed. You didn't have to be a psychiatrist to figure that one out, she thought. A painstaking investigation might have picked up evidence. No, she decided. Time to end it for the poor bastard.

"All right then, Harlan," Fiona said. "Accept our apologies." He calmed down, then slumped in the chair, looking like a large piece of pudding. "So you see. She was in a double bind. She couldn't have an abortion and she couldn't really say it was her husband's. Which could explain her suicide."

"I don't believe any of this," he muttered.

"I'm afraid it's true."

"Harlan," Cates asked. "Who the hell is the father?"

"Oh God," he stammered, then looked at them squarely. "You must believe this. I haven't the remotest idea."

They stood up. He seemed genuinely stunned. Fiona put out her hand. Foy ignored it, turning his face away. She wondered if he had begun to cry again.

"If you have any ideas we'd appreciate hearing from you," Fiona said.

He did not reply.

They left the office and walked through the corridors of the Rayburn Building. Cates was inordinately silent. At this point he would have been chirping away, offering comments and conclusions.

"What's with you?" she asked as they walked into the bright sunlight.

"I'm not sure," he replied, continuing his silence all the way back to their office. Assessing the interrogation herself, she was absolutely convinced that Foy was out of the picture. His shock had been genuine. Nor had she calculated on the stunning impact her revelation about Frankie's pregnancy would make on him. A clever lady, Frankie. She knew the womanly art of keeping things to herself. Fiona could relate to that.

When they reached the office, Cates startled her by making a beeline for his desk. He pulled out a sheaf of shiny papers, obviously FAX copies, then studied them for a few moments.

"God damn," he shouted. The office was deserted and the sound reverberated in the empty room. "It was bugging the hell out of me."

"What was?"

"This," he said. He shoved one of the papers in front of her nose and pointed to a name.

"B. Dellarotta," he said.

She looked at him.

"When?"

"The evening Frankie died," Cates said. "Near as I can figure she spent two hours in Washington. More than enough time to do the job."

"Well," Fiona said. "Do we have a believer on our hands?"

"Not in miracles," Cates smiled. "Could blow your theory. One thing is certain. She couldn't be the father."

17

THE DEAL BETWEEN the Boston and Washington Police Departments was for Fiona to meet with Jack McGuire and Beatrice Dellarotta. Beatrice Dellarotta was nowhere to be seen.

"This is not what we agreed on," Fiona said.

Bill Curran, Chief of the Boston PD, unsmiling and arrogantly pompous, looked at her with disgust. He was a spare man with thin skin as white as snow, a longish bony nose and little eyes that hid deeply behind high cheekbones. His lips were also thin, with a purple bloodless tint. He was one of those healthy men that look sick. Probably a jogger, she speculated. There was no attempt on his part to be ingratiating. His carefully cultivated deadpan expression made him one intimidating son of a bitch.

They were sitting in the living room of Jack McGuire's apartment overlooking the Boston Common, a spacious place, filled with wooden Colonial furniture that seemed, even to her unpracticed eye, to be authentic antiques. Except for tacky pictures of Jesus and the Virgin Mother scattered around the apartment, it might have passed muster as the residence of an old moneyed Brahmin.

It irritated her to think in such bigoted terms, but these Boston Irish invited the comparison. Her father would have clucked his tongue. An old story, he had told her time and again. Shanty Irish imitating the Protestant establishment without paying lace curtain Irish dues.

But her primary irritation was the way these old boy shanty types stuck together. Jack McGuire, sitting smugly in the leather wing chair opposite the forbidding and dour Chief Curran who sat stiffly, legs crossed, in a high-backed wooden chair, a match of the one in which Fiona sat. It was exceedingly uncomfortable. A metaphor floated into her thoughts. The room stank of collusion.

It had taken two days of contorted machinations to get this far. The Eggplant had greeted the revelation about Beatrice Dellarotta with a resounding slap on his desk.

"Now that is police work," he said pointing his panatela at Fiona.

"So what happens now?" Fiona had asked, reminding him that they hadn't a stitch of evidence that Beatrice Dellarotta had ever set foot in Frankie McGuire's apartment. No prints. No technical evidence of her presence.

"Juicy stuff," the Eggplant said, still smiling but obviously avoiding Fiona's question. "The pregnant other woman confronts the pregnant congresswoman. The stuff of soap opera."

"A field day for the media," Cates said, a note of caution in his tone.

The Eggplant looked at them and shook his head. His smile faded.

"Looks like we got us here a P.R. problem," he sighed.

She knew what he meant. He would have to talk to the mayor. The mayor would talk to Rome. It could wind up as the kind of story, once loose, that would slop over everyone, pro-lifers and pro-choicers, the cops, the Congress. Everybody would be made to look like assholes.

Ridicule was the media's most dangerous weapon. It would stick like molasses to everyone that came within spitting distance. Naturally, such a fiasco would require a prize goat, someone in the middle rung to be kicked and pummelled by those above and below. Someone like the Eggplant and his minions. A quick verdict of suicide would now be everybody's ideal solution, especially present company.

"So far, all we have is a red-hot lead," the Eggplant said, proclaiming the obvious. "And we're still in the area of the circumstantial."

Credit the bastard with stubbornness and pride, Fiona thought with grudging admiration.

"But it does explain a great deal about Jack McGuire's attitude,"

Fiona pointed out, deliberately refocusing the discussion. P.R. was one thing, saving one's ass was another, but the heart of it was: What really happened to Frankie McGuire? The fact was that none of them, she, Cates or the Eggplant would ever be able to live comfortably under the cloud of cover-up. And Beatrice Dellarotta did not come to Washington for her health.

"So what's your theory?" the Eggplant asked.

Fiona and Cates exchanged glances, Cates signaling his approval of her proceeding.

"McGuire came home from a meeting the night of Frankie's death," Fiona began, knowing that their joint theory was still far from conclusive. "He found the little lady gone, got nervous. Undoubtedly, she had threatened confrontation with Mrs. McGuire. When he discovered that Beatrice was not at home at that hour, he assumed the worst, meaning that she had gone to Washington loaded for bear. He immediately called Frankie, maybe to put his two cents in or somehow defuse the situation. He got no answer. Imagine what might have gone through his mind. Probably called again and again. Since Frankie had switched the calls from the desk to her apartment, indicating that she could be inside the apartment, he was doubly nervous. Finally, in desperation, he called Foy and persuaded him that there was enough at stake for him to go see what was going on in Frankie's apartment. He went."

"Then Beatrice arrived home," Cates interjected.

"Probably raised quite a ruckus," Fiona continued. "No shrinking violet that one. He was probably madder than hell. Enter Foy. He has gone to the apartment. He calls McGuire. Tells him what he has found."

"And the shit hits the fan," the Eggplant interpolated.

"His first thought has to be . . ." Cates said.

"That his bitch murdered his wife," the Eggplant said.

"Something like that," Fiona agreed with a frown of distaste. No point in challenging the epithets, she decided. This wasn't the time to change the world.

"Or harassed her to suicide," Cates said.

"Either way, McGuire chooses to stonewall."

"Can you blame him?" Cates said.

"Not at all. Wouldn't want to be in his place," Fiona said. "The woman he loves . . . somehow causes the death of . . . the mother of his children." Of course, such a supposition was the heart of the theory.

"Back to square one," the Eggplant snapped. "Murder or suicide."

"I said 'somehow,'" Fiona qualified.

"Too many women. That's the lesson here," the Eggplant said, half-facetiously. Once again she ignored the macho female baiting.

"Not at all," Fiona said coolly. "The lesson here is in the method. An emotional confrontation does not suggest a murder by poisoning. A knife, maybe or a bullet. Certainly the congresswoman would not be neatly tucked in bed with a glass of wine as she received her visitor."

"There's a big hole in the ice here," the Eggplant said. "Too many damned glitches to pin a rap on our Boston lady. Why the absence of clues? No prints. No visible shootings. Too much premeditation here. Too little emotion visible."

"Maybe that was the point."

"I don't get it," the Eggplant said, turning to Cates who shrugged. The idea had not been discussed with him. It had just popped into her mind.

"Maybe she and McGuire were in it together. Maybe it was a set-up. The lady is expected. She comes up to Frankie's apartment. They talk. All very civilized."

"And she pops the poison into Frankie's glass," the Eggplant said.

"It does have a bizarre logic," Fiona said.

"No way," Cates interjected. "If anything, the woman's presence, the confrontation, could have been a trigger for the suicide. The motive."

"Death by aggravation," the Eggplant sighed.

"That doesn't explain the absence of evidence indicating that the woman was even in Frankie's apartment," Fiona argued. It all came back to that. No clues. Nada.

"One thing we do know," the Eggplant said.

"What's that?" Fiona asked.

"We've got to feed this little rat some cheese."

She got the go-ahead the next morning. To keep the politicians out of it, the deal was worked out at the lowest possible authorized level. Thus, the Eggplant talked to his counterpart at Boston PD. The mayor had instructed him to put a routine face on it. He told the Boston homicide captain that they just needed a bit of informational material to wrap up the suicide. Had to talk with McGuire and Miss Dellarotta. There was absolutely no way to avoid it. The idea, subtly conveyed by the Eggplant, was to clean it up and put it away as quickly as possible. No tape recorders. No notes.

"Play it cool," the Eggplant had warned her. "There's bound to be paranoia so it will be rough." They were alone in his office. He had made it a point to call her in while Cates was not available. The Eggplant seemed weary and more harassed than usual.

"I want you to know up front, FitzGerald, time is running out on us."

"High noon?" Fiona snickered.

"The chorus is getting louder. Suicide. Suicide. They think they can just dump the thing into this nice little coffin and bury it forever." He studied his hands, avoiding her eyes.

"Are you asking me to be less than objective?" Fiona said with a touch of mock belligerence. She knew better.

"I may rag you sometimes, FitzGerald, but I never once asked you to cop out."

That part was true. His various strategies were sometimes convoluted but he had never pressured her to compromise herself. Whatever her private feelings about him, her distaste for his vanity, his sometimes calculated brown-nosing and his overt willingness to avoid blame at all costs, she knew him to have a hard core of integrity. Deep down. Sometimes very deep. This time he was taking the ultimate risk. Without a killer, they might force him to declare a suicide, which in turn would be challenged.

"I'll buy that," she said. Their eyes locked. "Are you still stonewalling them on the pregnancy issue?" she asked.

"It's my only ace in the hole," he sighed, sucking on his panatela. "We wrap this up, it's academic. We find a killer, it would be out of our hands."

"You're hoping then that this Dellarotta is the lady."

"With all my heart," he said.

He nodded, smiled and took a deep drag on his panatela.

"I'll do my best," she told him.

Homicide solutions needed as much certainty as possible. Human life was at stake. A killer at large was dangerous enough, but a falsely accused killer, especially one that was ultimately convicted, was a homicide detective's nightmare.

"A confession would do nicely, thank you," the Eggplant muttered as she left his office.

"You know she has to be talked with," Fiona said, her eyes darting between Curran and McGuire. She took the folded plane roster from her pocketbook, unfolded it and handed it to Curran. "It's irrefutable. She was in Washington around the time of the congresswoman's death."

"That doesn't mean that she was anywhere near Frankie's apartment," McGuire said.

They had checked, of course. They knew there were no prints or any other evidence linking Beatrice to Frankie's place.

"Then what was she doing in Washington?" Fiona asked.

"I'll admit this much," McGuire said. "She did go to Washington with the intention of seeing Frankie, begging her to grant me a divorce, make our child legitimate."

"Without your knowledge?" Fiona asked. Curran started to say something, but McGuire waved him silent.

"Do you seriously believe that I would have consented to let her go if I knew?"

"If it did the job . . ." Fiona began.

"Now that is uncalled for, sergeant," Curran snapped.

"And I'm doing my job," Fiona shot back.

"You have no evidence to suggest that Mr. McGuire had any knowledge of Miss Dellarotta's trip," Curran said with a glance toward McGuire.

"I don't need any evidence to ask the question, chief," she sucked in a deep breath. "And you know it."

Again McGuire waved Curran silent. He turned toward Fiona and smiled unctuously. His objective, she knew, was to be persuasive, to send her away without any suspicious feelings about his girlfriend.

"You could understand why she would want to do this, Fitz-Gerald," McGuire said. "You being a woman."

"And being a woman, I'd be more comfortable if she told me why herself."

"She's too damned upset by all this and is scared to death that you wouldn't believe her. What happened was, she got off the plane, and couldn't bring herself to humiliate herself. She's a proud woman, you see. But Frankie really was being a shit about it. Really. It wasn't a question of money. All Beatrice wanted was respectability. Was that so much to ask? Frankie's change of heart was a great blow to Beatrice. I guess she had it in her mind to make a last ditch effort."

"And you say she got cold feet?"

"He didn't say that, FitzGerald," Curran interjected. "He said that the lady simply changed her mind. Ladies do that. The congress-woman did it as well."

"And men don't?" She felt a sharp tug of anger. Irish macho was, to her, the most insidious of all. Too close to the bone.

"No offense meant to your sex, sergeant," Curran said, quickly backtracking. He was, she could see, one for testing the waters.

"It still would be better hearing it from her," Fiona pressed. She was determined not to give up on that point.

"Give her a break. Is it Fiona?" McGuire asked. He was trying his best to be ingratiating and she was beginning to buy his sincerity.

"It's Fiona," she said flatly.

"Good Irish name that," McGuire said. Don't overkill it, she thought. He looked at Curran. "Has a good ring, right, chief?" Curran grunted, his face without expression.

"I think the Scots favor it more," Fiona said, unable to resist. McGuire did his best to ignore the remark.

"Like I said. She went to Washington, decided she couldn't face Frankie, walked around, then took the plane back two hours later."

"Did she tell you why?"

"He already said," Curran interjected.

"You didn't know Frankie," McGuire volunteered. "She was tough. She would have chewed her up, turning it around on her. She had wanted to face her ever since Frankie changed her mind. I told her no. Absolutely no. She did this on her own. As it was, it turned out that Frankie wouldn't see her. Damned bitch. But you couldn't blame Bea for trying."

"Who said anything about blame?" Fiona said. From their expressions and the way they exchanged sly glances, she could see they thought they were winning. She sucked in a deep breath and cleared her throat. "If that's what she said, this business of not seeing Frankie. I just don't believe her."

Curran stood up and thrust a finger in front of her face.

"Now that's out of line."

"You men and your waving fingers."

She had meant something else, of course, but she held back. No sense in inflaming them beyond reason. She needed to pack a real wallop, one that hit them rationally, not just emotionally.

"We have two theories, gentlemen. One is that she did indeed get in to see the congresswoman. We don't know how." She looked at McGuire. "She might have used your key."

"Who told you I had a key?"

"Somehow she got past the desk man," Fiona said, ignoring his question. "and got into Frankie's apartment. There, she did confront the congresswoman. Frankie refused to reconsider her decision. Miss Dellarotta begged and cajoled. When finally Frankie was still unmoved, she appeared to backtrack, apologized, then consented to a cozy little drink. Then came the little episode of the cyanide."

Curran, who had sat down again, rushed out of his chair once again.

"I can have you thrown right out of this city."

"On what grounds?"

"I'll find them."

"Good. More grist for the mill. The media will eat it up."

"Who said anything about the media?" McGuire's complexion suddenly matched Curran's.

"Pregnant mistress begs lover's wife for divorce."

"Is that a threat, sergeant?" Curran said coolly. He was not easily intimidated.

"Of course, it's a threat. I strongly suggest you heed it."

"Goddamned little bitch," Curran muttered.

Suddenly Fiona stood up. She could feel the churning begin inside of her, the rising sense of indignation, the blood pumping in her temples. She was the same size as Curran and she looked straight into his eyes. There was no emotion there. The man was ice cold.

"This whole situation stinks of cover-up and corruption," she said, slowly and pointedly. Curran's response was merely to look at her, his expression a frozen wasteland. Considering how he had jumped up to protect McGuire, she had expected more emotion. Her insult had been calculated. It would have had a mule's kick for any police chief in the country. But this one was beyond that, hard as nails, as cold as a bear's cave.

"You got it wrong, Fiona," McGuire said solemnly. "Bob Curran is above reproach. Everybody knows that. If we have any weaknesses up here we take care of our friends. The man's a friend."

"Then it looks funny," Fiona said, unyielding, but believing him.

"I don't care how it looks, sergeant," Curran said. "The man's had his share. No need for any more. If he believes Beatrice, then I believe her."

She was, she knew, a sucker for this kind of loyalty among friends. In a political context it was rarer than a heat wave in winter. It softened her and she sat down again.

"I promise you," she said. "I'll be fair with her. I will not upset her. But you both know, I have got to speak with her."

McGuire lowered his eyes and looked at his hands. Curran looked at her, his features immobile. Suddenly McGuire raised his eyes.

"You be careful with her," he said.

"Of course," Fiona replied.

"It's all right, Jack. We'll see to it." Curran continued to stare menacingly at Fiona.

McGuire got up and left the room. He was back in a few moments with Beatrice Dellarotta. The contrast between her and Frankie McGuire was dramatic. She had a hawkish dark Mediterranean face. Large brown eyes with dark circles under them, lips that curled into a cupid's bow. Her jet black hair was long and shiny. She wore a blue silk flowing dressing gown, but it did not hide the fact that she was already showing her pregnancy.

Curran stood up when she came in. McGuire was surprisingly attentive, dancing around her, leading her to the leather chair, his touch and look reassuring. His devotion seemed truly without guile.

Fiona had also risen, accepting McGuire's introduction respectfully. She took the woman's hand, which was warm and responded to the pressure of greeting. McGuire pulled over another straight-backed wooden chair and sat next to the woman. Reaching out, he took her hand. It was, indeed, a tableaux of great affection.

"Believe me Miss Dellarotta, I . . ."

"McGuire," Beatrice interrupted, barely above a whisper.

"I'm sorry," Fiona said, somewhat confused.

"We were married three days ago," the new Mrs. McGuire said. It would have been less than a week after Frankie died.

"I didn't want it to happen this way," McGuire said. "But as you can see . . ." He waved his hand toward Beatrice.

"I'll be thirty-seven next month," Beatrice said, clearing her throat. Fiona reacted, of course, thinking of herself. She looked deeply into the woman's dark eyes. I know, she said to her silently, reminded of what she hoped might be happening to her.

"I understand," Fiona said sincerely.

"I wanted this child to enter the church with dignity." She looked toward McGuire, lifted his hand and kissed it. "We know how it looks. But what is one to do. It could have been . . ." She checked her words, swallowed, her eyes moistening. Fiona waited until she found her voice again. "God's will," she whispered. "That's the only way to explain it. I certainly did not want to see her dead."

McGuire patted her hand.

"Of course not, sweetheart."

Again she swallowed, took out a tiny handkerchief from the

pocket of her dressing gown and dabbed at her eyes.

"I did go to Washington. I was angry and hurt. It wasn't as if I was the other woman in its worst sense. Jack had already left her bed. It was over when we met." She took a deep breath to calm herself and wrapped her arms around her swollen belly and smiled. "He just jumped."

McGuire reached out and touched her belly, concentrating.

"There it is again."

"It's a miracle. A wonderful miracle."

Fiona nodded, but was too emotional to speak. In a few months, she hoped, she too might feel that miracle. A shiver trilled up her spine.

"As soon as I landed I knew I couldn't go through with it. I lost my courage. I could not bring myself to suffer the indignity of begging this woman . . ."

"I told her that," McGuire said.

"I took a cab. But as soon as we crossed the river I asked him to let me out. I walked around a little, had a cup of coffee. Then I walked some more and finally I took a cab back to the airport and went back to Boston."

When she had finished she looked at McGuire, as a child might do to a parent after a public recitation. He responded by nodding and patting her hand. Up to then, despite the presence of Curran, she had assumed that their overly protective stance was a kind of natural paranoia.

Fiona could understand McGuire's unwillingness to upset his pregnant sweetheart, keep her out of harm's way, exposing intimacies that both of them would have preferred to remain private. On that basis, she could accept Curran's presence.

But there was something in Beatrice's tone and manner which put her on alert, triggered her suspicion. She looked at Curran who caught her gaze and kept it. He had the look of a predator. She could detect not the slightest fear and uncertainty. Something is definitely wrong here, she decided.

"And you never set foot in Mrs. McGuire's apartment?"

"That's what she just told you, sergeant," Curran said.

"Do you remember where the taxi dropped you off?" Fiona asked gently.

Beatrice hesitated, then looked at McGuire. She seemed suddenly uncomfortable.

"I was so agitated . . ." Beatrice began.

"It was a strange city," McGuire added.

"Do you remember where you had coffee? What did the place look like?"

"Just an ordinary coffee shop," Beatrice shrugged.

"In what sense ordinary. Small. A counter. Do you remember what kind of person served you. Black? White?"

She saw both men exchange glances. Curran nodded as if to say: Don't worry. I'm here.

"Really, I draw a blank. I . . . I was so overwrought, you see."

"Do you remember anything about the taxi ride? Did you pass any familiar landmarks, any monuments. Could you see the Capitol dome, the Washington Monument?"

"I saw that. Yes I saw that," she said. McGuire still held her hand.

"Was it on the left? On the right?"

She seemed to struggle with that for a few moments.

"I'm not sure," she said. She looked at McGuire. "Is it important?"

"Not really," Curran said. He seemed to have determined that the best way to get rid of her was to let her do her number.

"When you got out of the cab were there many people around? Could it have been Georgetown?"

"I wish I was sure," Beatrice said, looking at Fiona. "I want to be cooperative. Really I do. But consider my condition and my emotional state."

"I am, Beatrice. I am quite sensitive to it."

"I want to do the right thing," Beatrice said.

"Of course, you do, my darling," McGuire said. He picked up the hand which he was holding and brought it to his lips. There was genuine affection here, Fiona observed, wishing she could dispose of her suspicions, feeling queasy. Unfortunately, there was no going back. She had to play out the string, follow her instincts.

She turned suddenly to Curran.

"We'll have to check out the cabs," she said. "You'd expect that of your people as well."

Curran looked at McGuire. Again there was the exchange of collusive glances, but neither made a comment. But Beatrice's eyes flitted between them nervously. She turned to face her.

"All I want is some geographical point that puts you far away from the scene. A witness, for example, who saw you at the coffee shop. Something. Anything. I can't go back and tell my boss that you simply forgot where you were." Again, Beatrice looked at Curran, her expression deliberately troubled and pleading.

Curran turned to her.

"Surely you remember something, Bea?"

"I was so overwrought," she began, then shook her head vigorously. "I just don't remember."

"Was it Georgetown? Did you walk in Georgetown?" Fiona asked.

"I don't know."

"She wouldn't even know where it is," McGuire said.

"Did you tell the cab driver where you wanted to go and then change your mind?"

"I . . ."

She hesitated and turned once again to McGuire.

"Believe me, I can check that," Fiona said.

"Well, then, check away, dammit," Curran said. "Stop harassing the lady."

Fiona ignored him and pressed on, concentrating her stare, trying to hold Beatrice's gaze.

"Did you get to the apartment house, then turn around?"

"I told you I couldn't go through with it," Beatrice said.

"So you went to the apartment house first, then turned around?"

"I won't have this," McGuire said, getting up, his face flushed. Yet, he continued to hold her hand.

"I did not kill her," Beatrice cried. Her body stiffened as she raised her voice. "I did not kill her. I did not." The veins stood out on her neck.

"Stop this," McGuire said, his rebuke directed now to Beatrice.

"I only talked to her," Beatrice whined. She had started to stand up then fell back on the chair. She had turned dead white. Fiona felt pity for the woman, ashamed for herself. Worse, she worried about the baby inside of her.

"Some water, please," McGuire screamed, rubbing Beatrice's hands. Curran ran out of the room.

"I'm so sorry," Fiona said starting to rise.

McGuire reached out with one hand, palm upward.

"No. You've caused enough trouble."

Curran came back with the water and gave it to McGuire, who lifted it to Beatrice's lips. Concentrating on Beatrice, they ignored Fiona who felt thoroughly guilt stricken. The sudden admission, although she had suspected what was in the air, had stunned her.

"It's all right," Beatrice said finally, waving them away.

"You had better go," McGuire commanded. Curran was silent, averting his eyes. The man showed no emotion at all.

Fiona got up. Her legs felt rubbery. Her mind told her she wasn't supposed to go. How could she explain it away?

"I'm sorry, Jack. We can't have this." Curran said.

"What could I do, Billy?" McGuire whispered.

"Too late now," Curran said. They were still ignoring Fiona.

"I'm glad it's out," Beatrice said. The color had returned to her face. "It's a relief. I knew at confession this morning. I couldn't tell anything but the truth."

"Goddamned priests," McGuire mumbled.

Fiona sat down again, waiting for some calm to set in.

"I did go there," Beatrice said. She looked directly at Fiona now. "But he didn't know that I was going. Not then. We talked about it weeks ago when she changed her mind. At first he did suggest I talk to Frankie. Then he decided it would be too much stress for me. You see, she didn't know I was pregnant. Finally, I said to myself, I'll go see her, talk woman to woman. Show her what was happening. Plead with her. She couldn't be as cruel as all that. She wasn't interested in Jack anymore. She couldn't be. I'm sure her constituents would understand. People are generous." She paused, smiled, touched her belly. "There he is again. See he knows I'm doing the right thing."

She looked at McGuire, reached out and held his hand. A sweet and loving woman, Fiona decided, knowing that a detective must always look beyond the personality, keep all options open, eschew quick judgments. The woman's face was suffused with joy and she envied her. Oh how she envied her. Perhaps she too . . . but she quickly put such sentiments out of her mind.

"I called her from the airport. I was quite determined, you see. We had never met and when she answered the phone I identified myself and there was a long pause. Please Frankie, I must see you, I told her, explaining that I was in town. I don't want to embarrass you in any way but we must talk woman to woman. At first she refused. But people do have a way of reaching across animosity and hatred. Finally, she did relent. But, bless her memory, she was still the politician, still protective of her image, still a bit fearful that I might be concocting something to deliberately embarrass her. She told me to have the cab drop me off at Wisconsin and M Street and she would pick me up there. True to her word she was there waiting and she drove the few blocks to the apartment house. We went in the garage you see. I didn't realize it until later, but obviously she did not want me to go through the lobby. Probably wanted to keep me a secret, something like that. When I found out about what happened . . ." She looked at McGuire. "We thought that her taking me through the garage was a blessing in disguise." She shrugged. "We were wrong as you can see. Anyway we went up to her apartment. I remember nobody was in the elevator. Inside she made some coffee and we talked."

She had been holding the glass of water as she talked, the words tumbling out of her, as if it were necessary to expel them as fast as possible. She raised the glass to her lips, finished the water, and gave the glass back to McGuire. He, too, appeared to be approving and relieved. Only Curran remained stolid and emotionless. All this was apparently news to him as well.

"We chatted for a long time, circling the subject. I told her how much I respected all she was doing on those issues that were important to me, especially on the issue of abortion. I would never, ever, contemplate such a thing. Never. She touched her belly with both hands caressing it. I told her how much I loved Jack . . ." She paused, her voice breaking. Gathering control, she cleared her throat and continued. ". . . how much it meant to me to have his child. Tears came into her eyes. She told me that it had been impossible to hold her marriage together considering her role in politics. Nor could she blame Jack. Early on, she said, it had been a good marriage, that both she and Jack had respected each other and that she appreciated Jack's willingness to go through the charade, she used that term 'charade', when it counted for her career. She was not the unfeeling bitch I had once thought she was. She was very kind, very thoughtful, very understanding and we had a good cry together. Finally I asked her why she had changed her mind after she had agreed to the divorce. She grew very depressed. The color drained from her face. Her lips trembled and for a moment she could not speak. I was very alarmed, afraid she was about to faint or something. Finally, she said . . ."

Beatrice looked up and turned for a moment to briefly face each one that was listening.

"I swear this to you. May God strike my baby dead, if I am not telling the truth. She said: 'I give you my consent and I give you my blessing.' I swear it on my baby's life. She said that she would call her lawyer in the morning and told me to tell Jack to do the same. She said they would explore the quickest way to do it. Then she took me downstairs and drove me to the airport. We kissed in the car. I told her that I was eternally grateful . . ." At that point she faltered. Her chest heaved and her shoulders shook as she covered her face with her hands. After awhile, she removed her hands and wiped her tear-stained cheeks with tissues. McGuire had hurried out of the room to bring her a box of them.

But she wasn't finished yet.

"When I came home I was so happy. So happy. Jack was upset with me, of course. I couldn't blame him. He had been terribly worried and he had called Frankie. You know the rest. That man Foy called. I can't believe it. I just can't believe what happened. She was so kind and considerate. I had no idea that she would do that. No idea at all. I tell you it will haunt me all my life."

"You can't blame yourself," Fiona said. She had been deeply moved by Beatrice's story.

"It's been a terrible burden for us, FitzGerald," McGuire said, turning to Curran. "Can you ever forgive me, Billy? I should have told you the whole story. But I was so afraid for Beatrice. So afraid that they would accuse her of doing this to Frankie."

"What do you think, Bea?" Curran asked. He did not look at Fiona.

"I tell you she was perfectly content when she left me at the airport," Bea said. "I keep thinking that maybe after she got home, she mulled it over, felt some sense of overwhelming unhappiness and did away with herself."

"I can understand sleeping pills, some other overdose, but cyanide." Curran shook his head and finally looked at Fiona. Although his face was still expressionless she could sense that the hostility had dissipated.

Fiona turned to Bea.

"What Chief Curran means is that the type of poison used implies planning. No one has cyanide lying around the house."

"Unless she was contemplating suicide for a long time," Curran said. "Then, of course, she would have to obtain the cyanide, have it handy. It's not something that lies around the medicine chest." He turned to McGuire. "I never knew Frankie to manifest the slightest tendency to suicide. Unless she just flipped out."

"Not Frankie," McGuire said. "Frankie was always in control."

"I don't know what to make of it," Beatrice said. "I've just been holding myself together for the sake of the baby. I'd never forgive myself if I caused her to do that. Never."

"I keep telling her," McGuire said. "She can't blame herself. We were hoping to keep a lid on this. Never works." He turned to Fiona. "I hope you can keep this out of the media. Be messy for all of us."

"Certainly we'll do our best."

She was tempted to tell them about how the mayor and important members of Congress were trying to do just that, but she held her peace.

"There are still some questions," Fiona said. She turned toward Curran and detected the faintest nod of approval.

"I told you the absolute truth, Sergeant FitzGerald," Beatrice said.

"It's just that these questions must be asked," Fiona said. Beatrice sighed and nodded. "Do you recall touching anything in the room?"

Beatrice grew thoughtful.

"Certainly the coffee cups."

"Apparently she washed those," Fiona said.

"I went to the bathroom," Beatrice said brightly. "Being pregnant you know. Yes, I went into the bedroom and used the bathroom."

"There was a guest bathroom. Why not that one?"

"She said it would be more comfortable for me to freshen up in the bedroom john. Better lighting. Things like that."

"Did you touch anything?"

"Of course. How could I do otherwise?"

"That's been the problem. The absence of prints."

"Believe me, Sergeant FitzGerald. I used the bathroom. I was there."

"In light of your story, Bea," Curran said gently, "they would want to establish that you were there, corroborate it."

"And if they did?" McGuire asked.

"Be a question of who believes what," Fiona shrugged.

"That's why it seemed that the best way would be to deny that she was in the apartment. If the police couldn't place her there what was the point of her telling everyone? Just because she was on the plane doesn't mean she was at Frankie's place."

Beatrice patted McGuire's hand.

"I'm happy I told them, Jack. Very much relieved. It's the truth, the absolute truth. You can't go wrong telling the truth."

"The car," Curran said suddenly. "Frankie's car."

"Of course," Fiona said, reacting instantly.

"They brush the car for prints?" Curran asked. He was all police professional now.

Her hesitation gave him his answer.

"We might have missed that, too," Fiona said, a bit ashamed of the oversight.

"That will prove it then," Beatrice said. "I didn't wear gloves." She looked up and smiled at them.

"On the one hand it will indeed corroborate your story," Curran said looking at Fiona. She picked up the message. They were a team now, two detectives on the job.

"And prove she didn't sneak in to Mrs. McGuire's apartment with bad intentions," Fiona said hopefully. She felt herself fully in their corner. "Unfortunately, it still wouldn't explain the absence of prints, or anything else to place her in the apartment. That could be a negative."

"How so?" McGuire asked with some concern.

"Could be argued that she wiped away the evidence. Forgot about the prints in the car," Curran said. He looked at Beatrice. "It's all right, Bea. Just cop speculations. Nothing to be alarmed about."

"Maybe we should have kept quiet," McGuire said.

"I couldn't live with it, Jack," Beatrice said firmly. "I don't care what they think."

"Suppose they just don't believe her?" McGuire asked.

"Don't worry, Bea, it's not enough to make a case," Curran said.

"I told the truth. That's all that matters," Beatrice said, turning to Fiona. "Do you believe me?"

"Without a shadow of a doubt," Fiona said.

At that moment McGuire bent down and kissed her hair. It was odd, Fiona thought. Her first impression of McGuire was that he was shrewd, devious and corrupt, all of which he probably was. But she was quite touched by his display of loving affection. Suddenly she thought of Greg. Perhaps loving covered a multitude of sins. Perhaps she had been too judgmental, too willing to see his public life of dissimulation and insensitivity as an extension of his private life.

Suddenly the room grew silent, each of its occupants lost in his or her own thoughts. It was the moment, Fiona decided. There was no way around it. They needed to know.

"Mrs. McGuire was pregnant," Fiona said quietly. No need for her to raise her voice. The information seemed to hit them like an earthquake.

"Frankie?" McGuire responded hoarsely. Even Curran, for the first time that morning, showed signs of emotion. His mouth hung open.

"How could she? She was . . ." Beatrice began.

"Forty-seven," McGuire said turning to Fiona. "That has got to be pure bullshit."

"This is an M.E. confirmation?" Curran asked, his voice strangely hoarse.

"There is absolutely no question about it," Fiona said. "Six weeks according to Dr. Benton, our M.E." She turned to McGuire. "She was in superb shape."

"Frankie pregnant?" McGuire said again. "Involved with a man? Jesus." He turned to face Fiona. "Who was it?" He looked down at his hands, then at Beatrice. "I can tell you this much. It wasn't me." Beatrice smiled briefly.

"That explains why she changed her mind," Curran said.

"Poor Frankie," Beatrice said. "Oh God, I hope I didn't push her to it." She stifled a sob.

"You didn't," Fiona said emphatically. An idea was forming in her mind, taking shape.

"How can you be so sure?" Beatrice asked.

Fiona pointed to Beatrice's belly.

"Would you kill that baby?"

"Never. Absolutely never." She shook her head repeatedly. "No way."

"Find the father . . ." Curran began.

". . . find the murderer," Fiona said. It came as a pronouncement, without strings or doubts.

18

THE MAYOR WAS livid with rage. The Eggplant had played his card. He had just revealed to him and Charles Rome that Congresswoman McGuire was pregnant.

"Why wasn't I told this earlier?" he shouted.

He turned in his big leather chair and looked at Congressman Rome, whose unruffled dignity contrasted severely with everyone in the room, including Fiona. The Eggplant, although immaculately groomed in his tan suit, chocolate brown tie with yellow stripes and cordovan tasseled loafers, was, she knew, fighting with himself to appear unruffled. Cates's complexion had turned to the color of clay.

"Frankly, it was such explosive information, I did not want to compromise you." He paused and glanced toward Congressman Rome. "Either of you." Rome had the air of a man for whom there were no surprises. Discipline and dignity were apparently the key to his persona. Quite obviously, he had harnessed these traits to the service of his political career.

"That was for me to judge, Captain Greene," the mayor said, somewhat mollified by Rome's controlled reaction.

"We needed to be sure because of the political implications. In this case, suicide might have been considered a rather crude form of abortion." The Eggplant said, turning to the congressman. "It wasn't the issue itself. The credibility of a dedicated congresswoman was at stake. I wanted to be sure before I reported it."

There he was doing his little jig for the powers that be, Fiona thought, resolving all guilt about her overuse of the derisive Eggplant monicker.

"Sure about the suicide?" Rome asked.

"Yes. I wanted to be sure."

"So, it was a suicide," the mayor said hopefully.

The Eggplant looked at him, then shifted his gaze to Fiona.

"We don't think so," he said.

"Shit," the mayor muttered through clenched teeth. Rome shook his head slightly and lowered his eyes.

The mayor was a big man whose former image as a street-wise protestor had been considerably softened by his three years as mayor. This latter incarnation might have been more to the point. The mayor, whose father had been a prosperous dentist in Pensacola, Florida, had majored in English Lit at Florida State. His ghetto intonation was a learned affectation for him, although the southern accents of the Florida panhandle were a good beginning for this argot tongue.

When calm, he was remarkably dignified with his grey cottony hair and eyebrows and penetrating green eyes. He was not calm now. A thin moustache of perspiration had popped out on his upper lip. On the surface, he was attempting to impress Congressman Rome with his sincere desire to keep a lid on this explosive scandal-ridden case. Congress was, next to the overwhelming black majority of the nation's capital, his most important and affluent constituent.

This had been billed as an informational meeting. The police chief was deliberately kept out of it. It simply confirmed what Fiona had divined. If down the line, they needed scapegoats, the Eggplant, Cates and she would fit the bill nicely.

They were lined up in a semicircle in front of the mayor's highly polished ornate desk framed by a standing American flag and one bearing the insignia of the District of Columbia.

The Eggplant, as man of authority and spokesman for the homicide division, then reported on Fiona's meeting in Boston with the new Mrs. McGuire. He was laying his case out carefully, knowing it would be unpopular.

But he had bought Fiona's assumptions that Mrs. McGuire had no intentions of committing suicide, assumptions based totally on Beatrice Dellarotta's observations of Frankie's state of mind shortly before her death. They had, indeed, found her fingerprints inside Mrs. McGuire's car, concrete evidence that Beatrice's story was, at least, partially provable.

Under normal circumstances, the Eggplant would have been completely skeptical, but Fiona knew that the assumptions she had made meshed nicely with his own instinctive belief about the manner of Frankie's death.

Now she was feeling slightly guilty for creating the Eggplant's predicament, wondering if she hadn't relied more on the emotion of sisterhood than the cooler reason of a seasoned detective.

Had she overreacted to Beatrice's story? Had she related too deeply, too personally, to Beatrice's motives? Were her instincts overpowering her logic? Had she taken advantage of the Eggplant's own gut feeling that Mrs. McGuire had been murdered? Had she manipulated him into going along with her arguments because Beatrice had touched something deep within her? Of course, she had, a conclusion that added to her present discomfort. She hoped she was right. For both their sakes.

"But what does that prove?" the mayor asked with some sarcasm, after the Eggplant had finished. "Merely that this Beatrice was in the congresswoman's car. How is that in conflict with a judgment of suicide?"

"We have a theory about that, Your Honor," the Eggplant said. They hadn't, after all, expected the meeting to go smoothly.

"They got theories," the mayor snapped with some contempt, swiveling toward Charles Rome, as if to solicit approval for his reaction. The congressman remained stoic and serene, blinking his eyes, a gesture that might be interpreted either as a signal to continue as well or a sign of approval.

The mayor swiveled back to face the Eggplant. "Seems to me that you've got a real problem here. Okay, you've got the lady in the car. But you admit you can't find any evidence to place her in Mrs. McGuire's apartment. Not a shred. What does that mean?" He lifted his hand to stop any reply. "It means that the woman was never inside the apartment. In fact, you have no proof that anyone at all was inside Mrs. McGuire's apartment. Ergo . . ." He paused now awaiting a reaction.

"With respect, Your Honor," Fiona interjected. She looked at the Eggplant who nodded his consent. "We're theorizing that there were no prints belonging to Beatrice . . . the second Mrs. McGuire because . . ." She sucked in a deep breath. "The murderer wiped them out."

"Theories again," the mayor croaked, shaking his head. "And how would he know exactly where they were . . . these prints." He turned toward the Eggplant. "Really, captain, the logic is awry." He swiveled back in his chair and looked at the ceiling. "Try this on for size. The lady, does indeed, tell her story to the congresswoman, who is shocked, appalled and guilt-stricken, her nerves worn thin because of her own condition. Her marriage has failed, her political career is in jeopardy, her personal beliefs make it impossible for her to abort her child. She is at the end of her tether. The other woman has been the catalyst for her final decision. Suicide. No question in my mind." He turned toward Congressman Rome.

No, she decided, the mayor was no dummy. Certainly a case could be made for his theory, despite their own rejection on it. She cut a glance to the Eggplant whose expression appeared to echo her thoughts.

"With respect, Your Honor, we speculate," she continued, "that Beatrice was telling the truth about her visit to Mrs. McGuire's apartment. We must assume, too, that she might not have actually touched many things. She said she and the congresswoman had coffee together. Well, the coffee cups were all washed. She said she did go to the bathroom, but had used Mrs. McGuire's, the one in the master bedroom. No prints were found there, either. Our technical staff was quite thorough . . . which indicates that someone had wiped them away."

"Did it ever occur to you, sergeant," the mayor asked, "that she might have done so herself . . ." Suddenly he stopped himself, realizing that he was adding fuel to the murder theory with the new Mrs. McGuire as the chief suspect. "Now you're making me crazy.

The fact remains that there is absolutely no proof that the woman was in the apartment. None whatsoever. I really think I've heard enough." He looked at his watch and started to rise.

"Don't you think we should hear her out?" Congressman Rome said.

The mayor shrugged and settled back in his chair.

"If you think so," he said grudgingly.

"Our theory . . ." Fiona paused and looked at the mayor. "I'm sorry Your Honor, but there's no other way to describe it. We think that Beatrice did indeed get the congresswoman to promise that she would grant Mr. McGuire his freedom, that she had every intention to carry out this promise. We believe that her original promise to do this had been broken when she discovered that she was pregnant."

"I don't understand," Congressman Rome said.

"Theory again," Fiona continued. "When she found out she was pregnant by a man other than her husband she broke the promise because she did not want her child to be born out of wedlock. Bad politics. Especially for her constituency. And she couldn't by belief or conviction have an abortion under any circumstances."

"Good politics, considering her constituency," the mayor interjected. "But odd reasoning. Why then would she make another promise to this Beatrice woman? She was still pregnant?"

"Because she was a decent compassionate woman," Fiona said. "She was doing what was right. Not necessarily political, but what was right."

People do that, she told herself suddenly remembering her father's excruciating dilemma over Vietnam. Like you Dad, she heard a voice within her say.

"Right for who?" the mayor asked.

She could feel the subtle patronizing that lay beneath the question, just as it lay beneath the surface of this overbearing male police culture. How they hated any pushy woman, especially one who raised the banner of feminist political courage. This is one for sisterhood, she heard her voice echo in her thoughts. Only a woman had the biological capacity to be in a fix like that. Therefore, she told herself, only a woman could understand such a plight, such painful decision-making. The idea buttressed her courage.

"For her, of course," Fiona replied in a deliberately respectful tone. She would not, she promised herself, blow this out of pique.

"You've lost me," the mayor said. Rome remained quiet and noncommittal but obviously interested. Their silence meant that she should continue.

"When she got back to her apartment, she called her lover and told him the news. It did not sit well with him. Don't ask us why. None of us are certain. Not yet."

"The hole in the doughnut," the mayor snickered.

"At that moment," Fiona answered slowly, nodding in tandem for emphasis. "It's only a question of time." It was always impossible to transfer one's instincts without raising hackles. She glanced at the Eggplant and grew silent.

"May I ask you a question at this point?" Rome asked. Of course, he could. The man exuded an air of distinguished solicitude and fatherly confidence.

"I think your theories are commendable," he began, rubbing his smooth strong cleft chin with well-manicured fingers. "Very imaginative and resourceful, sergeant. But with due respect for your professional experience, you're also presenting a scenario that could trigger a suicide," he said. "My first thought . . . when I heard poor Frankie had died . . . was that she couldn't possibly have taken her own life. For what reason? She was still young, successful, effective. She had everything to live for." He continued to rub his chin and studied Fiona. "Now you've given me a plausible reason that I understand. If you're theorizing, why not suicide? The absence of evidence, it seems to me, makes that theory more plausible." He looked toward the mayor. "Don't you think so, Bob?"

"As I've said, so far I've heard nothing that makes me think otherwise," he said agreeably.

"Then there's the question of the cyanide," Fiona interjected. These were tough men, used to being prevailed upon, used to all the tricks of persuasion. More important, they were used to saying "No." "Why would she have had cyanide lying around the house? Makes no sense. She had a bottle of sleeping pills in her medicine cabinet. She could have chosen a nice sleepy way of dying. A certain knowledge of poison is required to make such a choice. Cyanide is not even commonly available."

"I'm not so sure about that either," Congressman Rome said. "You'd be surprised what a resourceful intelligent person with strong desire can do. Especially a person like Frankie. As for information on poisons, we have available to us the greatest library in the world."

She glanced toward Cates, whose research and thoroughness was always impeccable. He smiled thinly. "My partner here, Sergeant Cates, checked the Library of Congress to see if her office had inquired about cyanide. Nothing. As a matter of fact we checked to see if any member of Congress had inquired about cyanide in the past year. We found only one inquiry and that was appropriate enough, a research assistant for a committee that dealt with mining." She looked toward Cates.

"It's used in gold mining. Beyond that there's not much use for it. Not in Washington," Cates said, then picked up on her explanation. "We also checked all obvious sources of information about cyanide. Libraries, computer banks, druggists, not for information about the substance per se. We just wanted to know if anyone had requested any information about it for the past year. Turned up zero of consequence. In other words we could find nothing linking Mrs. McGuire to the substance in any way."

"Nor anyone else," the mayor said.

"That's true," Cates pointed out. "But our theory . . ."

"Fucking theories," the mayor snapped in exasperation.

"The point is," Cates continued with some determination now that he had the floor, "that the use of cyanide implies some planning."

"Yes, it does," the mayor said. "She could have been planning this suicide for a long time."

"She could have been," the Eggplant interjected suddenly, obviously worried that his department's speculations were not cutting any ice with the mayor and the congressman. He glanced helplessly toward Fiona who had briefly retreated into her own thoughts. Poor old Eggplant, she thought. He had bought her theory with such enthusiasm. But the mayor and the congressman did have a point. It was all theory.

"I don't think you have enough to declare this case anything but suicide," the mayor said. He looked pointedly at Fiona. "Despite all your fanciful speculations and conundrums." He turned a withering gaze on the Eggplant.

The Eggplant averted his eyes, looked at his hands.

"Not yet," he whispered, his words barely audible.

"I would suggest then that you either shit or get off the pot," the mayor said. It was a sharp blow, crudely executed and she felt awful for having been partially responsible for it. Congressman Rome said nothing, his silence implying that he was totally in agreement with the mayor's assessment.

"There is still one compelling question," Fiona said, unable to remain unmoved. Her voice broke for a moment and she cleared her throat. An emotional loudmouthed pushy woman was anathema to these men. Such behavior would have totally destroyed their case, that is, if it could possibly be destroyed further.

"What is that, sergeant?" the mayor asked, his tongue thick with contempt. He looked at his watch. "I know you have to get back, Mr. Rome."

"We do have a vote on the floor." He, too, looked at his watch. "I've got a few minutes left."

"You were saying, sergeant," the mayor said.

"The question of paternity. That is still open."

"Let's face it, the woman was married," the mayor said, looking toward the congressman.

"In name only," Fiona said. She had already referred to the woman's anonymous lover. Were they trying to bury such a notion?

"One never knows what goes on between couples, even couples who are separated. Does one?" the mayor said with an intonation that suggested this was a piece of wisdom direct from the highest authority.

"You and your wife were good friends with her," Fiona said, turning to the congressman. She knew that, in some way, it was a breach of protocol to bring the congressman into it on such a personal basis. "Did her husband ever visit her in Washington?"

"Not for a few years, as far as I can remember. But she often went up to Boston."

"Had she been up there about eight weeks ago?"

"Really, sergeant, I wasn't privy to her schedule," the congressman said. "Besides, our relationship was social but not that intimate. We were colleagues, often together in the House, working on various committees. Barbara, my wife, felt sorry for her, living alone like that. All work. No play. We tried to include her in a great deal of our social plans. Beyond that . . . you're asking for more than I could give." He paused and studied her. "I can tell you this. I never saw her in a one-on-one situation with any man."

"It could have been a closet kind of thing," Fiona said. This time she could not contain herself. "It goes on very often with powerful men."

The mayor laughed.

"A cutie stashed under the desk."

"Something like that."

"Did you uncover something like that?" the congressman asked.

"Only Foy," Fiona said lamely.

"Foy?"

"He had access. He was her constant companion," she said without conviction. Her objective was to keep this case alive at all costs.

"That's really quite hard to believe," Rome said. "The man is obviously a homosexual."

She cut a quick glance at Cates.

"And so it seems. But we haven't been able to come up with a single bonafide homosexual incident." She was stretching it, of course, ignoring Foy's alleged pass at the apartment desk man. The mayor turned his eyes away and awkwardly shuffled papers on his desk.

"That seems to be pushing things a bit, sergeant. Really."

"One never knows in a murder case," Fiona said pointedly. "The least likely are often the guiltiest."

"But if Foy were the father," Congressman Rome said, "that only makes the case for suicide stronger. Why would he kill her? What possible advantage would it be to him?"

"Maybe . . ." Fiona hesitated. She had not really thought this one through. "Maybe he was upset that she did not want to marry him. Maybe he was wildly in love with her. Who knows?"

"Beyond the pale, sergeant," the mayor said. He was right, of course.

"People have motives, they . . ." She felt helpless, inert. Her theories were losing their power, even to herself. She looked toward the Eggplant whose eyes seemed to mirror his defeat.

"I really think you've done a grand job," Congressman Rome said. "You've established an excellent motive for Frankie's suicide." He shook his head. "It's fine, as far as we in Congress are concerned, to continue your investigation. Naturally, my own inclination would be to end this once and for all. I want you to be dead sure, of course. But so far nothing said here this morning indicates anything more than suicide."

"Seems that way to me, as well, congressman," the mayor said. He turned to the Eggplant.

"I'm sorry, captain. But we can't let this drag on indefinitely." The message was clear, succinct. Wrap up the mother.

"I understand," the Eggplant muttered.

"We're not saying that you should stop investigating Mrs. McGuire's death," the mayor said, growing more and more pontifical as he spoke. "I think I can speak for the congressman when I say that you and your staff should satisfy yourselves so that you can make your declaration without a shadow of a doubt. Only please, captain. Do it swiftly. We don't want this albatross around our necks. And, for God's sake, keep any waffling on the suicide issue out of the press."

"Especially the pregnancy," Congressman Rome said. "The media would have a field day with it. Above all, we wouldn't want Frankie's name to be dragged through the mud. Hard to tell if there's any real political fodder in this for the pro-lifers. I suppose both sides can twist it to their advantage. My own call on this is that the faster we get it behind us the better."

"Exactly my sentiments," the mayor said.

"If we had more time. More manpower," Fiona said.

"More manpower. More people know. More people talk. More media action," the mayor said. "I'm afraid I won't have that."

"I just feel . . ." Her frustration was stupefying.

"That's the point, sergeant," the mayor said. "Feeling. Emotion." He slapped the desk. "I won't have it. Bring me valid murder, complete with suspects or drop the damned thing." He looked toward the congressman who nodded and stood up.

He shook the Eggplant's hand.

"You are to be commended, captain." He looked at Fiona and Cates. "All of you. Believe me when I say your work is well appreciated. But I tend to stand with the mayor on the issue. I know you're trying your best to get to the bottom of this terrible tragedy. But murder is a very serious business. We must be absolutely certain. Absolutely."

He shook hands all around. His flesh felt strong, warm, reassuring. Everything about the man seemed reassuring.

The mayor waited for him to leave before turning to face the remaining group. His pose of solicitation had disappeared.

"I don't appreciate this, Luther. When you requested this meeting, I thought you had something a lot more definitive."

"I just wanted to leave the door open to other options."

"Bet you'd just love this to be a nice juicy murder. All that hot dogging on the tube." He looked at Fiona.

"And you, woman. There's no case here. I told the congressman you had a case. I looked like a goddamned fool." He bore in on the Eggplant and pointed a dark longnailed finger at him. "You got a week. That's about it. The media will be on our ass by then, so nothing, nothing comes from you or me other than: We are in the process of confirming suicide. I don't want them to get the murder bug up their asses. Hear?"

"I hear," the Eggplant said.

"And another thing . . ." the mayor began. But he looked at Fiona and Cates. "If you both don't mind I'd like to have a little private conversation with Captain Greene."

It was definitely a signal to leave. Fiona felt humiliated. She had been so sure that they would be able to convince the congressman and the mayor. Then, as she expounded her theories, her own confidence had wavered. Perhaps that's why they had not been persuasive. The failure was definitely her fault. Worse, from their point of view, she probably had made the case for suicide.

"In the absence of any real evidence it's tough to make a case of it," Cates said. "Sorry, Fi. But you know where I stand."

"Can't fault you for being a good soldier, though," Fiona said as they stood in the corridor waiting for the Eggplant to come out of the mayor's office.

"You did try. I'll say that."

"I can't much blame them," Fiona sighed.

"You were terrific," Cates said. "It was the case itself, I'm afraid."

"I feel like a damned evangelist," she sighed. "Trying to make people believers on faith alone."

"Well nobody can cry cover-up. Can't say we didn't touch the bases."

"Must be something we missed," Fiona said.

"I doubt it." He smiled. "I won't throw in the sponge, though. Not until you do. Until then, I'll try to keep an open mind."

"Loyal to the end."

"For better or for worse," he joked, looking at his watch. "I'm still beating leather for the cause. Got more appointments on the Hill."

She began to pace the corridor, wrestling with the problem. A missing link. There had to be. But why? Her confidence level moved like a pendulum. She sensed Cates studying her.

"I want to go back to McGuire's apartment," she said.

"Flanagan's been through that with a fine tooth comb. The Eggplant's sent him and his crew back three times. Nothing."

"We'll sit there, soak it all up. Maybe something will come to us."

"Doubtful," he shrugged, "but I'm game." Again he looked at his watch. "Take me about three, four hours. I'll meet you there, say, three."

"Got a deal," Fiona said.

A few minutes after Cates left, the Eggplant came out of the mayor's office, tightlipped and obviously unhappy. Probably had a real old-fashioned dressing down from hizzoner, she speculated. Nor could she deny what she felt for him now. Pity. Genuine pity.

"Time for a cup of coffee?" the Eggplant asked awkwardly. He was always uncomfortable socializing with the troops, although he had on occasion joined them for working lunches or dinners. Every year on New Year's Day, he and the formidable Loreen had "open house", a stiffly formal up-tight event in their large house on Sixteenth Street.

It was dress-up and egg nogs with finger sandwiches and quiet talk. Loreen was a part of the closed black society of Washington that had had debutante balls for a hundred years. The Howard University crowd, sometimes referred to as black snobs, but very much the elite. Poor Loreen had married the promising black law student Luther Greene, only to discover that he preferred police work to law, a move for which she never forgave him. Or so the story went.

To be appointed police commissioner was the only way he could ever satisfy Loreen and pressure at home was explanation enough for his occasionally hostile attitude, crankiness and the need to build around himself a great wall of protective ego.

They went across the street to the coffee shop of the new Willard Hotel.

"I don't know what to say, captain," Fiona began as they slid into a booth in the rear of the coffee shop.

"Not your fault," he muttered.

"It's not?"

She had already worked herself up to a dressing down.

"You were great in there."

"But I didn't do you any good, that's for sure. You'd think they'd be proud of the way we did business. Not going off half-cocked. Bet he really roasted you back there."

"He roasted me all right."

The coffee shop was practically empty. There wasn't much activity at that hour. Another half hour it would begin to fill up with the luncheon crowd.

"Tired of playing it safe, I guess," he said. The waitress came, took their order, and went off.

"You realize, of course, that they're right. We have been playing this case with our guts."

"It's the subconscious at work, FitzGerald. A lot more logic than

meets the eye. Sometimes you find out why much later." He watched
her through his dark cryptic eyes, offering a thin smile. He had
brought her there for a reason and she waited for it to be revealed.
The waitress brought their two coffees. He took a deep sip of his.

"My nose," he said. "That's what told me for sure. I smelled it on
her that first time, but I couldn't place it. Not until I was sitting there,
taking the man's shit. Amazing isn't it. Proves that instinct has a
reference point. Who knows why? Loreen wears the same perfume.
Goddess. I hate the shit. Can't wait until it goes away. Takes about
three hours. I actually timed it once. Nor would Benton have picked
it up since it was already gone when he got to her. But I could still
smell it when I arrived and it must have lodged in my memory bank.
I'm not saying it's not possible for a woman on the verge of a planned
suicide to put on perfume. But my limited experience suggests the
lure and lust department."

"She put it on for some man," Fiona said.

"Doesn't seem like the act of a woman on the verge of suicide.
But then a smell doesn't make a case."

"But it does explain your gut reaction," Fiona said. She wished
she could explain her own so candidly.

"There must have been something in your subconscious that made
you believe that Beatrice was telling the truth. That's a helluva leap
of faith. After all, you put her at the scene within a couple of hours
of McGuire's death."

"I believed Beatrice," she said. She wanted to say something about
the intuition of sisterhood, but held her peace. It was no time to test
his understanding. "And you believe me," Fiona said.

"She could have done it, though," he mused. "All she had to do
was get past the desk man on the way out, which is likely considering
the sloppy security in that place."

She watched the Eggplant sip his coffee. He was unusually sub-
dued. The fact was that Captain Luther Greene had been put down
in front of his subordinates. For a man of his ego, this had to be almost
unbearably painful.

"That woman was murdered, FitzGerald," he said after a long
silence.

"My sentiments, exactly."

"And I think we got it close to right."

"So do I."

"A man and a woman as secret lovers, they leave tracks, something. The whole world isn't blind. Somebody knows something."

"This is the kind of thing the media are good at. Getting the word out." She lowered her voice. "We could always leak it. See what bubbles out of the sewer."

The Eggplant lifted his lugubrious eyes and laughed. It was an empty hollow laugh.

"Plenty I'll bet. You heard them. Paranoid about the media."

"Nobody can be in politics for more than ten minutes without getting that disease," Fiona said.

The Eggplant finished his cup of coffee. A waitress came over and gave him a refill. Fiona refused. She was agitated enough. Caffeine would make it worse.

"I didn't take over homicide to call murders suicides," he muttered, peering into the dark shiny coffee. Then he looked up suddenly, as if someone might have heard. "I can understand their point of view. I really can. Nothing to go on."

"Nothing but our expertise," Fiona said. "And that should be enough."

He sighed.

"No skin off my tail if they call the damned thing a suicide," he snapped, mostly to himself. "Not worth blowing my future over it."

"Definitely not worth that."

"Except it's right. The right thing." He lifted his cup and looked over the rim. "Like you said about the lady. She did the right thing."

Which was really what he had brought her here to say. A little sob bubbled in her chest.

"Be careful, chief," she said, feeling the rush of sentiment. She felt her eyes grow moist.

"Hell, the old Eggplant knows how to play the game," he chuckled, smiling broadly. She blushed and he must have seen her discomfort and he quickly changed the subject.

"That Rome is a cool one."

"As soft and smooth as olive oil," Fiona said.

"Son of a bitch is playing his own political game. Probably sees any blow-up of the situation a negative for his side."

"Just remember, chief. Everything a politician does is all political. He pees, it's political. He snores, it's political."

The Eggplant nodded, then finished his coffee and slapped the cup back in the saucer. Lifting his hand he signaled for the waitress and mimed a writing gesture for the check.

"Well, FitzGerald. We got a week. You better get the lead out. We either wrap it or dump it. Right or wrong. Gut feelings or not."

"Might as well be a year," she said. It was her experience that cases either moved fast or withered. The longer a case stayed open the better its chance of being frozen in place. Interest wavered. Leads got cold. Indifference set in.

The waitress brought the check and the Eggplant looked at it and whistled.

"I just wanted coffee not a major investment." The check came to five dollars.

"You want a fancy hotel," the waitress said, turning snotty, "you got to pay for it." She was white, red-neck southern with a hairdo to match. They both knew where she was coming from.

"Too bad fancy service don't go with it," the Eggplant snapped. He gave the waitress a five dollar bill with the check. She could tell he wasn't going to leave a tip.

"You people," the waitress muttered. "Run everything now. Take our women."

"You ain't had black dick, you ain't had nothing'," Fiona sneered, enjoying the woman's reaction. She had opened her mouth, but no words came out, then she turned on her heel and flounced away.

"You didn't have to do that. It's not your battle."

"She insulted a cop. That's family."

Again he smiled broadly.

"For a senator's daughter you got a mouth on you."

"It wasn't meant as a compliment to you and your macho brothers," she snapped. "Just a put-down for the lady."

"Same old FitzGerald," he laughed.

"Same old . . ."

"Eggplant."

They walked out of the restaurant, went out the Pennsylvania Avenue side and got into the Eggplant's car. They headed back to headquarters.

"Back there," Fiona asked as they drove. She had been curious. "The mayor really blasted you."

"Comes with the territory."

He had thrown up his guard again, the tough gruff unfeeling Eggplant.

"I'm sorry, chief. I really am."

It was the second time she had apologized.

"Want to know what he said?"

She nodded.

"Said I was pussywhipped."

"That sexist bastard."

He turned to look at her.

"He was right," he said. He did not smile.

T HERE WAS A MESSAGE on her desk from Greg when she got back to the office.

"Confabulation necessary. Got to talk," the message read. He had been calling her more frequently than ever during the past few days and she had been deliberately cutting the conversations short, blaming it on her "busyness" which was half-true.

But evenings, when she had finally let go of her work and was left to her own thoughts, it was harder to keep him out of her mind. Was she or wasn't she pregnant? Obviously it was too early to tell, nor would she allow herself to take a do-it-yourself test. And she rejected the idea of seeing a doctor at this stage. Not yet.

Perhaps this reluctance had its roots in her early Catholic training. Concepts like God's will be done were ingrained, programmed into the mind, impossible to extract by a mere exercise of logic and scientific proofs. Not that she had any illusions about the technology of conception. But the randomness of fertilization did provoke ideas of mysterious forces at work, like fate and destiny. If it was meant to be, she had decided, then so be it, notwithstanding the fact that she had helped the process along. She would, therefore, await the decision of fate. It would come soon enough.

She had, however, made one decision out of pure reason. She would not tell him. It was a complication she did not wish to confront or burden a child with. Therefore, she knew that, if she were pregnant, she would have to wean herself from him. He must never know he was the father of her child. Never.

She was certain that she had thought it through. He was not divorced, nor did it seem that his wife would ever allow it. Aside from the woman's religious convictions which mitigated against divorce, being married to an important lawyer like Greg gave her a certain legitimacy and prestige. Washington, like all places where power counted, was a bad place for ex-wives of important players. No, she decided, even if bells clanged for Greg, his wife would never release him without a horrendous struggle.

Nor did she wish, under any circumstances, to be part of a closet family. Not that it was uncommon these days, but it was not her style to be a closet anything. Besides, the pressure on Greg would be destructive. He had his two young sons who were always on his mind, guilt trip enough for one man. It would have to end badly, she had decided.

On the other hand, the importance of fathering, she presumed, was not to be dismissed. Surely it had made a great impact on her life. Perhaps some day she would meet a man who would marry her and perform that function. But it was certainly unfair to both natural father and child to bring them together in a relationship that could be debilitating and destructive.

Therefore, she had assured herself, it was better to have the child by herself, mythologize the father in the child's eyes and bring it up as if she were a widow. In the black culture that surrounded her, it was a common practice to raise a fatherless child. It was, of course, economically foolish for those poor black girls, but emotionally, their argument that a woman alone needs a child to love was not without truth. Simplistic, she knew, but she had determined that it was also valid for her.

She, too, needed a child to love and the biological window of opportunity was closing fast. And, unlike those black girls, she was not impoverished. Her inheritance was substantial enough for her to properly raise and educate a child. She would not have to worry about day care or proper help.

She had prided herself on her independence and had always tackled the world on her own terms. Her choice of profession, her financial independence, her sophistication and her ability to choose her lovers were the envy of many of her peers. If she had not found a man to share her life forever, she supposed it was partly her own fault. This was the downside of the female mystique.

Her mother would have called this idea of being a single parent self-willed and impractical. But then she maintained a slavish belief in convention and appearances.

"I'd say I was married, Mother, and wear a wedding ring, for crying out loud," her inner voice said in its endless debate with her mother, a constant echo in her mind. "Besides, it's too late. I've already done it."

That would have stumped her. Like Frankie, her mother was a confirmed pro-lifer and this would have been too great a challenge to her hypocrisy. After all, the way the Catholics had worked it out, screwing out of wedlock was a sin, but it was never a sin to conceive in or out of wedlock.

"Then we'll just have to make the best of it," her mother's voice said. Fiona also heard the echo of a sigh, her mother's sure sign of surrender.

"So I do have your blessing, Mother?"

"Have I a choice?"

To fulfill the spirit of her plan, she would, if pregnant, have to say goodbye to Greg, cut it clean, but in a positive, civilized manner.

She dialed Greg's number and got his secretary who told her that she was instructed to put Fiona right through.

"In a meeting, Fi," he said. "Just hold while I get to another phone."

He was back in less than a minute, slightly out of breath.

"You okay?"

"Working hard. This is a tough one."

Her tone was clipped, hard-edged, the words sparse as if she wanted to prepare him for the inevitable, start the process of departure. But she was not totally comfortable with the idea. Suppose it hadn't happened. What then? She would need him once again.

"I need to talk," he said.

"About what?"

"Us," he said flatly.

"Sounds ominous," she said trying to be lighthearted.

"We've got to discuss the future," he said. "Our future."

The irony was troubling. She could sanction deception for ferreting out murderers, but it was quite difficult in her private life. She looked around the shabby squad room. At that hour most of the detectives were on the street. Even the Eggplant was not at his desk. She would have welcomed the hum of activity, the familiar sounds of interrogation and cajolery, the clash of accents and the still unfamiliar sounds of the electronic telephones, the comforting voices of friends and antagonists.

"Why now?" she asked cautiously.

"It's . . . well . . . because it's bugging me."

No, please, she wanted to say. You're making it quite difficult. She was silent. What response could she give? She had used him.

"Really Greg, this is not the time . . ."

"I've got to see you. We've got to talk. I'll be over tonight. Your place, tonight. Is that all right?"

Certain she owed him that. Besides, it was not yet time to burn the bridge.

"Not early, Greg. This case is overwhelming. Say around ten."

"I'll be there," he said. But he did not hang up. For some reason she, too, continued to hold the instrument to her ear.

"Fi?"

"Yes. Yes I'm here."

"I love you."

Only then did she hang up the phone.

20

FIONA AND CATES sat in the living room of the late Frankie McGuire's apartment. A film of dust had begun to settle on the surfaces of the furniture and a mustiness flavored the air. They had carefully gone over every inch of the apartment. Looking for what? She wasn't quite certain. Something that might trigger an idea, suggest a promising lead.

Nothing.

Cates had, by then, checked with almost all the tenants in the building. Many of them, especially those not associated with the government, had never met the congresswoman. Even when shown a picture most had not acknowledged ever seeing her.

There were eight other congressmen in the building, including Mr. Rome, also three senators and a number of government officials. Most, like the Romes were married, and those wives Cates had managed to question told him, in one way or another, that Frankie, when she was not accompanied by Foy or the Romes, always arrived at social functions alone.

Mrs. McGuire's apartment was on the fourth floor, at the end of the corridor, near the fire exit. The staircase ran from the roof to the lobby. With the exception of the desk man there was no elaborate security system, which was standard in most of the new buildings being erected in Washington. But this was an older building and since the burglary rate was comparatively low in the area, the building's owners apparently did not see the need to install an elaborate system.

It was conceivable that a determined intruder could get into the building undetected. The chances were, too, that he might even get past the indifferent desk people. But getting into the apartment would be a different matter entirely. The owners had installed a modern locking system that was well secured from inside the apartment.

"An exercise in futility, right, Cates?" Fiona asked after they had poked around the apartment for a half-hour.

"I'm from Kansas," Cates said.

"Missouri. The expression is 'I'm from Missouri.' "

"Same idea."

For her part, she felt herself digging in her heels, although she did not quite understand the underlying reasons for her surety. Frankie McGuire was murdered by her lover. Find the lover, find the murderer.

"There are no secrets," she mused aloud.

"Got to admit. That secret is the only airpocket in this case. Believe me, I've tried to get to it. She dealt with men all the time on the Hill. She went up to Boston every month. Every person with whom I talked put the idea down, however it was presented. Not the slightest hint, not an innuendo, not a breeze of scandal."

"That only meant that she was clever," Fiona said. "I never heard of a woman conceiving by herself." She paused, felt the brief pressure of her own situation, then chasing it away said: "Well, almost never."

She stood in the center of the living room, her mind focusing on details. Despite the dust and mustiness it was as neat as when she had first seen it. The technicians had put everything to rights according to their photographs of the scene at the time of discovery. Every chair, table and picture was in perfect placement, every knickknack carefully arranged. Nothing was out of place. The apartment was in effect, still in custody, awaiting a determination from homicide.

"It's here somewhere," she sighed.

Cates shrugged.

"It'll be over in a week," he said, as if that were a fait accompli. She ignored the comment. But she could not ignore the wealth of research he had amassed, all of it buttressing the suicide argument.

"How could she have kept it hidden from the Romes? They were her closest friends."

"I spoke at length to Mrs. Rome," Cates said. "She and her husband saw a great deal of Frankie."

It occurred to her that Cates, because he lacked conviction, might not have been asking the right questions. Quite often a bias made the difference between success and failure in an interrogation. If her theory were correct then Cates, too, was missing something.

"Think Mrs. Rome is home?" Fiona asked.

"That's easy enough to find out," Cates said. He looked up the phone number in his pocket notebook. He was extraordinarily thorough in finding and preserving information. She knew, too, that he often transferred such information into his home computer.

Finding the number, he reached for the phone.

"Busy," he said, looking at the useless instrument. "Let's just go on up."

By then, it was late afternoon. The Romes lived on the floor above on the tier facing Massachusetts Avenue. Frankie McGuire's apartment faced New Mexico Avenue and Fiona assumed that the layout was similar to Frankie's although reversed. Fiona was not a fan of apartment living, although she had occasionally rented her parents' place in Chevy Chase and had sublet an apartment for various lengths of time. Never again, she had decided. Too confining.

Mrs. Rome answered the door herself. A tall full-bodied and elegant-looking woman, she was smartly dressed, perfectly groomed and, as always, not a hair was out of place. Greying, with cheerful brown eyes and lips formed in what must be a perpetual political smile, Mrs. Rome, raised well-plucked eyebrows in surprise. Nevertheless she remained placidly calm, considering that they had barged in on her. Normally, guests were announced by the desk man.

"I'm terribly sorry to bother you, Mrs. Rome, but my partner and I have been going over Mrs. McGuire's apartment and would just like to clear up some loose ends."

"Of course," Mrs. Rome said, flashing a smile and standing aside to let them in. She was, Fiona decided, the epitome of proper conduct and reminded her of her mother, who was also always perfectly groomed and ready to admit guests to her home at any given moment.

Like her mother, too, Fiona noted, Mrs. Rome's apartment was sparkling clean. It had a polished look. Oriental rugs graced the floors. Where the hardwood floors were visible they were shined to a high gloss. In fact, wherever she looked everything was shined to a high gloss.

English and early American antiques were everywhere. A painting looking suspiciously like a genuine Remington on one wall and smaller paintings of western scenes, undoubtedly of equally illustrious provenance, hung on other walls.

"Just came in from an absolutely marvelous luncheon at the Jockey Club," she said as she led them through the apartment. "A sendoff for one of our foreign service wives. Her husband has been appointed Ambassador to Peru."

They followed her through the immaculate living room to a paneled den. From what they saw of the apartment it smacked of big money, old big money.

Fiona studied the room. To one side was a wet bar lined with bottles. Behind Mrs. Rome were floor to ceiling bookcases, filled on one side with antique leather bound books and on the other with modern novels in their dust jackets. Thrillers and mysteries seemed to be favored.

"May I get you coffee or tea? A soft drink, perhaps?" Mrs. Rome asked.

They both declined politely.

Sitting in a leather wing chair, she waved them to two soft leather easy chairs and primly crossed her legs. Here was a woman well used to entertaining constituents and making them seem important. Her mother reincarnated, Fiona thought.

Mrs. Rome smiled pleasantly offering herself with devoted expectation.

"Really nice of you to see us without any notice," Cates said. "But we were here and took the chance."

"No trouble in the least," Mrs. Rome said. "I can't get dear Frankie out of my mind. It baffles Charles and me. Frankie never, ever appeared suicidal. Not to us."

"Nor to anyone else," Fiona said.

"She had everything to live for," Mrs. Rome said.

"We met with your husband and the mayor this morning, Mrs. Rome," Fiona said, somewhat abruptly.

"Oh, yes. It's very hard on Charles, having to deal with the matter. But the Speaker is really anxious to expedite the disposition of the case one way or the other. Somehow it reflects on all the members when something like this happens. Casts a cloud."

"Have you spoken to your husband today, Mrs. Rome?" Fiona asked. It wasn't, after all, her place to impart the information about Mrs. McGuire's pregnancy.

A frown creased her forehead, although the smile remained fixed.

"Yes I have," Mrs. Rome said.

"Then you know about . . ."

"Mrs. McGuire's pregnancy."

Fiona nodded.

"I'm afraid so," she sighed. "I'm sure it's a mistake."

Was there a double entendre here? Fiona wondered. Whose mistake?

"Dr. Benton is the finest medical examiner in the United States," Fiona said cautiously.

"I didn't meant that," Mrs. Rome said, frowning. "I can only assume that to be accurate. But it is somewhat remarkable for a woman to conceive at her age. That part of her life seemed long over. After all they have four grown children. But these things happen, I suppose."

Something seemed off kilter in Mrs. Rome's remarks, as if she was reacting to a totally different stream of information.

"Of course, the way they lived, with Jack McGuire in Boston and she here most of the time, it wouldn't have been very good for the child, don't you think?" Her brown eyes sparkled as she spoke.

"Are you saying that you think that Frankie's husband was the father?"

Mrs. Rome raised her eyebrows indignantly and Fiona did all she could to resist exchanging glances with Cates.

"Isn't that the usual explanation for a married woman?"

"Mrs. Rome," Fiona responded, unwilling to let the statement go unchallenged. "The McGuires haven't been together as man and wife for years."

"Media nonsense," Mrs. Rome said.

"I'm afraid not," Fiona pressed. Mrs. Rome apparently also had her mother's habit of evading unpleasant truths. "I've spoken to Mr. McGuire. He confirms it."

"You can't believe anything that man says," she said fiercely. "We had them out to our ranch in Nevada. When was it? Six, seven years ago. I'm a Nevada girl, grew up there. Daddy was in the mineral business. Anyway, all that McGuire man did was booze booze booze. No wonder she wouldn't have him ever come to Washington. I can tell you that marriage was always strained. I couldn't imagine how she ever put up with it. I'll say this for her, she was always quite defensive about Jack. And overly tolerant."

"He's already married another woman, Mrs. Rome," Fiona said.

"Wouldn't surprise me," she said with a familiar huff in her voice. Yet Mrs. Rome's naïveté in this matter seemed genuine. Fiona felt her tolerance level descend.

"Which sort of buttresses the argument that they hadn't been living together," Fiona said. "It also suggests that it was unlikely that Jack McGuire was the child's father."

"I'm sorry," Mrs. Rome said with a smile. "This is not my expertise."

"But surely you would agree . . ."

"Gossip is simply not my ken," Mrs. Rome said, making an obvious effort to be pleasant.

"Surely you noticed something. Anything. Really, Mrs. Rome, this is very important. If you had the slightest hint . . ."

"Little blinders," Mrs. Rome said mimicking someone putting on spectacles. "That's what you wear in this town. Especially as regards those matters. I stay in my own vineyard."

"I'm asking specifically about Frankie McGuire," Fiona said with growing exasperation. "Did you ever have any indication that there was a man in her life?"

"Other than her husband?"

"I just told you about her husband, Mrs. Rome," Fiona snapped. The sudden pique elicited absolutely no reaction in Mrs. Rome.

"The answer to your question is no," Mrs. Rome said simply. "It is inconceivable."

"But the evidence of her pregnancy suggests otherwise. Surely you have to concede the possibility of her having a lover who impregnated her. Knowing who it was is really quite critical to this investigation. You and your husband were her closest friends in town. Think back. Review it in your mind. Was there ever anyone . . . ?"

"I suppose I haven't made myself clear," Mrs. Rome said politely.

"It's just that . . . secrets are so difficult to keep in this town."

"Quite true," Mrs. Rome said. "And I'll grant you that liaisons are, I suppose, quite common. Something about the aphrodisia of power. Any woman who leaves her husband alone for extended periods has to be mad. All those ambitious young ladies thirsting for excitement. It does go on, I'm sure. Makes for bad politics, not to mention bad morals." Her words were emphatic but not angry and the smile never left her face.

"Goes for the gander as well as the goose," Fiona said, studying Mrs. Rome's face.

"I really don't think it's the same," Mrs. Rome said. "I guess I'm an old-fashioned gal."

"Apparently Frankie McGuire wasn't," Fiona said pointedly.

"That's because you didn't know Frankie," Mrs. Rome said. "She was a hardworking, dedicated, brilliant woman. Her focus was completely on her work. My husband and she had tremendous differences. Her position on abortion, for example, is well known, as is my husband's."

"Can you ever recall seeing her with another man?" Fiona asked. Her question seemed almost desperate, obviously repetitive. She cut a glance at Cates who had remained silent and deadpanned.

"Why, of course," Mrs. Rome said calmly. "She was a member of Congress. You can't imagine how hard devoted members work. My husband is a case in point. Up at the crack of dawn. Off to the job while most of us are still locked in dreamland. Sixteen hour days. Show me a dedicated congressman and I'll show you a workaholic."

"I meant being with men in another context. Romantically, if you will."

"Never. How could she find the time?"

Her smile broadened with the little joke and she showed no sign of losing patience with Fiona's line of questioning. Undaunted, Fiona pressed ahead, although she was beginning to see this interrogation as a futile pursuit.

"When she went to a social gathering was it always alone?"

"On many occasions she went with us. There are so many events, of course. I presume she might have gone with one or another of her colleagues. But not in the way you suggest."

"Did she spend much social time with Harlan Foy?"

"Her AA?"

Mrs. Rome's smile broadened.

"Now really, Detective FitzGerald. Everybody knows about her Mr. Foy."

Fiona felt herself growing increasingly frustrated. Again she looked at Cates, imagined she detected a tiny gloating smile. Go ahead, he seemed to be saying, get it out of your system.

"You can think of no one . . . no one that you can even remotely consider as her possible lover?" Fiona asked. She felt like a broken record.

"If you must know," Mrs. Rome said with the slightest touch of haughtiness. "I can't even think of Frankie in that light."

"Well somebody had to be the father," Fiona said, detecting a kind of whining tone in her own voice.

"You have my opinion, officer. Perhaps she and Jack were separated, but knowing that man . . . and Frankie . . . I could imagine him deep in his cups demanding that she meet her . . . her wifely obligations. Besides, I never heard her utter an unkind word about her husband in the years that I've known her. Beyond that facade of the independent strong-minded woman was a very traditional and moral person. It would be unthinkable to see her in any other way." She looked pointedly at Fiona. "Really, I don't think that my husband or I can be of much help in concocting the kind of case you're trying to make in this matter. Frankie was our friend and she remains our friend even in blessed memory."

"We hadn't meant . . ." Fiona began, but it was quickly apparent that Mrs. Rome was not through. There was great toughness, Fiona observed, behind the persistent smile.

"Yes, you had. Frankly, I don't know what demons possessed poor Frankie. We did not see her as deeply troubled or unhappy in any way. I suppose in politics you learn to dissimulate. Perhaps she was so good at it that we never saw the truth." Mrs. Rome's attention seemed to falter, drift away. It became clear that the interview was over.

"Well, you've been very kind to talk with us again, Mrs. Rome," Cates said. It seemed a signal for the woman to rise. They also rose and followed her through the apartment to the front door.

"If I can be of any assistance, officers, please don't hesitate to visit or call." She held out her hand to Cates, then Fiona, shaking them in turn with a strong politician's grasp.

"Don't say it," Fiona snapped as they walked to elevators.

"I won't."

"She's living in a fantasy world," Fiona said, thinking of her mother. "Typical smiley-smiley. Political helpmate. Woman behind the man bullshit." Frustration had knotted her guts.

"All beside the point, Fi. Still no hits, no runs."

"Only errors," she sighed.

They moved down the corridor and Cates pushed the elevator button. As they waited they heard banging noises in the shaft and when none of the two elevators arrived after an inordinately long wait, they decided to walk down. They proceeded to the door marked exit which was next to the Rome apartment and started down the stairs.

But when they descended down two levels, Fiona stopped suddenly and ran back up the stairs. She opened the exit door and found herself in the corridor where Mrs. McGuire's apartment was located.

"What is it?" Cates said puffing obediently behind her.

She avoided an answer as she repeated the process of opening and closing the exit door. It operated smoothly making no sound. She stood for awhile just inside the landing, contemplating an idea that was emerging clearly in her mind.

"You're not thinking that?" Cates said.

"It's entirely possible," Fiona said, tapping her teeth with the longish nail of her forefinger.

"You're reaching."

"Think so? A quick run down the stairs. One flight. If he had a key, he'd be in her apartment in seconds with no one the wiser."

"Dangerous theory," Cates said.

"Worth pursuing," Fiona said. Again she opened the exit door and studied the empty corridor.

"Especially if you're looking for another line of work."

"A politician is a born opportunist," Fiona said. She closed the exit door and looked upward to the floor above. "And this is an opportunity."

21

"**Y**OU'RE LEADING ME straight down the garden path to hell, FitzGerald," the Eggplant said half-mockingly. It wasn't exactly what he had bargained for.

"Mrs. Rome could be the unwitting beard," Fiona said, spinning out yet another scenario. "He had proximity, that's for sure. Clever rascal, Rome. You can bet he'd find a way to get together with the lady without being seen."

"Talk about circumstantial," Cates said.

"Still the stubborn opponent," Fiona sighed.

"I'm not saying it couldn't happen," Cates said. "All I'm saying is that you haven't placed the man in the apartment."

"He found a way. He's a politician. Man like that always finds a way."

"Maybe," Cates agreed. "He'd have to be a really cagey bastard to evade the all-seeing Mrs. Rome."

"She certainly has a narrow view," Fiona said.

"Man with a hawkeye like her for a wife doesn't have too many options."

"Love always finds a way," Fiona said.

"We're talking here of place," Cates said. "Geography."

"They could have gotten it on up there," the Eggplant said pointing with his panatela in the general direction of Capitol Hill. "Horniness and power. Goes hand in hand in this town."

"No way. For Rome that would be geographically unacceptable,"

Fiona said. "Be like doing it in public. Too image-conscious. Too much staff around. Too many eyes and ears. Not foolproof enough for him. And her. No. If it was Rome, this would be strictly a closet thing. Their biggest consideration was obviously safety and discretion. If it did happen, they sneaked around."

"There's a contradiction there," Cates said. "There are no foolproof ways to sneak around. Not in this town."

"That would depend on logistics," Fiona said. "I may have solved that problem."

"Flanagan's boys are brushing the place," the Eggplant said. "We'll soon see."

"It would still be circumstantial," Cates said.

"Every great journey begins with but a single step," Fiona said.

"That still doesn't explain how he evaded Mrs. Cyclops."

"Well, for one, how about mornings? She said he got up at the crack of dawn. Pecks the little lady on the cheek, then pops down to Frankie and hops in for a roll in the hay. They'd spend an hour or so, then down he'd go to the garage and off to work."

"Sounds like you've been there, FitzGerald," the Eggplant said. Fiona blushed. For a brief time a few years ago, she'd had a morning lover, a man cheating on his wife. Of course, she hadn't known that fact. Although his habit of meeting her in the morning did strike her as peculiar. He said he worked for the CIA and his work kept him busy until late into the evening. She had checked that out. He did work for the CIA. Despite that he could not ultimately hide the fact of his marriage and that ended that. Nevertheless, from his point of view, it was a discreet, safe plan. The fact was, he never did get caught by his wife.

"Or he could have stopped by on his way home," Fiona said continuing her speculation. "Through the garage, up the elevator. If it was safe he'd get off on Frankie's floor. If not he would proceed to his own and dash down the stairs. Most likely, he would use the stairs to get back up. Chances are he wouldn't see anyone on the stairs. Wouldn't be a place for much traffic." Actually, she liked her morning theory better.

"Naturally, he had a key," the Eggplant said.

"Is the pope Catholic?"

"Then why no clues in the McGuire apartment?" Cates interjected.

"We could always get a warrant to search the Rome apartment," Fiona suggested. "Might turn up something."

"Now there's one that would wake the dogs," the Eggplant said. She watched him suck the end of his panatela saturating it with saliva.

"Part of the procedure for any ordinary suspect," Fiona protested.

"Are you suggesting that the old Eggplant is a chicken?" He tried relighting the panatela without success.

"Just figuring out ways to make a case here," Fiona said. The Eggplant shrugged and studied her.

"My father was a house painter. When I was a kid I worked for him. It's the only other skill I have. I do what you suggest, I start Monday with a brush and bucket."

"Just raising one small voice for justice," Fiona said.

The panatela was too wet to smoke and he discarded it in an ashtray and lit up another, sucked in the smoke, and blew it out in rings. His attitude, she sensed, was surprisingly philosophical.

"Justice, is it? You got movies of Rome in the sack with Frankie? Rome slipping the cyanide into the wineglass? Rome wiping off the prints and stealing upstairs to his nice cozy nest? You got that, FitzGerald, then I'm first in line on your parade."

"All I'm saying is that we have to start somewhere," Fiona muttered. "It's not our job to let him get away with it."

"Maybe we got here the makings of the perfect crime," the Eggplant sighed. It wouldn't, of course, be the first time. She had encountered a number of situations where someone who had with absolute certainty committed a murder but could not be brought to trial for lack of sufficient evidence. It was one of the main frustrations of all homicide detectives.

"No crime is perfect," Fiona countered. "Every solution depends on the diligence and commitment of people like us," she said with lofty assurance. "I truly believe that this thing is bustable."

"Might bust us, too," the Eggplant muttered.

He was remarkably sanguine. In other circumstances he would have insisted that she lean heavily on a suspect, play with his head to extract a confession. He was holding back now. It was too risky. They needed more, much more.

"Maybe we could dig up the body, do a DNA print," Fiona said.

"Still experimental. Maybe someday," the Eggplant said wistfully.

The telephone rang. The Eggplant answered it, barked out some order, then hung up.

"You get him to confess, FitzGerald, we got us a case," he said, as if he had read her mind. He smiled and watched a smoke ring rise to the ceiling.

"He's too damned shrewd to let me take him," Fiona said. "He's an expert in manipulation. He'll see through me in a minute."

"With due respect," Cates said, clearing his throat, a tic signaling a coming profundity. He looked at Fiona. "I'm not saying it didn't happen exactly as you suggested. Or variation thereof."

"Well, thanks for the seal of approval."

"Don't misunderstand, Fi. I really do believe that Rome could have been the woman's lover. But killer. That's a whole different ball of wax. Still nothing I've seen or heard rings that bell. All I've been getting is a motive for suicide. Nothing more." He shook his head. "Sorry."

"Motive for suicide, is it?" Fiona asked. "Old Rome refuses to divorce the lovely Barbara. Maybe he even suggests the "A" word. Because of that, she does herself with cyanide. That it?"

"Something like that," Cates said.

"Soap opera bullshit," Fiona shot back. She felt a bubble of anger expand in her chest. "She was an independent strong-minded woman. She was perfectly capable of accepting the reality of the child." She looked at both of them pointedly, pugnaciously. She thought suddenly of Greg and her own situation. "Married or not, dammit."

Her burst of anger seemed to surprise Cates and the Eggplant.

"Cates has a point, FitzGerald," the Eggplant said calmly.

"The only point he has is on his head," Fiona said, fuming.

"What we are seeking here," the Eggplant said, ignoring their verbal joust, "is a possible cover story for an ungraceful exit. We declare suicide. Name no names. Case closed."

"You're kidding," Fiona said, startled.

"It's a perfectly logical option," he muttered.

"Politically speaking," Fiona said.

"In the absence of evidence, as good a resolution as any you've offered," the Eggplant said. She couldn't tell if he was serious or not.

"You were the one who pushed the murder theory. I arrived later on that one. And him . . ." She looked at Cates who met her gaze head on. ". . . he's still at the station."

"I'm only going on what we have at the moment," the Eggplant said. The man gave us one week, remember. Far be it from me to dampen your enthusiasm." Was he mocking her? Or goading her on? She was getting mixed signals. Maybe he was setting her up, letting her go out on a limb on her own.

"Gentlemen," Fiona said standing up. "We have a problem here. Neither of you know shit about women."

"I won't deny that one," the Eggplant said, obviously being patronizing. She could imagine his interpretation. This was the last line of defense for the harassed female. When in doubt blame the boys for not understanding the girls. She felt suddenly like a cliché, an object of ridicule.

Cates avoided her eyes.

At that moment the telephone rang. The Eggplant answered it, looked at her and mimed "Flanagan."

"Are you sure?" the Eggplant asked. He shook his head, grunted into the phone and hung up.

"Sorry, FitzGerald. No good prints near the exit doors, on the railings or walls."

She was disappointed. But it didn't shake her theory. Not one bit.

"It was, I will admit, an intriguing idea," the Eggplant said, his voice trailing off.

"He gave us a week," she stammered. "I want the time." She looked at Cates who shrugged.

"You got it," the Eggplant said. "Only I want . . ."

"To be apprahzed," she said mimicking the way he said it.

He nodded and puffed a line of smoke rings in her direction.

22

S HE HAD BEEN sitting in the den for two hours nursing the day's many inflicted wounds. The ashes of anger still smoldered, but high emotion had receded. What difference did it make? She had finally concluded. No skin off my tail.

Try as she did, all protestations ended in defeat. That woman was murdered. Of that she was now certain, dead certain. Never mind that it was purely intuitive. Never mind that she had superimposed her own highly individualized emotions on the lady's motivation.

Frankie McGuire was tough, strong, independent and courageous. She had chosen career over family. She was a fighter. Nothing that Fiona had heard about her indicated that she would deliberately take her own life. Certainly not the fact that she was pregnant. Especially that.

But that conclusion could not manufacture evidence of foul play. Cates wasn't much help either. All his research had only buttressed his own view of the suicide argument. She was furious with him, but she couldn't blame him.

She heard Greg's car rolling up the gravel driveway. She had forgotten. Also her mental state was such that she was not up to any more confrontations. She wished she could send him home.

It was too late, of course. She opened the door for him and he immediately embraced her and, despite her reluctance of a few moments ago, was glad he had come. She responded to his kiss.

"God, I've missed you," he said.

She led him to the den and he sprawled beside her on the couch. A fire was burning happily in the fireplace.

"I told you," he had joked between kisses. "We had to talk."

"This is talking," she said.

"Not right away. I never said first thing," he whispered. By then, it was already too late to turn back.

"It's a fine way to greet somebody," she said insinuating her body under his.

"Very friendly," he said.

They were silent for a long time as the embrace accelerated to culmination.

"I love you," he whispered, as they cooled down, remaining intertwined. "It's important for me to say that to you, Fi. I love you with all my heart and soul. I love you. I never want to be without you. Never."

She did not respond and after awhile, she got up and put on her robe and went off to the bathroom. When she came back she poured out two Scotch and waters and handed him one.

"I can't get you out of my mind, Fi," he told her after he had sipped some of his Scotch. She had sat down beside him and he took her hand and kissed it.

"Just what does that mean?" she asked.

He took a deeper sip on his Scotch, then looked at her through his long black lashes. His face was conventionally handsome, high cheekbones, strong chin, eyes that could pierce the veil of any woman's indifference.

"It means," he said, after studying her for a long moment. "That I want us to live together."

That again, she thought, wondering if, under all those layers of fear and caution that she had contrived, she really loved him. Yes, she liked being with him, adored and appreciated his sensuality. In that way, he was delicious. If that was love then she loved him deeply. He could make her swoon with pleasure.

But there were barriers, principal among which was his marital status. Then there were her own instincts about his reliability, his morality, his value system. His choice of clients, for example, was a measure of his corruptibility, despite his protestations that he was only a professional advocate. Didn't that mean that he was a hypocrite? Easily bought and sold to the highest bidder.

And yet she had chosen him to be the father of her child. Corruption, after all, was an environmental malady. Not something passed on by the genes. Now, after their lovemaking, there were soft moments when she grew more reflective, more open to possibilities. In his arms, she felt warm, secure, protected against the afflictions of the day. He put his arms around her shoulders, hugged her closer. She nestled herself in the crook of his arm. Gently, he caressed a breast while she rubbed an inner thigh. Easy, intimate, sensual, she thought. Rejecting such pleasures suddenly seemed unthinkable. Yet, she persisted.

"I've tried living with someone before. It hasn't worked yet."

She thought briefly of Bruce Rosen, saw his grey curly hair, remembered its touch. It was all she wished to remember about him with fondness. That, too, was a matter of reality over fantasy. Reality had, thankfully, been the victor.

"So have I," he mused. "Wrong combinations is all." He gently squeezed her breast. "Not us. We're peanut butter and jelly."

"I hate peanut butter," she countered.

"But you do like jelly?" he asked.

"You were referring to the combination," she said, hoping he would understand the symbolism.

"Seriously, Fi," he began. "We have got to face this."

Please, she begged him in her heart. No confrontations. Not now. Not yet. She maneuvered herself out of his arms and sat up stiffly. Then she drank half of her Scotch, feeling its shock as it hit her stomach.

"You can't evade it," he pressed.

"It's the timing," she countered.

"Timing? What's that got to do with it?"

He certainly was forcing things. She took refuge in silence.

"It can't go on forever, Fi. I've had it out with her. She's agreed to give me a divorce. It couldn't go on like this."

"Is she giving up religion?" Fiona asked.

He sat up stiffly and looked at her.

"That all you can say? I thought you'd be elated. I thought that's what you wanted."

"You seem to be taking a lot for granted," she said, her anger beginning to rise. This was totally unexpected and she had no time to prepare a response.

"I can't believe this," Greg said. "We're lovers. Look at us. We're perfect together. I love you. My life is dominated by thoughts of you." He was obviously confused by her attitude.

"It took me by surprise," Fiona said, still trying to come to grips with her confusion. "I hadn't thought of you in that context. You're talking marriage. That's a whole different kind of commitment. I had accepted that in my mind. The legalities of your marriage. The kids."

"My kids will love you, Fi."

She was immediately sorry that she had raised that issue. His devotion to his children was commendable and redeeming.

He stood up and began to pace the den. He had put on his pants, but was barefoot and his shirttails hung down over his waist.

"Look, Fi. I know what I bring to the table. I'm forty-one years old. And I do have baggage. I've lived. I've had a number of prior relationships." He paused. "So have you, Fi." Then he resumed his pacing. "It's also true that I represent some of the biggest bastards in the business. I do that for money. People do things that they detest for money. I have children I adore and I have one first-class fourteen karat cruel bitch for a wife who has finally agreed to let me divorce her. Don't ask me how I married her in the first place. Maybe I wasn't perceptive enough. Anyway, it was wrong. People change. She became someone else. I changed. She is a miserable woman who hides behind her religion and her causes to absolve herself of responsibility. She has been a rat to me. And, as a consequence, I have had to fight back. But Fi . . ." He stopped again and turned toward her. "I am a good man, a good person. And I love you. I want to live with you. I don't want this to be some casual temporary thing. I want to marry you."

He stopped pacing, turned his back to her and looked into the crackling fire. Naturally, she was moved. His appeal had been passionate and heartfelt. She felt that the barrier had been breached, that there was a lot more to him than she had imagined. Still, the central issue that concerned her now was the fact of her hopefully impending pregnancy. She had deceived him and he would have to confront that fact. And there was more to it than that.

At the beginning of their relationship, he had averred time and time again that his fathering was complete, that he had quite enough offspring, thank you. There had been no mistaking his tone and the air of finality.

But that was before love had arrived. No longer did she detect the arrogance of manhood. Love changed things. Love, as they say, could move mountains. He turned suddenly and looked at her.

"Of course, if there's no mutuality here then I'm shouting in the wilderness."

"I'm not sure, Greg," she said honestly. Of course, she would miss him, would long for his nearness and the comfort of his presence. Aloneness was not necessarily an ideal condition although she had managed to come to grips with it, even enjoy it at times.

Yet, her nature required the occasional intimate company of a man. Perhaps, she thought, she was judging him too critically. Years of disillusion with men and independence had created too tough a hide. Maybe, too, she was misinterpreting what love meant to a thirty-six-year old single woman. Maybe the bells changed their tone in the fourth decade of life.

"Don't be a fool, Fiona," her mother's voice echoed in her mind, rebuking, guilt-inspiring. More than a fool, she told herself, berating herself for her deception. Immaculate deception. She heard the echo of her own laughter in her thoughts.

"The thing is, Fi," Greg said. "We're a perfect fit physically and intellectually." He was being cerebral now, making lawyer's points. "I have no hang-ups about your work. In fact, I think it's great, exotic and satisfying."

"Not too blue collar?" she asked, testing his level of snobbery. Most of her past serious men friends had, sooner or later, frowned on her work. Not for reasons of danger, which she could understand, but for the usual class reasons. Greg was an exception.

"If I have any real quarrel with you, Fi, it's your hyperactive sense of political idealism," he said.

"Runs in the family," she responded, although her father had played the game at the beginning with great helpings of bullshit and blarney.

"I know you detest my clients. But I'm only a hired gun and you know it. Besides, it shouldn't be grounds for turning me down. All I'm asking is a try." He moved toward her and lifted her from the couch. "Experiment. Gamble. Take a chance on a guy that loves you." He embraced her and whispered in her ear. "Fi. I'll do anything you ask. If my clients' causes bug you I'll trade up. I want your respect as much as your love."

She could feel the persuasive pressure of his words. Her resolve was weakening. Why not? If he loved her that much surely he would respect her desire for motherhood, her need. All right, he would have to reevaluate his feelings about fathering any more children.

Naturally, a two-parent family would be a plus for her child, she decided. He would have to make a commitment irrevocably to the idea of fatherhood on an equal basis with his two other children. That would be far more important than marriage. No. She would not pressure him on that point. That would be her commitment to him.

"I'm not half bad as husband material, Fi. I'm easy to get along with. I'm not overly argumentative, although I do have a tendency to be a bit sensitive. Maybe that's because the little boy in me just won't grow up. I make plenty of dough, enough to go round. I guarantee no economic problems. I'm also an exceptionally neat guy as you've seen. I fold up my clothes, keep my closets perfect. Comes of being the son of a Craig's wife type. I never leave a room without picking up after me."

"Has something to do with toilet training," she laughed and knew he was winning her, breaking down all resistance. Still he continued. His suit was relentless.

"And believe it or not, I was a true blue faithful husband until . . . well that's all beside the point. I would always be faithful to you. Always. You're more than enough for me, Fi."

As if to emphasize the point, he grabbed her buttocks with two hands and pushed his hardening penis against her and kissed her neck and ears. No question about it, Fiona thought, we are totally compatible in that department, which was no small thing.

"I have a healthy lust for you. I love you. I cherish you. I promise to bring you nothing but joy. Live with me, Fi. Please."

"You must be one helluva lobbyist," she said, feeling all resistance crumble. She ground her pelvis into his.

"That has a bad connotation. I am a soft and loving man. And, as you can tell, wildly romantic. If you won't move in with me now, we'll wait until we marry. How about that? Real old-fashioned. Any which way you want."

She kissed him long and hard on the lips, her tongue caressing his.

"I couldn't leave here, Greg," she said.

"Wherever you want. It's your call. I'll even pay the mortgage," he joked.

"There's no mortgage," she said. "My father saw to that."

"I'll give you anything you want, my darling. Anything."

It was, she knew, the moment.

"I want a child," she said.

She felt him stiffen. His erection subsided. She had obviously hit a raw nerve. Slowly he released her and walked across the room, peering into the fire, which was ebbing.

"That's what I want, Greg. I'm sorry it offends you. That's the place I'm in now. I've given it a great deal of thought."

She could not now tell him what she had done. A great stone weight seemed to be growing in the pit of her stomach. Suddenly, he turned to face her.

"I wish I could," he said, sucking in a deep breath. She could tell he had fought back tears.

"You did ask," Fiona said.

"I can't," he said.

"I suspected as much," she said. "I know how you feel about your kids. And I do respect your decision on this. But it's what I want." She dared not tell him the truth. "It would always be between us."

"It's not what you think, Fi."

She was confused. He came toward her and held her by the shoulders.

"I did it out of self-protection. My wife wanted to live as a true Catholic, have a giant family. As many kids as God provided, she would say. Then she became this fanatic. I no longer knew her. I hated the idea of a huge unplanned family. Worse, I began to hate her and her ideas." He paused and looked into her eyes, pleading. "I tried to keep us together as a family. It was the only weapon I could muster. I needed to fight back. I had a vasectomy."

A sinking feeling engulfed her and she felt on the verge of fainting. She turned away, hiding her face. Her sense of defeat and humiliation was acute.

"In some cases it is reversible," he said. "But there are no guarantees and the percentage is minuscule."

She could find neither the will nor the courage to answer him. Her sense of self-delusion was intense. She had brought this down on herself. She had victimized herself with false optimism, wild assumptions and mad fantasies. She assailed herself for her naïveté, her vulnerability.

"Oh Mother, Mother," her inner voice whined. "I am such a fool."

"You can't always get your own way," she heard her mother respond, her voice larded with that unmistakable tone of self-righteous surety.

"I never told you. I never even thought it might be a factor between us," Greg said. He could not hide his disappointment. "All I can promise, Fi, is my love. Surely that's a valuable thing."

She felt herself approaching the outer cusp of hysteria and was fearful that she might erupt, lose control. Then she heard herself laughing, a hollow false note.

"I'm sorry, Greg. No. You're right. It shouldn't have been a factor. I'm not so sure I'd make a good mother anyway." She paused, letting the words linger in the air. "I don't think I'm good marriage material either."

"Only one way to find out," he persisted. He was amazingly, infuriatingly tenacious. But hadn't he been devious as well?

She shook her head, walked toward him, and came within range of a potential embrace. He held off, watching her face. She most certainly must have been a puzzle to him.

"I say . . ." she began, hoping her voice reflected an airiness that

she did not feel inside. "I say we leave well enough alone, Greg."
"But really, Fi . . ." he began.
Moving closer to him, she put a finger on his lips.
"You know what too much familiarity breeds."
"I'm not going to give up, Fi," Greg said.
But she had already written it off. His cause was hopeless now.

23

S HE WATCHED HIM stand for a moment in the entrance of the Marriott Restaurant. For a brief moment as he stood there, she saw him without his political mask of surety and reserve. Then he caught her eye and the mask quickly reappeared and he walked toward her with a broader smile than he usually wore, compensating surely for his inner anxieties.

She had deliberately chosen the Key Bridge Marriott on the Virginia side of the Potomac, counting on the symbolic separation to suggest confidentiality and secrecy. The view, one of the best in town, was also symbolic. Through large picture windows one could see the whole panorama of official Washington with its monuments and wedding cake buildings, the seat of power in all its physical glory.

Her call to Rome had been a compulsive idea. Last night's episode with Greg had shaken her equilibrium. Her fantasy had exploded leaving her angry and humiliated with most of her enmity directed against herself. All that angst and rationalization. All that convoluted logic. It hadn't mattered. None of it.

To get her mind off her appalling miscalculation, her childish foray into mindless wish fulfillment, she had forced her thoughts to near total concentration on the McGuire case. Perhaps her call to Rome was motivated by some subconscious effort to balance the scales, to pursue a moral imperative. Enough, she berated herself. Enough of this psycho-babble.

She had, indeed, talked from both sides of her mouth and her disappointment was not only in her lack of conception but in her own lack of insight and scruples. Served her right. In the end she found a tiny shaft of humor in the predicament. She had misappropriated some dead semen. How was she to know the son of a bitch was shooting blanks?

Poor Charlie Rome, she snickered without pity. She had appointed him surrogate whipping boy.

The fact of meeting him was an act of defiance. She hadn't asked permission. She had "apprahzed" no one. This was her own call. She knew she was flirting with danger. If nothing came of it the Eggplant would be apoplectic. Cates would be appalled. The mayor would be vindictive. If it backfired she would be out or, at the least, relegated to the Siberia of traffic control. There was absolutely no upside for her in this, even if she cracked the case wide open. They'd put it down to just another pushy broad going off half-cocked during her monthlies. Never mind that she was doing the right thing.

Rome offered his hand as he sat down, a pol's natural reflex and she took it, felt the flesh's pressure and heat. At this proximity in the bright morning sunlight, he showed his age. His skin, which looked pink and healthy from a distance, revealed a sprinkling of brown sun damage spots. There were nests of wrinkles beside the eyes and the rings of his contacts were clearly outlined over moist brown eyes.

But his grooming was impeccable. His navy suit with white pinstripes was obviously custom made. Presidential cufflinks peeked out of crisply folded shirt cuffs. The fellow knew how to put himself together. She'd give him that, although somehow it suggested his wife Barbara's passion for a style based on crisp orderliness.

"I couldn't resist an air of mystery," he said. The waitress came with coffee. As he thanked her with his pol's smile, he looked surreptitiously around the room with what she thought were furtive eyes. No one here to misinterpret things, he seemed to conclude, with obvious relief.

"I'm really sorry about the sense of urgency, but I did feel it was necessary that we meet."

He looked at his watch.

"I was due at a prayer breakfast," he said with a chuckle. "I hope the Lord will forgive me." He took a sip of his coffee and looked cursorily over the menu, then moved it aside with an air of indifference.

She sipped her coffee. It tasted bitter and turned sour in her stomach. Swallowing hard she began.

"This is strictly between us, congressman."

"I thought as much from our conversation."

"No one knows. This is my own idea."

"You have my complete confidence."

Her voice was shaky and it surprised her. The weakness seemed to relieve him somewhat, which she took as a good sign. She wanted him to be relaxed, less on his guard.

"I believe I know who Frankie McGuire's lover was."

She looked for signs, involuntary cracks behind the wall of outward serenity. None were visible.

"You make it sound earth-shattering."

"In a way it is."

"I want you to know up front, that I doubt she had one. Certainly not Foy. If I were a betting man, I'd say that she and Jack got together. Despite their differences, they were still husband and wife."

The waitress came back and took their order. Rome ordered scrambled eggs and she whole wheat toast. There was no way she could eat it and she suspected that what she was about to say would take away any appetite that Rome had mustered.

"We have evidence . . ." She cut herself short, a tactic to deepen the sense of ominous mystery, and studied his face intently. No sign of fear or anxiety. No reaction either way. It began to worry her. If she was wrong, she could kiss her career goodbye. Rome would never forgive her, go for the jugular.

"Evidence of what?" he asked blandly.

"We know how she and her lover managed their trysts without apparent detection." The word "apparent" was the tease, implying witnesses. It crossed her mind that perhaps the man was wired, making a case for police entrapment. Nevertheless, she pressed ahead.

"Why tell me this?" he asked, smiling pleasantly. Not a nerve seemed awry. There wasn't the slightest sign of tremor or palpitation.

"Because," she said drawing it out. "I think I can trust you to know."

"That's a tall order," he said, his smile collapsing. "Maybe you shouldn't tell me either."

He wasn't fooling her one bit, she decided. He knew the parameters. She had told him on the phone that she had something "new" to impart on the McGuire case. For his ears only. She had made that perfectly clear. The very fact that he had accepted her invitation proved his special concern.

"On the contrary," she said. "Because of your extreme interest in the case, I think you should be the first to know."

She was deliberately crawling up to the revelation, dancing around it. To spark his curiosity, a buildup was essential. Her object was to get him all shook up to the point where he couldn't keep the mask intact.

"Not Foy, I hope." It was intended as a stab of levity but it fell flat.

"Not Foy," she said.

"Am I supposed to ask?" he said with just the slightest flareup of annoyance.

She shrugged, then looked directly and deeply into his eyes. For the very first time she saw the fear. Now, she decided.

"You were Frankie's lover, Mr. Rome."

She said it softly, watching its impact. She saw his expression change, the wavering of surety, the first faint signs of a terrible vulnerability. He stood up and flung his napkin on the table. But he made no move to leave.

"I don't think you would want to create a scene, Mr. Rome," she said coolly. She was into it now, strong and confident, studying him for clear signs of her theory's validation. She hadn't expected him to crumble without a fight. After glaring at her for a long moment, he sat down.

"There are heavy consequences in false accusations," he said, lowering his voice.

"I know."

She watched as he forced himself under control. This was a man of enormous discipline. Through willpower and imagination he had literally shaped himself into an image of what apparently passed for a "statesman." He projected dignity and bearing, especially with his greying hair and superb grooming. Combined, these attributes gave his words the tone of wisdom. It was fair to say that he was long on style. As for substance, she knew little about his performance, but a good guess would be that he was more of a power broker and a "force" rather than an imaginative conceptualizer of new legislation.

If his head were transparent, she was certain, she would see the patterns of a computer program set to trigger a kind of charming indignation. It was really his only option. The fact that he had not stormed out of the restaurant was a hopeful clue that she had not guessed wrong.

"You realize, of course, that that is the most absurd notion I have ever heard in my life. I am a happily married man, a constant and devoted husband. I suppose I should be flattered to be accused of infidelity with such a lovely woman as Frankie. The idea is fascinating, even attractive, but I'm afraid a clandestine affair is not my cup of tea."

He was ladling out the charm from a bottomless inner bucket, slopping it over her with what he must have thought was elegance and finesse.

"Just hear out my fantasy, Mr. Congressman," she said. She hoped he noted the sarcasm and contempt in her tone. She didn't care. She was encouraged now, her gut instinct vibrating like a tuning fork with sympathetic certainty.

"I'll listen, of course. But I would appreciate it if this bit of fiction stopped at the door of this restaurant."

Despite his calm exterior, she continued to sense his fear.

"We found a latent fingerprint," she said, sucking in a deep breath, wondering if her nose was growing. "Yours."

"Wouldn't be surprised," he said calmly. "We visited Frankie often."

"On the toilet seat, at that point where a man's hand is used to lift the seat."

"And yes, I most probably did use the facility," he said with contrived bemusement.

She was strictly improvising now, jockeying for position, waiting for the moment of vulnerability. Since he was a man of vast talking experience and a heavy reliance on wit, it would be natural for him to best her in any rebuttal and deflect accusations.

"You reached her discreetly through the exit stairway. A cautious man could effect such an operation without being seen. Unfortunately that was not a foolproof operation."

"Of course you have a witness for these fictional assertions," he muttered.

"Yes, we do. Two in fact. Both quite credible. They saw you in the corridor on Frankie's floor. They're dead certain. I showed them pictures. They didn't know your name, only that they saw you often coming out of the exit door and proceeding to Frankie's apartment."

"That's sheer madness," he protested. Still, he made no move to leave. She noted, too, that despite his control, he could not quite dominate his fingers, which shook, and his skin, which had grown pinker.

"What is, your being Frankie's lover?"

"And this is your own brilliant theory?"

"I do not believe it's theoretical," she snapped.

"Your superiors know nothing of this?"

"Nor my partner."

"And the technical people? The fingerprint."

"That doesn't mean an accusation. Prints are often identified without comment. And you were a visitor to Mrs. McGuire's apartment."

"With my wife."

He shook his head and forced a smile.

"On occasion."

"Sounds to me like something in someone's dirty tricks department. Who are you really working for, FitzGerald?"

"Now it's a conspiracy," Fiona said. "Mr. Rome, you have a very safe seat."

"No one is immune to reckless slander, especially in politics." He thought for a moment. "I get it. You're part of the pro-lifers. They've been trying to get me for years. So old May Carter has finally found a weapon." His face reddened further revealing his accelerating anger. "The old bitch finally found a way to get me. How utterly disgusting." He had, she could tell, truly believed he had found a way to get off the hook.

He certainly knew how to wiggle. She started to say something in protest, but he interrupted before she could get the words out. "It's all quite clear to me now. You won't get away with this. You know why?" He pointed a finger at her. "There's a basic flaw in your theory. Nothing you have said can prove that Frankie was murdered by me and that is, apparently, what you're suggesting. Even if I were her lover, which I deny categorically, you still have to prove that I murdered her, which is impossible and untrue."

He stopped, sucked in a deep breath and seemed quite satisfied with his explanation.

"There is a baby involved here," Fiona said, feeling her own emotional system ride into high gear.

"Fetus," he corrected.

"A life."

"And it was Frankie's choice to decide what was right for her. She chose to eliminate both herself and the baby."

"Your baby," Fiona said quietly. It seemed suddenly, to her, the profoundest issue in the case and for the first time she discovered the true nature of her own personal policy on that issue.

If it happened to someone else it was a moral issue only, abstract and high-minded, on whichever side one came down. If it happened to you it was a matter of life and death. Last night, tossing and turning in bed, she must have subconsciously debated the point with herself. She had, in effect, lost her baby. Albeit it had been in her imagination but it had been just as real to her as any biological conception. And she had experienced the same psychic hollowness, the same sense of despair and loss, as if something had been stolen from her body by forces outside of her control.

"I don't know why I'm listening to this," Rome said, but something in his tone lacked conviction. For the first time she noted that a moustache of perspiration had grown on his upper lip. Also, his clear intense eyes had grown suddenly vague as if he were looking inward.

"Because you know I've got it right."

"This is preposterous. I have a good mind to call the mayor," he said.

"I'm sure they can bring you one of those cordless phones." She began to look around for the waiter. Seeing one, she raised her arm and he reached out and brought it down.

"I don't want to embarrass you, FitzGerald," he said. "My advice to you is to have our coffee, then leave here and forget about all this."

He started to raise his coffee cup, but his hand shook so hard that the cup slipped into its saucer, spilling the coffee on the white tablecloth. He was quite obviously losing control and knew it.

"I've made a mess," he said, his voice breaking.

"Yes, you have," she said. She was noting other physical signs of a crumbling facade. His lips were trembling. She knew what she had to do now.

"Do you and your wife have any children of your own?" Fiona asked. He had been studying the coffee stain on the table, his eyes lowered. Suddenly he looked up as if his face had been slapped. She knew she had struck a deep nerve.

"No, we don't," he whispered, clearing his throat. "That's all public record."

Where he had sought her eyes, he now shifted his gaze to his hands. Then he shrugged and spoke, his tone low, as if he were addressing his fingers. Slowly, he lifted his head, but his look was still vague. "The doctors said I had too low a sperm count."

The assertion came as a shock. In a court of law such evidence could rule out the possibility of his being the father of Frankie's baby. Then why all this display of angst? she wondered.

"So you see I couldn't have been the father," he sighed.

"Not necessarily, Mr. Rome. All it takes is one."

"Yes," he said vaguely. "Just one."

Her long shot, she knew now, was paying off, but in an entirely different manner than she had expected.

"You were pretty proud, weren't you, Mr. Rome?"

He looked up at her, his eyes lugubrious, moist with tears. The facade had suddenly disappeared. What was left was a terrible psychic nakedness.

"I couldn't do that to Frankie," he said, swallowing hard, obviously trying to assert control over his emotions.

"Or to your baby."

He averted his eyes and wiped his face with his napkin, still fighting for control, but obviously losing the battle. Halfway home, she thought with relief. Unfortunately his revelation had underscored her principal fear, that Frankie's lover might not be her killer.

"I loved her, you see," he croaked, clearing his throat.

Despite the visible evidence of his surrender, Fiona was shocked. Watching this strong confident man crumble so quickly came as a surprise. But she knew that it often happened this way, a spear of truth hitting that tiny nerve of vulnerability.

"I was proud as hell," he whispered. His shoulders shook and he again picked up a napkin as a kind of prop, bunching it in his hands as he dabbed his face with it. All pretense of dignity had disappeared.

She sat watching him, feeling genuinely embarrassed, wondering if this was not simply another performance. It was, she knew, a time for silence, a time to respond to his need for confession, even in this unlikely setting. A compulsion to expiate was a powerful force and she knew from long experience when to get out of its way.

"It had no logic. It wasn't preconceived. I am not a philanderer. Nor was Frankie a loose woman. It simply happened between us, at first without our knowing, then finally as an epiphany. We fell in love. Imagine that. We were, in fact, on opposite ends of the political continuum but we fell in love. Despite everything. Love is a blind madman." He shook his head, blinked his eyes, squeezing out a few more tears which he wiped away with his napkin. By then, she had recovered her surprise. The fact was that the man had roused her compassion. She could empathize with his pain. Love, when it happened, was ruthless and demanding.

"We found a way," he sighed. "Early mornings. It was quite simple. I had always risen at the crack of dawn, headed for the office early. Always the first in. Get a great deal of work done before everyone arrives." He laughed self-mockingly and, of course, she understood. Barbara had confirmed his habit of rising early. "Dawn to midnight. A congressman's work never ends," she had said.

"We found a precious hour or two to be together," he sighed. "It was the happiest time of my life. And hers."

Discreet as well, she thought. It was unlikely that he would meet anyone at that hour on the stairs or in the corridor. Getting out without being seen would be slightly more risky. Obviously he had managed it.

He became suddenly contemplative and she sensed it was time for her to encourage him.

"Did you know about the child?"

"Yes. She told me." He nodded in emphasis, offering a clown's smile, the kind which indicated that you were crying on the inside. "I was the happiest guy in the world."

"And she?"

"Confused. And yet . . . joyous at first. We were like kids, you see. In love." He sighed deeply. "Then, of course, reality set in. We are rather high-profile political figures. The scandal would be devastating. At our age, it would be hard to portray us as romantic lovers, which we were in fact. Abortion, of course, was considered."

"But she was a pro-lifer by conviction."

"Yes she was. But you also have to understand that she was in a powerful position to serve her cause. With Jack McGuire pressing for a divorce, she would have made herself a laughing stock to her constituents. The media can be quite ugly. There is a way to rationalize things, FitzGerald. She was thinking, I suppose, of the greater good, a kind of self-sacrifice for the ultimate end." He shook his head. "In this case I was the more passionate naysayer."

"You? I thought you were an abortion advocate."

He paused.

"This would have been my only child, FitzGerald," he said, recovering, for a moment, his earlier commanding vigor. "It was unthinkable."

"What about marriage?"

"That, I'm afraid, was another problem. I couldn't leave Barbara. Why should Barbara be punished? I couldn't bring myself to do that. Not after what we had been through together. Barbara wanted children more than anything else in the world. We could have adopted early on, I suppose. But the doctors always held out hope. Then suddenly we were older and it was too late."

"But she had given Jack her permission for a divorce?" Fiona asked. "Then changed her mind."

"She was still contemplating things, you see. When I vacillated, unable to find the courage to leave Barbara, she decided to change her mind about Jack. At least the child would have legitimacy."

"Then she did opt against abortion," Fiona pressed.

"More to it than that," Rome sighed. "She loved me, you see. The child would be ours. She knew how important that was to me. It would have been her gift."

"With a minimum of political risk," Fiona added.

"That, too." He looked toward the windows for a moment. "To us politics is everything."

Fiona remembering her parents, knew exactly what he meant.

"Did she know that Beatrice, Jack's mistress, was pregnant?"

"I don't think so. It was you who told me that she was informed that night. By Beatrice. Damn. How tawdry it looks from the outside. How awful it sounds." He chuckled drily, bitterly. "All this conception. My whole adult life was dominated by the idea of conception. My weak sperm. God, how vulgar. Then suddenly, as if God had chosen it, Frankie and I . . ." He caught her eyes again, looking deeply. "How unfair it all is."

"What exactly happened that night?"

Suddenly, he was back in character, the consummate picture of the dignified congressman and politician father figure. He put the napkin aside. Apparently, he had great powers of recuperation.

"We had a late staff meeting at the Monocle restaurant. Every month we do this. It broke after eleven and I was home before midnight."

"You never talked to Mrs. McGuire?"

"I would have seen her the next morning."

"She never called your apartment?"

"Not at that hour. We both knew better than that. Barbara, you see, didn't know about us. Dear Barbara. She didn't have the slightest suspicion. Thank God for that."

He seemed calmer now. The confession had unburdened him. And, of course, she had tested him on the question of the call. She knew that Frankie had not called. They had, indeed, checked. Despite the emotion and her own reaction to his confession, his veracity had to be confirmed. It was, or seemed to be.

"Did you actually attempt to see her that morning?"

"I started to. You people got there first, I'm afraid. There was a policeman at the door."

"Did you return to your apartment?"

"No. I went to the garage, got in my car and rode around. I was quite upset and anxious. I knew something had happened."

"What did you suspect had happened?"

"I . . ." He hesitated, vacillating back to vulnerability, the mask of calm command removed once again. "I suspected that she had killed herself."

"You did?" There was no end to his surprises.

She looked around the restaurant. It was almost totally empty. Most people had left. He became silent, turning to look out of the window. She followed his gaze and saw the panorama of Washington.

"Had she ever talked about suicide?"

"Not in so many words." He turned to face her, his expression deeply pained, his lips trembling. "She was under very heavy pressure, caught in a triple bind. The woman was a member of Congress, for crying out loud. She was carrying another man's child. Not your usual political scandal. Abortion might have been a solution, but neither of us wanted that. Her career was on the line."

"And yours."

"Possibly. But she was a woman . . . under all the hullabaloo the fact was that she represented a very conservative district. The truth would have spelled disaster. A baby by the liberal Charlie Rome. Blasphemy. The reality of her husband's mistress's pregnancy could have been the straw that broke the camel's back. She might have felt that there was only one way out."

"Suicide?"

"Look, FitzGerald, I'm quite sick about all this. Do you know how it feels to grieve alone? I told you the truth. Frankly, you have it in your power to destroy my career. The idea that my actions might have . . . in fact did . . . precipitate Frankie's suicide would not exactly make me a sympathetic figure. By the time the media were finished with me, I'd probably have to leave for some remote South Pacific island. I have to tell you, though. I feel a lot cleaner having told you. I'm a politician, but I'm really not very good at carrying heavy burdens and dark secrets. So you have the gun in your hand. All you have to do is pull the trigger. Oh yes. There's more. The idea that you people were considering that Frankie was murdered panicked me and I did consult the Speaker on the issue. He did empower me to make a quiet investigation. Yes I manipulated him to do this. I knew that the longer this case was kept open, the better the chance of having all this come out. I was right."

"But how do you account for the use of cyanide, the absence of a note, the lack of fingerprints . . . ?" It was too late to swallow the word. Her lie was out now.

"I suspected as much," he shrugged. "Also the bit about the witnesses. The fact is that I didn't murder her. I loved her. In the end, the truth will out."

"But that still doesn't explain the complete absence of any physical clues."

"I've thought about that, sergeant. All I can say is that Frankie was enormously clever and resourceful. She probably figured it all out. Wiped away anything that might implicate me or anyone else. As for not leaving a note. Maybe an explanation was too painful. And how was she to realize that an autopsy would be performed? Maybe she wanted her life to speak for itself. She was quite independent. Her work was her life. Her children were grown and on their way. Her husband had chosen another woman. She wouldn't have dared leave me a note. I understand that. If you knew her you would, too. As for her choice of poison. She'd find a way to get it."

In a strange way, Fiona was also relieved. Deep down, she suspected, she had chosen to attack this man because of what had occurred with Greg, as if he were a surrogate for extracting revenge.

"In a way," Rome said clearing his throat, "you might say I did

murder Frankie. I'll have to live with that for the rest of my life."
Again tears welled in his eyes and he could no longer speak.

"I want you to know, Mr. Rome," she said with deep conviction,
choosing her words carefully, adopting a clearly official tone. "I will
respect this confidence. I'm really sorry to have intruded. Unfortunately, it's the nature of my work. I did, however, go beyond the
bounds of propriety, for which I apologize."

He reached out and took her hand.

"I forgive you, FitzGerald . . . is it Fiona?"

She nodded.

"I was less than forthcoming myself. Every once in a while, I guess,
people need to cleanse themselves. I guess you helped me choose the
moment."

She thought again of her father who had also chosen his moment.

"Maybe I have been wrong," Fiona said, feeling the warmth and
pressure of his hand's response. "Frankie McGuire may have committed suicide after all."

24

M AY CARTER'S VOICE boomed into the squad room
from the Eggplant's office.
"Lardass bitch," Briggs muttered. He sat at a desk near
the door to the Eggplant's office and was hunting and pecking his
way through paperwork. Fiona had just arrived after her meeting
with Congressman Rome. She felt unburdened and relieved. But was
she convinced? Away from the power of Rome's personality, nagging doubts surfaced again. Why no fingerprints? Why perfume and
face cream before retiring? Was she to believe Beatrice about
Frankie's state of mind? Or Rome's version?

But her agonizing also had another dimension. Could she bring
herself to reveal what Charlie Rome had confessed? And what was
she to tell the Eggplant about her reasons for choosing suicide?
Would he accept her conclusion, one professional to another? Perhaps, considering his own wavering, he might welcome her reinforcement. Certainly Cates would. And the mayor and members of Congress. Everyone involved, except maybe May Carter. Justice would
be done.

May Carter's intrusion was an irritation. Fiona did not wish to
postpone presenting her conclusions any longer than she had to.

"I say cover-up, captain," May Carter's voice boomed. Nothing
will convince me otherwise. You people have been less than diligent.
I have reason to believe that Frankie McGuire was murdered by a
very clever hit man contracted by those opposed to our movement.

People who believe in killing are not discriminating. For their God-less immoral cause they will stop at nothing. I demand that this office be mobilized to break this case."

Her words rang clearly in the squad room as they sailed through the thin inside walls of the Eggplant's office.

"There is absolutely no evidence to . . ." the Eggplant's words trailed off as he lowered his voice. But whatever strategy he might have used to placate her hadn't worked and she was soon at it again.

"I came here to warn you that I fully intend to go to the media on this one. Your mayor has great faith in your department's ability, captain. 'Satisfy yourself,' he told me. 'Speak to Captain Greene.' Well, here I am, and all I get is more lip service."

"Can of worms, the whole goddamned case," Briggs said. "And what does the little white princess think?"

"Shut up and play with your Johnson," she rebuked, straining to hear the conversation in the Eggplant's office. They had apparently reached a civilized decibel level.

"I've given you the motive. Mrs. McGuire was simply getting too powerful for them. I tell you this woman was murdered for that reason. Murdered. Not a suicide. Murder. Pure and simple. Bloody calculating murder."

Not bloody at all, Fiona told herself with rising indignation. She stood up and strode toward the Eggplant's office.

"I wouldn't, FitzGerald," Briggs said. "He'd be looking for a goat and you'd be walking right into goat heaven."

"He shouldn't have to take her shit. Her theory's off the wall."

Without another thought of the consequences, she ignored Briggs's warning and strode into the office. Both faces turned to her. Immediately she noted the Eggplant's relief at her sudden presence. May Carter's face was beet red with anger.

"You know Sergeant FitzGerald." He waved his hand toward Fiona. "She's one of the detectives on the case."

"We've met," May Carter said, sniffing, as if Fiona gave off an unpleasant scent.

He signaled for Fiona to sit down and she took a chair beside the woman. Her indignation was palpable.

"Where are we on the McGuire case?" the Eggplant barked officiously.

"Nowhere, that's where," May Carter harumphed. "Not that she hasn't nosed around." She turned to Fiona. "Understand you were in Boston," she said smugly, to illustrate the extent of her knowledge.

"Nice town," Fiona said offering a smile of innocence.

"She was murdered by them. Absolutely. There is simply no room for doubt."

"Mrs. Carter intends to go to the media with this case, tell them it's the work of a hit man for the other side."

"The abortion killers," May Carter snapped, lifting her chin pugnaciously. "Just another way of killing." She was well practiced in the art of intimidation. The Eggplant looked very repressed. The effort to hold his temper had apparently taken every ounce of his willpower. Help me, his eyes pleaded.

"Mrs. McGuire committed suicide," Fiona said cutting a glance toward the Eggplant. Frown lines of confusion appeared on his forehead. In his gut, she knew, he didn't buy it. She sensed his anger boiling just beneath the surface. Also, in the face of this persistent woman, his resignation.

"So, you're all in this together, are you?" May Carter said. "You're all going to pay for this one day. What you should be doing is putting all those baby killers behind bars."

"The issue here is the death of Frankie McGuire," Fiona said, suddenly heating up.

"Exactly. And Frankie McGuire was murdered by a contract hit man hired by the baby killers."

"That is complete nonsense, Mrs. Carter," Fiona said firmly without looking at the Eggplant who must have been mortified by her candor. After all, May Carter was a powerful and credible national figure who had threatened to go the media with an explosive accusation. Obviously such an action was to be avoided at all costs. Fiona's arrogant assertion, she knew, must be giving the Eggplant, notwithstanding his inherent disbelief in her assertion, nervous palpitations.

"We shall see about that." Mrs. Carter said, standing up.

"I'm sorry, Mrs. Carter," Fiona said. "You're only going to embarrass yourself and your movement."

"You had better watch your step, lady," Mrs. Carter snapped. She made no attempt to leave the office.

"And I don't appreciate your attempt to intimidate me. Or my superior."

"Thanks, but no thanks," the Eggplant said.

"No one murdered Frankie McGuire," Fiona said slowly, emphasizing each word. "She committed suicide. There is no evidence to suggest otherwise." She avoided a glance toward the Eggplant.

"That's absurd. I knew the woman, perhaps as well as I know myself. She was not remotely suicidal."

"She had compelling reasons," Fiona said flatly.

Mrs. Carter sat down again, her chin lifted aggressively.

"I doubt that."

"She is absolutely a suicide. Without a shadow of a doubt," Fiona said, finally looking toward the Eggplant. Skepticism was written into the deepening lines of his forehead, emphasizing her own. Was she really? Fiona wondered, once again assailed by nagging doubts. But May Carter had goaded her into drawing this conclusion, although it did challenge Fiona's comfort level.

"I warn you, I don't intend to accept that verdict and will do everything in my power to squelch it. I swear it."

"Are you certain then, Sergeant FitzGerald?" the Eggplant asked, in a tone that revealed a forced formality. It was clear that her sudden conclusion had left him confused. Worse, she was not certain that she harbored the conviction that could privately persuade him of its validity.

"Yes. I am." I think, she thought.

"I have a question for you, FitzGerald," Mrs. Carter said. It seemed like an attempt to be ingratiating. Fiona knew better. The woman was setting her up.

"Do you believe in abortion?"

"That's a loaded question, Mrs. Carter," Fiona said. It had come as a bolt from nowhere, completely unexpected. Fiona hesitated as she drew deeply from her recent experience. She needed time to recover herself, regain the momentum.

"Why is that so relevant to this discussion?" Fiona asked.

"It's important to know where you stand," Mrs. Carter said.

"I don't think it's any of your business," Fiona said belligerently.

Mrs. Carter nodded, as if illustrating her superior wisdom. She turned toward the Eggplant.

"You don't need a compass to know where she stands," Mrs. Carter harumphed, turning to stare at Fiona. "Of course it's my business. What happens in our society is everybody's business. More important, the creation of human beings is God's business."

She was, Fiona realized, launching into a polemical diatribe, whipping up the inner passion of the zealot. Again she glanced at the Eggplant, who looked upward at the ceiling in a gesture of frustration.

Fiona held herself in check. No point in arguing with a fanatic. Besides, her personal turmoil over the matter with Greg had reminded her about her own inner consensus, which had surfaced yet again, like a sea lion that must rise periodically out of the deep for air. For her, every issue, personal and public, required this inner consent and the litmus test of its personal validity was how it affected her own independence. Selfish but necessary in a hostile world, she had decided.

When Mrs. Carter had concluded, Fiona looked at her and said, "In your opinion, then, abortion is nothing more than murder."

She turned to the Eggplant.

"Good Lord, this woman is thick-headed." She looked back at Fiona. "What the devil do you think I was just talking about."

"And life begins at the very moment of conception?" Fiona asked.

"This is ridiculous."

"And if you had conceived a child you would never, ever make an effort to abort that child?" Fiona pressed.

"Are you hallucinating?" Mrs. Carter frowned.

"I take it the answer is no. Under no circumstance?"

"Don't you think this is a rather pointless exercise?"

Again, Fiona looked at the Eggplant. A thin smile had erupted on his face and she caught his barely perceptible nod of consent.

"And Frankie McGuire shared this attitude?"

"With her soul," Mrs. Carter said angrily.

"All abortion is murder, right?"

"Beyond a shadow of a doubt. Abortion is murder. Pure and simple."

The interrogation had developed a rhythm. Point counterpoint.

"After conception, a woman's will means nothing, her choice is out of her hands?"

"In the face of that miracle it has become God's choice. God's will."

"Exactly."

"And violating that will is a sin. In lay terms, it's nothing more than murder?" Fiona felt the fire rise in her gut. She sensed that Mrs. Carter was now operating out of both rote and morbid curiosity, wondering where Fiona was leading her. The woman's eyes had fixed on hers, steady and demanding. She was prepared to give no ground, a female Horatio astride the bridge, daring the enemy, to pass.

"Frankie McGuire committed an abortion on herself," Fiona said, her own glance unwavering. Mrs. Carter blinked in confusion. "How does that grab you?" Fiona said between compressed lips.

May Carter glanced at the Eggplant who met her stare with his own. But Fiona gave her no chance to gather her defenses.

"For her it was the only way out. She was carrying a baby by a man other than her husband."

"I don't believe it," Mrs. Carter said. "It's a trick."

"Medically confirmed," Fiona said crisply. Then, unable to resist. "Perhaps also the work of a new type of hit man."

Mrs. Carter's face flushed. Her eyes seemed like glowing coals.

"Why wasn't I told?" she asked, her voice tremulous, her surety broken.

"Because, Mrs. Carter . . ." Fiona began, resisting the temptation to seek the Eggplant's signal of approval. "It was none of your goddamned business."

Mrs. Carter started to rise from her chair, but apparently the revelation had sapped her energy.

"I can't believe it. Not Frankie."

"It's true, Mrs. Carter," the Eggplant intervened. His task now, Fiona assumed, was for him to defuse the situation.

"Who was the man?" she asked.

Fiona felt her stomach tighten as she exchanged glances with the Eggplant.

"We don't know," the Eggplant said.

"It's not the issue," Fiona interjected. "We are now certain her death was suicide."

"But it's so out of character . . ." Mrs. Carter sighed. "Besides, we all would have stood by her. Surely, she knew that."

No point in belaboring the issue, Fiona thought, keeping her silence, letting Mrs. Carter work it out in her own mind. The fantasy of the "hit man" was obviously over. Also, the opportunity for making political capital out of Frankie's death. No sanctity of life argument would stand muster now.

After a long silence, Mrs. Carter rose slowly out of her chair.

"Guess it took the wind out of my sails," she said, making every effort to achieve a dignified exit.

The Eggplant stood up behind his desk.

"Our object here is to dispose of this case as rapidly as possible." He lowered his eyes. "Without in any way damaging Mrs. McGuire's reputation."

"Yes," Mrs. Carter said with a nod. "I suppose we couldn't ask any more than that."

She started toward the door, turned, and faced Fiona.

"We're going to win, you know," she said, her bluster restored, then she turned and left the office.

25

"**N**OT BAD," the Eggplant said after Mrs. Carter had left.

"For a woman," Fiona replied. She had, indeed, experienced a tiny moment of elation. But that had quickly receded as she faced the prospect of having to justify her shaky conclusion about Mrs. McGuire's death.

Out of respect for the visitor, the Eggplant had let his panatela die. He lifted it out of the ashtray and fired it to life. Gobs of smoke swirled out of his mouth and nose as he assumed his favorite feet-on-the-desk position.

"No way out now," he said.

"None intended."

The Eggplant blew some more smoke.

"We had a week. You surprised me."

Fiona forced herself to lift her eyes toward his. She wondered if he saw her lack of confidence.

"Why prolong the agony?" he said, watching her. "We were spinning our wheels, wasting manpower."

"The issue here was murder or suicide," she said. "Not conception." She averted her eyes now. "We haven't come up with a single clue, not the slightest warm lead." She paused. It wasn't working. Her earlier conviction was evaporating. She hadn't thought it through and it was showing. "But we could still continue . . ." Her voice trailed off. After that little discussion with May Carter, she had boxed the

MPD into a bit of a hole. Under the Eggplant's gaze, she felt transparent.

"I guess I need hip boots to wade through all this bullshit," the Eggplant said calmly blowing smoke rings. His expression needed no interpreter. Storm clouds were gathering. "You found out who the father was?"

"Yes," she said meeting his gaze.

He waited, sucking in more smoke, blowing it out.

"I gave my word," she said sheepishly.

"You giving words now," he mocked. "You got no authorization to give words."

"I know."

She felt him studying her. It wasn't supposed to work this way. Then suddenly, instead of an eruption, he smiled.

"Sheet." He shook his head. "In the face of that bitch, what choice had you. In a way, I guess you saved our ass. Press would have crapped all over us. Everything would come out in the wash. Yeah, sergeant. I guess you had no choice."

"At least, I couldn't think of any," she admitted.

"You spoke to the man, right?"

She nodded.

"He sold you."

She nodded again.

"No way he could have done it?"

"I . . ." She hesitated. She hadn't actually checked his alibi, his assertion that he had been at a meeting until late. And she had believed his story totally. With her gut. In her heart. Emotionally, she had gone the whole nine yards.

"Don't say it," she said.

"Say what."

"Just like a woman."

They were talking in shorthand, nor did it surprise her how much was being communicated between them.

"That chip just hangs there," the Eggplant sighed. "Just Mr. Big Black Macho sitting here playing with his Johnson." He shook his head, then sat up and shot her an angry look.

"My word worth shit? Is that what you're saying? Think the old Eggplant's gonna blow it in a moment of extreme vulnerability." He pointed the panatela in her direction, smoke oozing from his nostrils. "Gotta remember, sergeant. It's your badge gave that word, not your person. There is a chain of command here. You give your word, you speak for me. For all of us. Capish?"

"It wasn't like that. I didn't want to destroy . . . oh shit."

"I don't want to hear, woman," the Eggplant hissed through clenched teeth.

"I was just buying your point of view," Fiona said, caught in the web of her own making, unable to extricate herself. Just like a woman, she mocked. Again, her mother's voice tumbled from the void. Women *are* different Fiona. Never forget that.

"You are procedurally correct," Fiona said, uncomfortable under his scrutiny.

"Which supersedes your personal word."

"All right then," she said feeling her throat constrict. Once removed, he would never be constrained to protect Charlie Rome if his own career demanded it. Information was ambition's most effective weapon, a double-edged sword. He would use it if he had to.

"Don't tell me," he snapped, taking a deep pull on his cigar. Again he pointed it in her direction.

"Is that an order?"

He pulled his wallet out of his back pocket, opened it, showed his badge, then flung it into the wastebasket.

"Hell, no." He smiled. She got the obvious symbolism.

"You can be one hell of a ball buster when you want to be," she sighed, relieved. He fished his badge out of the basket.

"Next time. No word. Nobody gives words without authorization from on high."

"Got it, chief."

"Question is, sergeant. Can we sleep nights on this one?"

"I'm not sure," she said.

At that moment, the telephone on the Eggplant's desk erupted. He picked it up.

222

"Yeah," he barked, handing her the instrument.

"Sorry, Fi. We've got to talk." It was Cates, agitated and secretive.

"Sure."

"We clear?"

The Eggplant had directed his attention to some paperwork on his desk.

"Yes."

"I got something. It'll knock your socks off."

"So have I," she said. Had her word included Cates?

"Where?" she asked.

"Sherry's. Leave now."

She hung up.

"Cates up to something?" the Eggplant asked indifferently.

"Not really," she said calmly. The fact that Cates had insisted on rerouting the call to the Eggplant's office had obviously increased its level of importance.

"You get the paperwork ready," the Eggplant said without looking up. "First thing tomorrow. I've got an appointment with hizzoner and I want to lay it on his desk."

"I'll do that," she said, hiding her agitation.

"All in all, sergeant. I'm pissed off . . ." He paused. "But I got no complaints," the Eggplant said, looking up briefly. "Our game is catching the bastards."

"And leaving the politics to the politicians."

"You got it . . . sister."

It was as near as he ever could get to a meaningful heartfelt spoken compliment. He quickly returned his gaze to the papers on his desk and she let herself out of the office.

26

"LEACHING," Cates said. It was his first word of response, except for a muffled greeting. He looked brooding and introspective when she first spotted him sitting at a back booth at Sherry's. Nor had he brightened when she came forward and slid into the booth facing him.

"That's it," she said. "All this angst for leaching."

"It's an industrial process." He caught Sherry's eye and she waddled from around the counter to pour them two cups of coffee, offering no greeting. Surliness was her trademark. But she did know cops, could read their faces and body language and had often proved her loyalty by generosity.

"You know leaching?" Fiona asked Sherry.

"Yeah. Pain in the ass deadbeats," she snapped, not cracking a smile, parading her outward pose of nastiness as she waddled back behind the counter.

"It's a process used in gold mining," Cates said, taking a sip of coffee and watching Fiona's face.

"Metallurgy. You called me in the chief's office for metallurgy?"

Part of the game, she knew. He was deliberately drawing it out, requiring such a put-down comment, warming up the information, setting the stage, preparing her. Instinctively, she knew he was getting ready to throw a bomb.

"I think I was wrong," he said. "From the beginning. Dead wrong."

She felt the heartbeat in her throat. You can't, she thought. "Call it an accidental discovery. The unexplainable meant to be." "Will you cut the horseshit, Cates," Fiona hissed.

"I was just sitting there," he said ignoring her comment. "In Rome's outer office. Waiting to see this fellow who could explain the mysteries of abortion politics. Maybe, as you said, we were missing something. Keep an open mind. The slogan of Fiona Fitz-Gerald. Always an open mind. Did you know that in Congress, the abortion battle lines are drawn around funding abortions for poor kids."

"Next thing you'll start reading me Roe v. Wade, Cates, for crying out loud."

"I was just sitting there shooting the breeze with this cute little black receptionist . . ."

He never shoots the breeze, Fiona thought. Nothing he does is without purpose. She did not interrupt.

"You know chitchat. She started to give me opinions about her boss."

"Rome?"

"She worshipped him. Thought he was real cool. He has a truly gung-ho staff." He shook his head and smiled. "It's her they can't stand."

"Mrs. Rome?"

"Herself."

"What can't they stand?"

"Calls ten, twenty times a day. One of these real possessive ladies. Gets mad when this kid says the congressman is out. 'Well, find him.' Kid's a real mimic."

"Does she call mornings?"

"Mostly." He looked puzzled. "How did you know that?"

"Just tell it, for chrissakes," Fiona said curtly.

"Well, this Rome lady, according to the receptionist is apparently real rude. The kid comes in at seven-thirty. When she first came to work for Rome about two years ago, Rome was always in the office ahead of her. Real early bird. That stopped about a year ago. He started to stroll in about nine, nine-thirty. By then, Mrs. Rome had called six or seven times, getting nastier and nastier."

"Then it began again," Fiona said. "Rome coming in early. Say about right after Frankie died."

"On the money. You're clairvoyant, Fi." He looked at her with mock suspicion, cocking his head. "Now when Mrs. Rome called the receptionist could put her right through. No more lip from Madame Nasty. Not in the mornings, anyway." He looked at her and his eyes narrowed. "How did you know that?"

"That confirms it." Fiona said suddenly elated. "Mornings he spent with Frankie. After her death he was back on schedule."

"I was heading in that direction," Cates said, genuinely surprised. "But you said confirmed. That implies a lot more than theory."

"I did better than that. I got a confession. Heart to heart. Person to person." She lowered her voice. "The man emptied himself, poured it out."

"Rome?"

She remembered her earlier discussion with the Eggplant. We don't give word without authorization from on high. She nodded.

"You're kidding. He went that far?"

"As far as you can go," she said.

"Official. In writing."

"Wasn't necessary."

"He turn himself in?" Cates asked. He was acting oddly, stunned. "Why would he do that?"

"I thought you said he confessed."

"He did. He was her lover. They met mornings. I think you've just confirmed it. I hadn't checked that part, you see. It did worry me a little. But now you've settled that point." Something continued to nag her. Rome had told her that Barbara did not know, had never found out. How had he put it? He was "thankful" that Barbara had never given him grounds for suspicion. Thank God for that, he had said. According to him that was the part that had troubled him most. It wasn't only his career. It would hurt Barbara. Why punish Barbara? he had said. The conversation with Rome only a few hours ago was recycling at high speed.

"So Barbara Rome was indeed suspicious," Fiona said.

"I still don't understand," Cates replied, obviously confused. "You said, 'confessed.'"

"To being her lover, yes."

"We're talking murder here," Cates said. "Did he confess that?"

"Afraid not," Fiona said. "But you just put a whole new complexion on the case. You implied that Mrs. Rome suspected that Mr. Rome was catting around. She waved her hand suddenly like a traffic cop stopping traffic. "Did the girl, the receptionist, say anything else about Mrs. Rome's morning calls?"

"Only that during that period, when Rome was coming in late, the calls had gotten progressively persistent and rude."

"That had to mean that she didn't know," Fiona said, somewhat relieved. "If she knew she would have rushed downstairs to Frankie's apartment with a rolling pin. You had me going for a moment, pal. We've just declared the matter suicide. The Eggplant and I. Before a witness, no less. May Carter." She paused. "And tomorrow we give him the paperwork to present to hizzoner."

"Some partner," Cates said. "Least you could have done was consulted me."

"I had no choice. She was threatening to go to the media with her cockamamie theory about a hit man. I needed to unload her wagons. Besides, you were suicide's number one fan. From the go." She felt her venom rising. She needed support from him, not opposition. "You should be happy to end the damned thing. Stop spinning our wheels. Get off the political trolley. I can tell you one thing. The old Eggplant was relieved."

Cates watched her over his coffee cup. He had taken another deep sip, but instead of replacing the cup in his saucer, he held it, looking skeptical.

"Well she could have committed suicide," Fiona pressed, her anxiety level rising. "She was in a triple bind emotionally. She couldn't have an abortion. Her husband wanted to marry his pregnant mistress and her own lover wouldn't marry her. Political dynamite. She saw her political career heading down the tube, her personal life exploding. She was a woman on the edge with one way out."

God, Fiona thought, was she trying to convince herself? She felt hyper and surely sounded it. Finally, after he had apparently concluded that she had wound down her story, he slowly put the cup back in the saucer.

"The kid was moaning about the rudeness of this rich bitch," he said, "wishing that she would stay away longer than overnight when she goes to Nevada."

"A gambler?"

"Hell, no. I was telling you about leaching, remember."

"Okay, Cates. Time for a straight line. What the fuck is leaching?"

"It's a process of separating gold."

"You said this was something important. I didn't come here for a metallurgy lesson." She sensed that his bomb was coming at last and that there was no place to hide.

"Cyanide is a key ingredient of the leaching process."

"For chrissakes, Cates," Fiona cried.

His nostrils quivered as he drew in a deep breath.

"The rich bitch inherited a gold mine in Nevada. Ergo, she knew how and where to get the cyanide," Cates said, his eyes glowing like hot coals.

"Talk about circumstantial," she snapped. She felt her shaky conviction begin to crumble.

27

"ONLY US AGAIN," Fiona said pleasantly, hearing Barbara Rome's voice from the other side of her apartment door. They were obviously being inspected through the door's peephole.

"Just some routine loose ends to wind up," Fiona lied. "We'll only take a moment of your time."

A burning debilitating anger had kept her awake throughout the night. She had roamed the well-kept garden in the clear moonlit April night, huddled in her mother's old mink, which had hung unused in the hall closet for five years.

Her mind seethed with self-doubt. Few things ever were the way they seemed at first. Emotion had a way of brutalizing. Lies and betrayals were everywhere, hidden in the nooks and crannies, the camouflaged orifices of the human soul.

"I know," she spoke aloud, as if responding to her mother's imaginary rebuke. Think only good of people, her mother had preached. Nonsense, her father had countered. Too many sly bastards plotting infamy and evil, waiting for their chance to own a pound of someone else's flesh.

Ironically, her mother's demeanor was dour, her father's devil-may-care, Irish, lighthearted. His crying was on the inside. Stop this, Fiona, she bayed to the full moon. Stop this silliness, this stupid exercise in trying to sort out her genes, looking for clues to her lack of insight. What was she in this business for in the first place? Her mother had berated her for that decision as well. You, Fiona, are a traitor to your class, turning your back on privileges honestly earned by your forebears, groveling in the filth of human degradation.

"To see justice triumphant," she shouted into the spring-scented night. Her mind's echo sobered her into silence and she thought of Frankie McGuire, cold in her grave along with her dead fetus.

"Can we sleep nights on this one?" the Eggplant had asked. Well here, by God, was the answer to that question. Me floating like an apparition through the night, searching for advice from the ghosts of my progenitors. She laughed aloud, like some cackling witch.

By the time she had crawled back into bed, she had roused a bellyful of anger. No one, by God, no one, fucks over Fiona Fitz-Gerald. Echoes of her father surfaced. It had been his own muttered theme. You'd have to get up damned early in the morning to do that. And since she hadn't gone to sleep, she had them beat on that score.

And after all the angst and internal pub-crawling, Fiona knew what had to be done. It carried a deadline as well. The Eggplant had asked for the paperwork, "First thing in the morning. I have an appointment with hizzoner and I want to lay it on his desk."

At the crack of dawn, she called Cates.

"Okay, so we slept on it," she said. "You game, Cates?"

"We don't shake her tree, we'll never sleep again."

She knew, of course, that that had to be his response. The irony was that they had ended their speculations the day before with "let's sleep on it."

All yesterday afternoon and evening they had considered possible scenarios, all of which reached legal, political or public relations dead-ends.

"So we place her in Nevada," Fiona had speculated.

"At the mining site."

"An office, a physical place. There would be a manager and materials, including the cyanide."

"Inventories, too. This is a substance that begs for control." Cates had grown thoughtful. "Or maybe not. Maybe it was just lying around available."

"So she gets it, brings it back with her."

"We don't know that."

"We're assuming."

"We'll have to do better than that. Half a loaf won't fly. It boils down to the old chestnut. Too circumstantial. This one needs proof positive."

"But we do have her accessible to the poison," Fiona had pressed.

"She would be clever. Keep far away from local sources. Too risky. This way she could get her hands on it without ringing warning bells."

"It makes all the sense in the world," Cates had pointed out. "She finds out that hubby and Frankie are a duo. She gets this idea to eliminate the competition. She concocts this plan. She goes to Nevada on her regular run. Brings back the poison, then goes downstairs for a heart-to-heart with the lady, drops the cyanide in her glass. Two and two make four."

"Five," Fiona had countered. "Lots of logic but not a shred of evidence."

"It's there somewhere, Fi."

"In the hot and guilty mind and black cold heart of Barbara Rome."

By then the scenarios had gotten repetitive and Cates had suggested they sleep on it. Not long, though. He was going to drop the paperwork on hizzoner's desk in the morning. Except that he wasn't going to have it.

Barbara Rome opened the door to them. She was wearing a blue satin dressing gown. Not a hair was out of place, despite the hour, which was barely 8 A.M. Her make-up, too, was immaculately applied. She was a perfect accompaniment to her apartment, which was as shiny as a new penny. Fiona wondered if the bed she shared with Charles Rome had already been made. Tight hospital corners for the sheets, she speculated. There was no sign of a maid.

Fiona's study of both the lady and her surroundings was intense and she was certain that Cates was equally as diligent. Her mind was a receptor now, a blend of scrutiny and memory. And something was already nagging at her, lurking in some dark corner of her mind, waiting to emerge. For some reason, too, her mind had also dredged up inchoate thoughts of Greg, something about him or something he had said. It was an odd intrusion and she tried to dismiss it.

"I have coffee," Mrs. Rome said, leading them to the living room. As before, it was scrupulously clean. A white-gloved inspection would not have garnered even a microscopic speck of dust.

"That would be fine," Fiona said. It was important for their purposes that the woman not feel threatened. Cates also nodded his acceptance of her offer.

They waited in the living room, silently inspecting. The damask drapes were pulled back, letting in the morning light. Even the windows, Fiona noted, were immaculately polished. Books on their shelves were arranged neatly, like shiny soldiers in formation. On the floor was a fringed oriental rug. With her foot, she flipped a corner aside. Beneath was a parquet floor polished to a mirror shine. Even what was hidden was carefully tended.

Barbara Rome came into the living room holding a bright silver tray, milk white cups and saucers and a matching coffee pot, which she placed on the cocktail table. Then she poured out the coffee with what seemed like elaborate ceremony.

From where she sat on the couch, Fiona could see the western landscape that she had seen earlier, but now it had far more significance. Orange-tinted in the late afternoon sun, the painting depicted a dry desert beauty and startling rock formations. In the cloudless grey sky a predatory bird circled, seeking prey.

"Nevada?" Fiona asked casually.

"Yes," Barbara Rome said. "Isn't it lovely?"

"You're from there, aren't you?"

No sign of caution. She was more relaxed than on their first visit.

"Just a western cowgirl," she said lightly. "Cream or sugar?"

"Black is fine," Cates said.

"Fine for me, too," Fiona said. "You go back often?"

"Every few months," Mrs. Rome said. "Family business interests have to be looked after. I was an only child of a driven man."

"Mines?" Fiona asked.

"That and real estate. Also cattle. My late father was a brilliant entrepreneur."

"Gold mines?" Cates asked.

"Not quite like it sounds. It's an old claim we're still working. Believe it or not, I have a degree as a mining engineer. Father was one as well." She turned in her seat and motioned with her head to a portrait of a forbidding man with a moustache that drooped at the ends. "Quite a man."

"Mr. Rome off to the Hill?"

"Man gets up with the roosters," she said, smiling. "Now what can I do for you? Charles tells me that this Frankie thing might be settled once and for all." She clucked her tongue. "But I'll never understand it. A woman like that taking her own life."

"She didn't," Fiona said quietly, her eyes probing those of Barbara Rome. Her only reaction was a slightly speeded-up blinking action. She lifted her cup and saucer.

"But I thought . . ."

"So did we," Fiona said cutting a glance at Cates.

"Are you saying . . ." Mrs. Rome began, then trailed off.

"Frankie McGuire was murdered. It is beyond a shadow of a doubt."

Barbara Rome still held the cup and saucer, but a clattering had begun as her fingers began to shake. Suddenly, both the cup and saucer fell on the cocktail table. The cup broke and the oriental rug got the full brunt of the coffee.

"Oh, my God," Mrs. Rome squealed. She ran into the kitchen and was out seconds latter with a roll of absorbent paper, a sponge and some cleansing compound. Down on her knees, she began to blot up the stain.

Only then, seeing her on her knees zealously sopping up the coffee stain, did the thought seep out of her subconscious. Greg had advertised his neatness as a great plus for their relationship. Nothing ever out of place. Everything shipshape and clean. This woman was obviously a fanatic about that, obsessively compulsive. Of course, Fiona thought, and suddenly an answer to a mystery had arrived on the wings of Greg's remembered voice.

Mrs. Rome frantically worked to remove the stain. After a full ten minutes of rubbing and applying cleaning materials, the stain appeared to be defeated. Then she went back to the kitchen with the cleaning materials and reappeared soon after and sat down again.

"Now what is this nonsense about Frankie being murdered?" she asked, making an effort to appear calm.

"It's not nonsense, Mrs. Rome," Fiona said gently, pausing for a moment. "As you well know."

The woman was sitting on her hands now, but a tremor in her jaw gave away her inner agitation.

"I . . . I shouldn't be talking to you. I . . ."

Barbara Rome was trying desperately to gather her forces. Sensing this vulnerability, Fiona pushed ahead. Show no mercy, give no quarter, she told herself, feeding the blue flame of anger. She glanced toward Cates. Now, she told him with her eyes. He signaled his understanding with a nod.

"Mrs. Rome," Fiona said. "It was no secret to you that your husband and Mrs. McGuire were having an affair. Am I right?"

"What!" It was an effort at indignation. The woman tried to stand, then sat down again.

"For a year," Fiona said, her voice steady, carefully modulated and controlled. ". . . he would leave her bed for yours. You found out, Mrs. Rome. And when you did . . ." Fiona allowed herself a long pause. ". . . you took action."

"No," she shouted, her voice tremulous. "I won't stand for this." She managed to rise unsteadily. There was a telephone on a table nearby and she managed to reach it. With shaking hands, she picked up the phone, punching in the numbers with clumsy fingers. She had to do it three times to get it right. Fiona and Cates watched, but made no move to stop her.

"Mr. Rome," she said into the phone. Her voice was wispy, agitated, but she seemed to be recovering her poise. "This minute. Dammit. I don't care. Interrupt him then." Her facade was collapsing and her inherent bitchery could no longer be hidden. As she waited, she put her hand over the instrument.

"You had better leave this minute. Both of you. I'll see to it that you're charged for this. You'll never hear the end of it as long as you live." Her voice trembled with anger as she lashed out. She was a woman well-versed in intimidation. The crust of charming superiority had been shattered. Fiona and Cates stood their ground.

"Charles. These people are here again," she said into the phone. "That woman detective and that black man. They are saying crazy things. All sorts of crazy things." Her voice rose on a wave of hysteria. "I want them out of here this minute. I want you back here. Now. Do you understand? *Now.*" Her face had become pasty under her make-up. "And I want these people charged. You can't imagine what they've been saying." She looked suddenly at Fiona and said to Charles, "Here tell her yourself." She then thrust the phone into Fiona's hand.

"You filthy bitch," Rome shouted into the phone. "I'll have your ass for this. You gave me your word . . ."

Fiona replaced the instrument quietly in its cradle.

"We'll wait for him," Fiona said.

"Not I," Barbara Rome said. "I'm getting dressed and I'm getting out of here." She started to leave the room. Cates blocked her way.

"A little calm, Mrs. Rome," he said.

"You do have a choice," Fiona said. "We can pull you in for Murder One now. Or you can wait until your husband arrives."

Her determination seemed to seep out of her. Her shoulders hunched and her body wavered as if it had been hit by a heavy gust of wind.

"I'm not saying anything to either of you," she muttered. She groped her way to the couch and sat down. Hands folded tightly, she lowered her head slightly and stared at them.

Fiona had seen it before. She had stiffened herself for stonewalling. A cornered suspect wants to appear to retreat from reality, except that it was not that simple a task to stop the ears from hearing.

Fiona moved toward the couch and stood over her, feeling the pressure of time. The impending presence of Charles Rome would stiffen her resolve. She had to be broken before Rome arrived.

"You've got to face it, Mrs. Rome," Fiona began.

She waited. The woman showed no sign of answering and Fiona continued.

"You planned it to perfection. You had access to the cyanide and you knew the way you were going to get it. No sweat there. Mrs. McGuire had stolen your husband. You confronted him. He confessed. Worse, he told you she was pregnant by him, something you were never able to achieve together."

She shook her head, unclasped her hands and brought them to her ears. Fiona reached out and pried them apart. Still holding them, Fiona continued.

"He wanted to divorce you and marry her."

Her ploy hadn't worked. Fiona was reaching her, driving the message home.

"He was getting ready to dump you, Mrs. Rome, have what he always dreamed about. His own child, which you couldn't provide him with."

She felt the impetus of relentlessness. She felt no mercy, thinking only of Frankie McGuire and her baby.

"No. No!" Mrs. Rome cried.

"You asked for time. Planned and plotted. In Nevada you got the cyanide. Then you chose your moment. That evening, with your husband at his staff meeting, you went down to Mrs. McGuire's apartment. She was already in bed. You had a real heart-to-heart, probably consented to the divorce, sealed it all with a toast."

"I won't listen to this," the woman protested, struggling to put her hands back over her ears. Fiona felt her strength. She shook her head when Cates stepped forward to assist her.

"You murdered her. In cold blood. To protect yourself and your marriage."

Again the woman shook her head vigorously. Fiona looked toward Cates, who stood by now, watching patiently, nodding approval. Still the woman hadn't broken.

"You killed that woman, Mrs. Rome. Admit it. We know too much now. You're finished."

"Lies. It's all lies," she screamed.

The woman was stonewalling beyond her emotional strength. Soon her husband would arrive to buttress her resolve. Greg's voice roared back.

"There were no fingerprints because you erased them, worked the apartment over, made it sparkle, cleaned every corner with your usual fanatic zeal."

"Just wait. Charles will know what to do," the woman said. "You can't trick me."

Fiona had been holding the woman's arms apart and now she let go.

Human beings, Fiona had learned, worked in patterns with surprising aberrations from the norm. This was one of those cases. The woman was holding back. Nothing was working. Or, Fiona thought, was she failing to see something? an essential ingredient overlooked. She heard movement in the vicinity of the apartment's front door. Only then did the idea occur to her.

"He told me you did it, Mrs. Rome," Fiona said calmly, bending over the woman, talking calmly, gently. "And he'll never forgive you. Never."

Slowly Barbara Rose raised her head, her eyes spitting black hatred.

"He's a damned liar."

"He's coming in now. Ask him."

A pale and angry Charles Rome confronted her from the living room entrance. He was out of breath. Behind him was the Eggplant.

"Don't tell them a damned thing, Barbara," he shouted. He turned to the Eggplant, who looked harassed and angry.

"I demand they be relieved of their duties as of now," Rome snapped. "They are harassing my wife." He moved toward his wife and put his arm around her. She shrugged it away, looking at him fiercely.

"You got something to say?" the Eggplant said, directing his attention to Fiona and Cates. Although he had the demeanor of an angry man, his eyes told Fiona that he was dissembling, playacting.

"This man," Fiona said calmly, taking her cue from the Eggplant's attitude, "was Mrs. McGuire's lover."

"You gave your word, you lying bitch," Rome said pointing a menacing finger at Fiona. Any pretense of control had vanished. Again he turned to the Eggplant. "Captain, I want them dismissed. I want their badges taken away and thrown into the Potomac."

The Eggplant stared at him, but did not respond.

"I can have you chewed up and spit out as well, captain. I demand that you act. Or would you prefer I speak to the mayor?"

"I told her what you told me, Congressman Rome," Fiona interjected pointedly.

"What did you tell her, Charles?" Mrs. Rome asked.

The congressman seemed suddenly trapped by competing forces, confused as to who to address next. He turned to the Eggplant.

"I want these people out of my home," he shouted.

"What did you tell her, Charles?" Mrs. Rome persisted. Rome turned to her impatiently.

"I told her the truth," Rome snapped.

"And what was that?" Mrs. Rome asked.

"That . . ." he began.

"That you killed her," Fiona said directly to Mrs. Rome "You poisoned her with the cyanide that you brought from Nevada."

"What the hell are you talking about?" the Eggplant pressed. He was growing genuinely angry now. Above all, he hated to be in the dark, especially at a so-called moment of truth. She pressed forward.

"She brought the cyanide back from Nevada. She owns a mine there."

"I don't have to stand for this," Rome said, rushing over to the telephone. "I'm calling the mayor instantly." He picked up the phone.

"Send him my regards," the Eggplant said.

Rome looked at him for a long moment, then put down the phone.

"Maybe we can settle this between us," he muttered. His complexion had turned ashen.

"What did you tell her, Charles?" Mrs. Rome asked.

"I told you. I told her . . ." Again he lost his voice.

"The truth you said," Mrs. Rome snapped.

"He told me you killed her," Fiona said, knowing she was gambling her career. But she was certain now. Dead certain. The Eggplant's glance shifted to Rome's face.

"Can't you see what she's doing . . ." Rome said, his voice sputtering to silence.

"You told her that it was me?" Barbara Rome asked.

"Can't you just . . ." Rome managed to reply, but he was being defensive now, treading water, on the verge of panic. "Don't say another damned thing, Barbara. I want a lawyer immediately. I know my rights. We do not have to say anything. Nothing. Say nothing, Barbara."

It was unraveling now. Fiona, the Eggplant and Cates had seen it before. Conspirators falling out. There was nothing for it but to let it happen.

"He was the one," Mrs. Rome said, her eyes narrowing with hatred.

"I told you to shut your fucking mouth," Rome screamed, lashing out with his fist, hitting her full force on her nose. The force of it threw her off balance and she fell against the bookcase and slipped to the floor bringing a shower of books with her. He started after her, but Cates caught him before he could strike her again and held him in a hammerlock. He squirmed and shouted obscenities, but Cates held him fast.

Mrs. Rome began to bleed from the nose.

"You dirty bastard," she cried, the blood trickling over her mouth onto her spotless clothes. "He did it. He was the one. It was all his idea."

"Shut your fucking mouth," Rome shouted.

"Cuff the son of a bitch," the Eggplant said. No sooner ordered than Cates had his cuffs on Rome, who had been forced to his knees.

"You bastards. I am a member of the Congress of the United States," he screamed.

"God help the Republic," Cates said. He lifted Rome's arms behind him until the pain quieted him down.

Still bleeding, but paying no attention to the blood trickling down to her chin, Barbara Rome stared at her husband with abject hatred. She had struggled up to her feet and was now looking down at her husband.

"I caught him," she said between clenched teeth.

"She's crazy," Rome whimpered. Then he looked up at her and found his strength. "Filthy rich cunt."

She sneered at him, spitting a wad of bloody mucus in his face. "My turn now, you animal," she shouted, then turned to the Eggplant, growing strangely calm.

"I followed him one morning. Wasn't the first time he had been with other women. But Frankie. Of all people, Frankie. Our so-called friend. And making her pregnant after all those years . . ." She paused to clear her throat of blood. "He begged me to help him, get him off the hook. He made promises, you see. Promises. He made lots of promises. All I did was get the cyanide. Everything else was his idea. No way people would find out. He was sure of that. It was he that laced the wine the morning before. Sure I had to give him one more chance. You see, he knew she always took a wine nightcap in bed. Oh, he knew all her intimate secrets. It was disgusting. But I stood by him, believed his promises." She turned to Fiona. "You're right about one thing, I did clean the place. I believe in cleanliness." The condition of her face and dressing gown was an ironic contradiction. "I must have done a helluva good job. He had it all planned out. Of course, he was at a staff meeting at the time. His alibi was airtight."

"You goddamned fool," Rome shouted through his pain. "We had it made. Perfect. I never told her you did it. They tricked you."

She paused, then turned to him.

"My father warned me about you," she said. "He told me you were too ambitious, would stop at nothing to gain your ends, that you would use me." She nodded, as if to herself. "Well, you used me alright."

"Used you," Rome sneered. "Spoiled bitch." He shook his head. "What choice did I have? She was going to expose us, ruin us both."

Fiona felt nothing but disgust for this ruthless poseur.

"What about all that sentimental horseshit, Rome?" Fiona asked. "The stuff you handed me yesterday about being so proud of having this child of your own?"

"He told you that?" Mrs. Rome sneered. "All that bastard was ever interested in was power. Power over everybody." She smiled suddenly. "Well I unloaded your wagons, didn't I, Charlie?"

Justice triumphant, Fiona sighed. Amazing how much scum bubbled to the top.

"Read 'em their rights and bring 'em in," the Eggplant said. While they did that, he used the phone in the den. They could not hear what he was saying. After awhile, he came back into the room.

"Hizzoner," the Eggplant said. "He was real pissed this morning." He looked at Rome. "That one raised hell, made the mayor rush me down here. Threatened he'd take my badge if I didn't move my ass."

"And now?"

"I just told him where he could put it," the Eggplant said, his face breaking suddenly into a broad grin. "He said he was going to spend the day practicing his pucker."

They started to move through the apartment. Cates first with Rome. Fiona following with his wife. They were docile now, zombielike in their obedience.

"FitzGerald, Cates," the Eggplant called after them. They turned. He raised a finger and waved it at them.

"I'm not finished with either of you." The Eggplant said. "When the Eggplant says he wants something on his desk in the morning, the Eggplant means it."

"Sorry, chief," Fiona said. "We should have kept you . . ." She paused. "Apprahzed."

He nodded and shook his head in what they both knew was mock exasperation.